Amerissance

American Renaissance

David F. Palmer

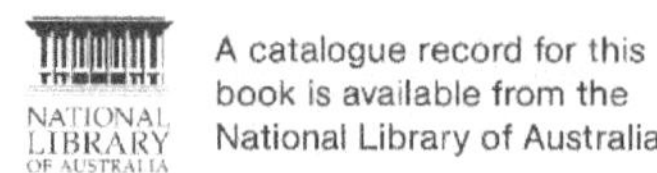

A catalogue record for this book is available from the National Library of Australia

This book is a work of fiction
and any resemblance to any persons
living or dead is purely coincidental.

Linellen Press
265 Boomerang Road
Oldbury, Western Australia
www.linellenpress.com.au

Dedication

In memory of the late Dr. Frank Legge, Ph.D.:
A great Australian, and the man who opened my eyes to the truth
about 9/11.

"Whereas it is essential, if man is not to be compelled to have recourse, as a last resort, to rebellion against tyranny and oppression, that human rights should be protected by the rule of law"

Extract from the Preamble of the
Universal Declaration of Human Rights

Contents

Prologue

Fall, 2039

Lot Solamonson never knew what hit him. One minute he was walking towards the black limousine parked at the front of the synagogue and the next his brains were sprayed out in a neat oval mosaic on the glistening white snow several yards behind him. The shot had clearly come from the right and probably from the fourth or fifth floor of the boutique hotel across the street.

Rabi Coleman froze as he took in the full horror of what he'd just witnessed. Then his Israeli military training kicked in. He threw himself to the ground and scrambled to the only meager shelter available, a low boundary wall about three feet high around the grounds of the place of worship. It was topped by a six-foot wrought-iron perimeter fence that offered little protection from a bullet travelling at over a thousand yards per second. There was no second shot. Clearly Solamonson had been the sole target. Coleman stayed crouched there for a further ten minutes anyway just to be sure.

High above him in Room 517 of the Majestic Hotel, a young Montanan disassembled the sniper's rifle and packed it into the oversized briefcase lying open beside him. He scooped up the single spent cartridge case and slipped it into the felt bullet container in the floor of the case, snapped the case lid shut, grabbed the case handle, rose and headed for the door. Twenty minutes later he was a mile away heading for the Brooklyn Bridge driving cautiously and trying to look like a typical New York motorist on a Saturday morning drive.

As he headed north the driver extracted a list from his top left-hand shirt pocket and glanced at it. Ten names were on it: Solamonson's the first.

"One down," the driver muttered. "Who's next?"

All listed were male but seemed to have no other common theme by way of nationality, ethnicity or religion. The assassin was also unaware of the particular indiscretion each had committed to justify his inclusion on his target list.

His instructions were to hit the names, in order if possible. More important than sequence though was consistency. He was to try to eliminate one victim each month until all were dispatched. He knew he was not alone in this endeavor. He knew there were numerous assassins with similar instructions across the United States and elsewhere in the world. He did not know how many. Nor did he know the magnitude of the total list of all targets assigned to this execution army. He had not heard of any other similar high-profile strikes either in the United States or anywhere else so he presumed that, in this late Fall of 2039, the Solamonson hit, his handiwork, had the honor of being the first strike in this new phase of the war.

Betrayal

Eleven years earlier, 2028
Jackson Parnell brushed the dust from the portrait photograph of a middle-aged man wearing a United States Army uniform bearing a single silver star on each shoulder. It had been taken five years earlier, in the Spring of 2023, shortly after his promotion to Brigadier-General. It had been taken at the insistence of his mother who, like mothers everywhere, considered her son to be handsome, with his 'baby-blues' as she called them, his athletic build, his five feet eleven and a half-inch height and his still thick, neat cut, mousey-brown hair. He smiled to himself. 'Perhaps he was', he mused. How would he know? There was no other significant female in his life to render an opinion on the subject.

"Mothers," he muttered, with no particular sentiment in mind. He placed the picture carefully back on the mantelpiece above the open fireplace; glanced back at it one more time. Even back then it portrayed the quiet confidence of a man who carried the burdens of command with a natural and well-trained competence.

He glanced up at the mirror above the polished slab of mahogany to compare it with the image of the man that stood before it.

Not too different, he thought. *A little thinner on top, a few more expression lines on the face.*

He could have added: *perhaps a little more composed …* perhaps the image of a man confident that he had done his duty and done it well and who could reasonably look forward to a comfortable, well-earned retirement with an adequate but not lavish pension in the near term — that was provided he didn't ruffle the feathers of his superiors and did not fail in whatever mission he was assigned in his last few years of service. *You never know*, he thought, *they might even settle another star on my shoulder as a farewell present.* That was not uncommon for officers with impeccable records like his; it added a few more dollars to a military pension as a reward for long service and good conduct.

His thoughts were interrupted by a discrete tap on the door leading to the hallway. It was Lieutenant Inglis, his aide and driver, the man elevated to a commissioned rank upon Parnell's promotion to star rank since Parnell had insisted on retaining the old warrior's services in that personal role. The two had been together for over a decade and could anticipate the other's every move.

"Car's ready, sir," said the veteran warrior.

"Fine," said Parnell in his quiet-spoken, courteous and respectful manner to the other man whose chest was as full as fruit salad as Parnell's. He reached for his cap, placed it on his head, adjusted it with the aid of the mirror, picked up his briefcase then turned and followed the other soldier to the door.

Parnell sat in the front seat next to Inglis as they drove to the base. They did not engage in small talk, Parnell mentally going over the material in his briefcase, thinking of the morning's meeting schedule, and planning what he would say to his staff as they prepared for the coming exercise regime. What could he say to whom? Who needed to know what?

The car swung into the headquarter's parking lot and drew up at the entrance to the brigade administration block.

"Pick up same time as usual?" queried Inglis.

"Yes," said Parnell, "although I'll need you again tonight at 1900 hours. There's a function at the officer's club tonight and I'm expected to attend ... shouldn't be too late tonight though, I'm hoping to get away by about 2130."

"Yes, sir," said Inglis.

Parnell exited the car, briefcase in his left hand so he could return any salute a subordinate might pay him as he entered the building and walked to his office.

The evening event was the usual: a soiree of medal-bedecked officers, some with their wives, the usual gaggle of minor bureaucrats and junior politicians, contractors and their secretaries networking with quartermasters and other supply officers, plus the occasional foreign dignitary someone was trying to impress. Parnell felt bored but tried not to show it.

Standing off to the side of the main bar area, he nursed a small beer from which he'd just taken his third sip when a young woman approached him. She extended her hand in a polite introductory manner.

"Good evening, General," she said. "Francoise Toulemont, visiting fellow at Columbia University."

The accent was European, 'French' guessed Parnell.

"Jackson Parnell," he said, taking the hand and shaking it, somewhat more delicately than usual. Parnell was not comfortable in the presence of women, particularly young attractive ones.

To his surprise, the young woman proved to be witty, intelligent, and a little mischievous, and Parnell found himself enjoying her company. Until, perhaps provocatively, she steered the conversation to a discussion of the terrorist attacks that had taken place in New York City and Washington DC on 11th September 2001, commonly referred to as '9/11', which had occurred some twenty-seven years earlier. She had broadly insinuated, in line with a popular conspiracy theory that had achieved some notoriety over the previous two decades, that the whole affair might have been 'an inside job'. She even insinuated the three buildings that had collapsed in New York City that day had been demolished rather than 'collapsing' as the official account had proclaimed.

"What?" Parnell spluttered incredulously, quickly shielding his mouth with his hand to avoid spitting his latest sip over the smiling woman. "Are you telling me the twin towers were brought down by a controlled demolition?"

"Yes," said Toulemont, flicking her hair slightly to defy his implied challenge.

"Oh, come on," Parnell argued. "Rigging a building like that for demolition would take weeks, maybe months. You'd have to place the charges and partially sever most support columns beforehand. How could you hide that?"

"You couldn't," she agreed, "not in the time between when the planes hit and the buildings fell. But what if the buildings had been prepared for demolition beforehand? What if it had been the people who owned, or were in control of those buildings? What if it was the people in authority who were doing the demolition?" She said this matter-of-factly. "You could do it then."

"Oh, that's ridiculous! Even if it was them doing it, there would still be a lot of people looking on. Someone would smell a rat. Someone would ask awkward questions. Someone would blow the whistle."

"Would they?" said Toulemont, her eyebrow rising. "Would they *really* be curious about what appeared to be normal maintenance? Would they *really* challenge a group of workmen dressed in overalls carrying out what they'd been told was renovations, building upgrades, or overhauling the lift systems? How many office workers *really* know what explosives or fuse wires or any of the other paraphernalia of the demolition industry really look like? Not many I'll bet."

"You wouldn't need many. You'd only need one person to see that things didn't look quite right before that one person started asking questions."

"And what would they be told? It's all been approved by the highest authority? It's all in the schedule? Go check out the building approvals if you're not happy about it? Talk to the maintenance engineer; or the city engineer; or management; or the landlord?

"You would have to be pretty sure of yourself before you would be game enough to challenge what appeared to be an approved schedule of building maintenance or renovation. This sort of thing goes on in high-rise buildings all the time. Most people just accept it and put up with the inconvenience."

Parnell glanced around nervously, checking that no-one in earshot was overhearing what might be considered amongst his military colleagues to be a strange conversation.

"No," said Parnell, shaking his head. "It's just too fantastic. It can't be true."

"That's what I thought at first too," said Toulemont. "That's what most people think. And that's where most people are prepared to leave it. It's a perfectly normal reaction; unless you have read the Harrit nano-thermite paper, that is."

"Is that what you think? That this is just another one of those outrageous conspiracy theories? Who is this person you mentioned anyway, this Harry fellow? Is he from your side of the pond?"

"His name is Niels Harrit, and he's Danish," said Toulemont. "But, 'yes', he is from my 'side of the pond'." She smiled at the idiom. "He used to be Professor of Chemistry at the University of Copenhagen, quite well regarded in academic circles, I understand. That was before he published his paper. Now he is avoided by most of his former colleagues. No-one wants to get labeled a nutcase along with him."

Parnell jerked his head back and nodded. "So he's a nutcase?"

"I didn't say that," said Toulemont. "I said that's what some people are calling him. But that doesn't mean he's crazy. To make a judgment on that, you *really* need to look at his work; his evidence, how has he analyzed his data, check do his conclusions flow from his analysis? You have to look at his paper critically, from a scientific point of view. Then you can make a judgment about whether what he is saying makes sense or not."

"Well, you would need to know something about the technical aspects of this particular field to do that," said Parnell.

Toulemont edged a little closer towards him to allow a steward carrying a plate of canapés to squeeze behind her and offer them to a small group of officers engaged in deep conversation immediately to their rear. Parnell stepped back as far as the bar behind him would permit. He felt a little more uncomfortable at her closeness as the scent of her distinctively French perfume wafted to his nostrils.

"Yes, I understand that," said Toulemont. "So what is it you want to know"?

"Well," said Parnell, "does it make sense to you, from a scientific point of view? Do you think he is talking nonsense?"

"No," said Toulemont. "To me, it looks like good science. You could probably criticize his work on some minor technical aspects. Scientists do that to each-others' work all the time. What you can't do, from a professional scientific point of view, is dismiss someone's findings just because you don't like the implications of what their research suggests. That's what politicians do. Scientists accept or reject conclusions on the basis of how they were arrived at, on the quality of the research work. And, as I said, as a scientist, this looks like good science to me."

"But if you accept the implications of this paper you're talking about," said Parnell, "you would be accepting the notion that the American Government was implicated in the murder of thousands of its own citizens."

"Yes," said Toulemont bluntly. "Scary, isn't it?"

"You can't expect me to believe that," said Parnell.

"Why not?" she asked, "… because it would be unpatriotic?"

Parnell didn't respond, and the silence became awkward. Then Toulemont said softly: "Listen, General, I'm not going to tell you what you should think or what you should do. Make up your own mind. But put aside the implications for a moment and just look at what the evidence is telling you. Let the evidence guide your judgment."

"You're saying that you *actually* believe this stuff!" Parnell pushed further. "I thought you were an ally."

"I am," said Toulemont. "That's why I'm not going to say

anymore. Other than perhaps to suggest that you should type in the words 'Chute Libre' and '9/11' into your internet search engine and see where that takes you."

"Chute libre?" queried Parnell. "What's that mean?"

"It means 'free fall', and if you link it with '9/11', the terrorist type not the emergency number, you might find it throws up some interesting reading. Follow your nose from there."

When Parnell made no response Toulemont added: "Get back to me if you need any help with any of the technical evidence you come across. And now, if you will excuse me, General, I have to catch up with Colonel Gross before he disappears."

Parnell bowed slightly and Toulemont departed, leaving him alone. He stood silent for a few minutes, not knowing what to think. Doctor Francoise Toulemont, the brilliant young French physicist the Army Headquarters had sent a memo around about earlier in the week was now here, talking conspiracy theories. Headquarters had praised the young scientist as being the new vanguard of European enlightenment. Now she was effectively endorsing a paper that challenged the very foundations of everything he believed in. He hadn't expected to meet this young woman here tonight. Now he had, he didn't know what to think.

"I believe you spoke to that young French scientist last night?" Parnell asked Gross, his second-in-command, the next day.

"Yes," said Gross.

"What do you think of this 'nano-thermite' paper she was going on about?"

"Nano-what?"

"Oh, never mind," said Parnell yet, with so much on his plate with the upcoming exercises he couldn't get the French scientist's theory out of his mind. It didn't make sense. Headquarters had endorsed her lavishly, but in her conversation with him, she'd practically espoused blasphemy. What was going on?

After a week of restless nights thinking about the exchange, Parnell keyed in the words 'nano-thermite', '9/11' and 'Harrit' into the search engine, as Toulemont had suggested. He hit 'Enter'. The search engine generated a list five pages long of articles headed by "9/11 Mystery Solved - Nano-thermite discovered in WTC remains". He started reading; first, that article then followed a few more links to some of the sources referenced. He read them then followed links from those pages to others.

Two hours later he located the paper Toulemont had referred to. It was titled: *Active Thermitic Material Discovered in Dust from the 9/11 World Trade Center Catastrophe*. It had initially been published in *The Open Chemical Physics Journal*, in 2009. In addition to its lead author, a Danish chemistry professor, it had been co-authored by eight others, among them American physicists and engineers, and an Australian chemist. The paper described the analysis of four dust samples taken from the lower Manhattan area shortly after the collapse of the World Trade Center's three towers on 11th September 2001, a collapse that resulted in the launching of the "War on Terror" by the Bush administration.

The 9/11 Truth Movement called the paper the "smoking gun" and claimed it proved that explosives were involved in the collapse of, not only the Twin Towers – the North and South towers, WTC1 and WTC2 – but also a third building, the forty-seven story World Trade Center building number seven. WTC7 had not been hit by aircraft but had collapsed eight hours after the twin towers came down.

Parnell bookmarked the paper. He would get back to it later. For now though, he needed sleep. It would be a busy day tomorrow.

Parnell came back to that paper at least a dozen times over the next three months. He learned that most 'sensible' people had dismissed those who gave credence to the 'Controlled Demolition' hypothesis as being 'Conspiracy Theorists', a not-too-subtle euphemism for 'nutcases'. Certainly, official accounts of these events dismissed them as such. Even President George W. Bush had warned the American people not to give credence to what he called 'outrageous conspiracy theories', and most 'patriotic' Americans had done so, including Jackson Parnell.

But then, most Americans had not read "the nano-thermite paper", as Toulemont had called it. And nor had Parnell until he met her. Now he had. And now it had practically been endorsed by the brilliant young French scientist Parnell had come to hold in high regard, he was not so sure.

Truly, he did not want to believe in the veracity of this paper. More importantly, he did not want to accept the implications of it if it proved to be true. As he'd pointed out to Toulemont, these buildings housed various agencies of the United States Government, particularly WTC7 which housed both Department of Defense and Central Intelligence Agency offices in New York City. It was difficult to see how such preparation could have been undertaken without the United States Government knowing about it. So if explosives had been used to bring down these three buildings, it seemed reasonable to assume that at least some individuals in some agencies of the United States Government must have been aware of the preparations; that they were complicit in the crime.

Parnell indeed had a hard time getting his head around that particular proposition.

Not usually given to flights of fancy, or prone to accept some of the more bizarre beliefs like UFO sightings, ghosts, spirits, and mythology generally, Parnell's military training and subsequent thirty-four-year career had molded him into a hard-nosed, shrewd and seasoned decision-maker. He had never – never before, that is – seriously had to question his fundamental belief systems. The nano-thermite paper, and particularly Toulemont's effective endorsement of it, challenged all that.

After Gross, Parnell rarely broached the topic with other American officers. It just seemed too bizarre. Showing interest in this type of thing could be a career wrecker, and he knew it. When he did broach the subject, it was always with a trusted confidant and always in circumspect.

But the evidence was compelling.

When he did get around to Googling 'Chute Libre' in conjunction with '9/11', it led him to a twelve-minute video clip about the events of 9/11 that culminated in the bold French pronouncement: "C'est un demolition controlee" – "it was a controlled demolition".

Parnell noted the nano-thermite paper was co-authored by an Australian so he rang his old friend Andy Wilks, who he'd served beside in Afghanistan back in the early 'noughties'. Wilks was now a politician in the Australian Federal Parliament. Parnell remembered their push towards Kandahar with Wilks' 'diggers' on his right; they'd performed well together that day and each had gained much respect for the other. He leaned back in his study chair just as the bugle sounded "Taps". It was 0800 hours in Australia.

He sipped at the Scotch he'd poured a few moments earlier.

"Have they heard about this 'Down Under'?" he asked Wilks.

"Yes," said Wilks. "Some guy sent us all a paper he called *9/11 Research Report, An Australian Perspective* back in 2010. It contained a reference to *Chute Libre* and to numerous other European works, and also works by some prominent American authors. There was also a video documentary by the same American physicist who'd co-authored the nano-thermite paper.

"At that time, the Australian Defence Force was re-equipping its forces with new American gear, so Defence didn't want to upset your people, so members of both houses of the Australian Parliament were briefed by the Australian Security Intelligence Organization not to get involved in the issue ... and to ignore any of their constituents that raised the matter with them.

"If Uncle Sam wasn't prepared to investigate the allegations then we sure as heck weren't going to upset the apple cart," Wilks added, "even if we did lose ten Australian citizens in the 9/11 incident."

Parnell spent much of his spare time the following few months 'doing his homework'. He spoke to Toulemont several times over that period and asked Wilks to dig out a copy of the Aussie perspective paper he'd been instructed to ignore. He read American writers' views on the 9/11 event that Wilks had mentioned and learned that belief in the basic falsehood of the US Government's narrative on 9/11 was widespread throughout the world. Even in America, suspicion about the veracity of the official story was widespread, with one survey reporting over fifty percent of the American people doubted it, or believed the government was hiding something. But no-one amongst the American academy, government, mainstream media, or, what might be loosely called the 'Elite', seemed to have publicly expressed such doubts.

Within a year of meeting Toulemont, Parnell arrived at two main conclusions from his research: The official version of what happened on 9/11 was seriously flawed, and, the 'controlled demolition' hypothesis was a more plausible explanation for the collapse of the three World Trade Center buildings than the 'progressive column failure' hypothesis.

Having arrived at those two conclusions, Parnell was now a worried man. A patriot, Jackson Parnell believed in America and all it stood for. His very calling demanded his dedication to protecting his beloved homeland and its people. But he was not a blind patriot. He could think for himself. He knew there was injustice, suffering, and want in America but was optimistic that most of its shortcomings would be remedied, in time. He had never doubted the core values of his upbringing – not until now, that is. Now he had doubts. Serious doubts.

Empire

Meantime

"Seventeen, eighteen, nineteeeen, twenteeeey."

John Davyd Darcy the Fifth lowered himself to the floor. He reached for the towel and mopped his forehead and under his arms then headed for the shower.

Known to his closest associates as "Fifth", he oozed style; the tanned, impeccably groomed, blue-eyed 67-year-old stood five feet nine and a half inches tall with slight to medium build topped by a full head of straw-colored hair, features that betrayed his Swedish ancestry. Urbane, cultured and self-disciplined, this American aristocrat was faultlessly courteous, fabulously rich, insatiable and relentless. He was supremely confident in almost all situations, feared practically nothing and reveled in command.

On emerging from his morning ablutions, Fifth, dressed in a light grey business suit with a plain, pale-blue shirt, headed to his balcony where a light meal of two boiled eggs, a slice of toast, and a glass of freshly squeezed orange juice awaited him. He ate slowly, glancing over the morning paper with mild interest as he did so. He finished the meal and poured a cup of lukewarm coffee which he sipped as he scanned the financial pages. He smiled to himself. Most of the core stocks of any interest to him were up a few points. No problems there.

On completion of breakfast, he rose, retrieved his coat from the chair opposite, and headed for the private lift that took him directly to his office three floors below. He entered the lavishly appointed room and sat behind the oak desk opposite a large picture window with a panoramic view of the Hudson River. He reached for the inward correspondence that awaited him.

Fifth's status and pedigree arose from the wealth accumulated initially by his great, great, grandfather John Davyd Darcy, who had made his fortune in the early days of the oil industry in America. This was enhanced through diversification into other natural resources like base metals and rare earths and support industries to service those basic extractive industries by his son of the same name. By the time Fifth's grandfather assumed the role of family patriarch, the cash flowed so profusely it became necessary to diversify into the financial industries, so the Darcy family also became bankers, investment managers, and risk managers. By the time Fifth became involved in the management of the family's commercial empire he was faced with a smorgasbord of career opportunities. Fifth had a flair for numbers so he gravitated towards money management and eventually ended up as president of the family's banking business.

A trim, immaculately dressed woman in her mid-thirties entered the room. "Good morning, Mr. Darcy," she said. "Is there anything you need from me at the moment?"

"No, I don't think so," said Fifth. "I believe we have the Mayor at ten but nothing else this morning." Fifth glanced at his gold Rolex: it said '9.05'. Plenty of time to finish his inward mail and make a few notes about tomorrow's board meeting. The secretary nodded, turned, and departed without further comment.

Fifth's role at the head of one of the world's most well-endowed financial institutions resulted in his counsel increasingly being sought by all manner of other ambitious 'wannabes', including a whole raft of aspiring politicians, including mayors. It was not an attention he craved, or even cultivated but, whether he liked it or not, he was in command of significant economic resources and those who wished to have those resources deployed to their particular areas of interest actively sought him out. Fifth absorbed the attention with his usual grace and competence, and he exercised power naturally but, with his innate ability and his privileged upbringing, he exercised it with skill and aplomb.

Fifth sat on the boards of seven other corporations, three of which, as well as the bank, were listed either on the New York Stock Exchange, the London Stock Exchange or both. He chose not to hold the presiding role in any of them but, in every case, the Darcy family held the controlling interest, not necessarily greater than fifty percent of the equity, but sufficient to ensure no other shareholder could dictate policy contrary to Darcy interests. The majority of the remaining shares were held by mutual funds which in turn held the accumulated equity investments of hundreds of thousands of small investors, pension funds, mutual funds, hedge funds and the like, managed by loyal and reliable allies of the Darcy family. In that way, a shareholding of only around fifteen to twenty percent ensured no other shareholder, or potential coalition of shareholders, could effectively challenge Fifth's grip on corporate control.

Fifth glanced over the last of the letters addressed to him personally and placed it at the top of the 'Filing' tray. Nothing needed his attention from that small pile of papers – those that did he had assigned to their respective managers and placed in the 'Out' tray. He reached for his leather-bound notebook and jotted the title 'Fidelity Board Meeting – 25th March' and underlined it. He began his list of agenda items.

The Darcy family's holdings comprised the leading, or at least major, holding in American banking, oil, and gas, defense contracting, mass media, information technology, insurance, and agro-chemical industries. Each of these parent companies also held substantial subsidiary holdings in numerous corporations in similar industries in foreign countries particularly in Great Britain, Germany, and Japan. As a result, Fifth held a high level of influence in the decision-making of over one hundred global corporations and near control of at least fifteen global industry groups. The House of Darcy was the modern-day equivalent of the House of Medici. None of these corporations or groups needed Fifth's direct management. All needed his oversight.

So what did the mayor want this time, he wondered, pausing as he noted down agenda items? *Money undoubtedly*. Fifth sniffed at the thought of the groveling politician. *Of course, money*, he thought. *Why else would he call? But he will pay for it one way or another.*

Fifth needed planning approval for a new real estate development on the Lower East Side, but there was also that Democratic candidate who'd sought his support for the Queens Borough Council. He would, of course, support the homeless appeal, but which reciprocal benefit should he imply would be more welcome? Whichever he chose would have the added bonus that these 'charitable' donations were also a useful tax deduction from whichever corporate vehicle Fifth chose to make his contribution from.

Fifth gave nothing away for free, especially to charity, and rarely left anything to chance. He often worked through non-for-profit organizations which he effectively controlled through initial endowments and ongoing corporate and personal donations. This strategy was not a Darcy family invention. It had been around for centuries. Physical goods, services, money, and influence could be controlled and deployed almost anywhere in the world, where ever he thought they should be deployed, by appointing the 'right people' to the boards of trustees and to the key executive and managerial positions of those charities, not-for-profits, service institutions, and businesses, all of which were beholden in one way or another to him. Fifth liked to win, always, and philanthropy was a time-honored mechanism for doing so.

Fifth's influence did not extend to just business matters. With key holdings in the American and foreign defense industries, he was an influential participant in the National Security lobby in Washington DC and the security institutions of key American allies in London, Berlin, and Tokyo. His influence in American banking also made him a key influencer in such international organizations as the Bank of International Settlements, the International Monetary Fund and the World Trade Organization. The Darcy family's holdings in the Information Technology and Mass Media industries also gave Fifth considerable influence in American politics and the manipulation of American and Western European public opinion.

His role in agrochemicals gave him influence with American agricultural policy and also within the United Nations, particularly in its Food Program. The family's interests made it one of the wealthiest in the world, and its financial structure enabled the capital leveraging of its funds to over fifty times the family's personal fortunes.

"Mr Fernadez," announced the secretary, breaking his attention just as he finished his agenda.

"Ah, Sean," said Fifth as he rose and skirted the desk. "Do come in."

Fifth handed the completed agenda to the secretary, who nodded back then withdrew. Fifth's short notice of his meeting agenda was his usual ploy, designed to keeping meeting participants off balance and in the dark until the last moment. It was just one of his many control techniques.

Turning to the small balding man, he inquired: "Coffee?"

The mayor declined.

"How can I help you, Sean?" said Fifth as he sat back behind the desk.

"Well, Mr. Darcy," said the mayor, "our annual homeless appeal is coming up in a few months and I was wondering if we could rely on your support again this year?"

Fernandez left almost precisely thirty minutes after he'd arrived, his pledge of support from Fifth secured and his assurance that planning approval for the South Side development would not be a problem.

As with all good leaders, Fifth had surrounded himself with able lieutenants and competent staff. Key among them was his deputy and close friend, Prince Gerhardt of the royal house of the

Netherlands, born into the power-wielding classes and presiding over a commercial empire as diverse as that of the Darcy family. It held prominence on the European continent. Gerhardt was a rather shy and retiring person so he preferred to allow someone else to assume the burdens of leadership. In conversation with Fifth, he often opened his sentences with: "You know, John, I was wondering if ..."

Gerhardt was one of the few people who ever referred to Fifth by his real name. He admired Fifth's easy assumption of the leadership role given the American's obvious suitability to it plus the latter's natural charm, ruthlessness, and inherent competence.

Fifth was also well served with talented staff: his two principal servants were Henri and Biggy, descendants of more recent immigrants to the United States. Both spoke English heavily laced with the accents of their ancestral homelands. Both had been accomplished scholars but had been wooed into Fifth's employment through the Global Security Commission, the GSC.

The GSC was Fifth's and Gerhardt's brainchild and creation. There the work was practical and hands-on rather than academic. With Fifth, they were able to do impressive things. Henri wrote the briefs for the 'think tank' inquiries that delved into key geo-political issues and made the recommendations to governments that emanated from them. *With our Guiding Hand* was a common attachment to his advice.

Biggy often input the wisdom into those 'think tanks'; made the recommendations that influenced American and NATO military and defense strategy. He often preceded his contribution with: "With your permission, sir", a habit he'd picked up as junior cadet in the Warsaw military academy in his pre-emigrant youth – he had however never actually attained any significant military rank on either side of the Atlantic.

Other professional researchers and administrators sought to influence those policies too, but Henri's and Biggy's recommendations, backed by Fifth's power, lent an authoritative air that few politicians dared ignore.

Fifth and Prince Gerhardt were not the only members of the elite's peak policy committees. Van Kleist, the Dutchman, also represented a major multinational group, the largest mineral resource company in the world. This company had close ties to the Dutch royal line, although van Kleist was largely on the council because of his natural talent. Fifth could almost relate to him as an intellectual equal, something he could definitely not do with the haughty Englishman, Hardigan, another multinational mining magnate.

"See if van Kleist can join us," he often said to Henri and Biggy whenever some real thinking was needed to resolve a particular resource problem.

Fifth busied himself with a few minor chores until eleven when the large video screen to the right of Fifth's great oak desk sprang into life. An image of Fifth's head and shoulders occupied the top center of the screen. Twenty smaller, irregular-sized squares surrounded it, blank initially, but one by one a head and shoulder image of the other members of the GSC council appeared as they joined the electronic meeting. Gerhardt and van Kleist flanked Fifth with Henri and Biggy to the right and left of them respectively as consultants to the council. Each of the remaining occupants of these images had a similar pedigree to Gerhardt but from amongst the British, Dutch, French, German, Italian, Japanese, Middle Eastern and Latin American elites.

Fifth lavished praise, flattery, and charm, each according to Fifth's own judgment as to what would encourage, motivate or persuade each of them. He also rebuked them when he felt the need but rarely in public and never with a raised voice. One of his favored putdowns was: "Really? Are you quite sure of that?"

The meeting lasted only ten minutes. It was initiated by a motion proposed by Fifth and seconded by Gerhardt.

"You have each received a detailed submission on this proposal," said Fifth. "Are there any questions?"

There were none.

"Do we require further discussion on this motion?" Fifth inquired.

Multiple heads shook in response.

"Fine," said Fifth. "All those in favor?"

All hands rose in the affirmative.

"Those Against?"

There was no dissent.

The motion was promptly followed by a second motion for the matter to now be delegated to the Executive Committee for implementation. Again, agreement was unanimous. Fifth then thanked all for their participation and each member signed off in quick succession.

That was all Fifth really needed: authority to proceed with the venture under consideration. The matter would henceforth be managed by the inner sanctum of the GSC, the real governing clique that drove the elite agenda of the world's leading potentates. It was comprised of just five individuals: Fifth, Gerhardt and van Kleist, ably supported by Henri and Biggy. That's where the real power lay.

Fifth was the undisputed leader of the Global Elite, the essential oligarchy that ran the world and owned most of its wealth. Anyone who was anyone knew of him, feared him and accepted his domination and his rule. Fifth's enemies included anyone who challenged his status, his authority, or his sense of superiority and he ruthlessly destroyed anyone who got in his way. Fifth made sure only he really knew the full picture about anything he considered important. Motivated by a sense of superiority, and a sense of entitlement, his primary goal was to stay on top – at the very top.

But the vast majority of the human race had never heard of him.

Demotion

Later that month

Standing back from the map on the large table that filled a substantial portion of his brigade command tent, Parnell assessed the current situation in 'Exercise Daring Eagle'. His brigade, now fully engaged and moving cautiously, pressed forward to its objectives. So far things were going pretty much as planned. His 'blue' units were arrayed in a rough semi-circle across a flat terrain dotted with the occasional knoll. This higher ground would make a good observation point for forward surveillance if they could be occupied before the 'red' 'enemy' units could capture them. So far only half a dozen red tokens dotted the map but he was certain more would be detected.

"Deploy one company of the 2nd to Hill 57 Alpha to the northeastern slope just below the summit," he ordered. "Get the exact co-ordinates and draft the order for my authorization!"

"Yes, sir," replied the officer standing to his right.

Parnell took a half a step further back; glanced up at the area map on the tent wall. "Send the Chinooks in from the southeast," he added. "There's a marine unit flying in from the southwest with their tiltrotor birds and we don't want to get mixed up with them when our choppers exit."

"Yes, sir," the officer repeated. Parnell heard a low throat-clearing noise off to his right and glanced that way.

"Message from Division, sir," said a young lieutenant, handing him an A4 buff-colored envelope.

Parnell took it and tore it open. He extracted the message form, flicked it open, and scanned its one-line order: "Report to Officer

Commanding 1st Cavalry Division immediately."

"In the middle of an exercise?" he exclaimed aloud.

"Sir?" queried Colonel Gross who stood at the left-hand edge of the map table.

"Take over, XO. I've been ordered back to Division," Parnell said, raising his eyebrows.

As a senior military officer, Parnell was privy to many secrets and the occasional professional intrigue. He had few private ones mainly because his quiet, sober nature reflected his straightlaced protestant upbringing. He did drink alcohol, but only in moderation, and he had never indulged in illicit intoxicants. His professional enemies were those of the United States of America which were now as plentiful as ever. Beyond those he had no personal adversaries save perhaps the odd colonel who thought the star should have gone to him, or her, instead of its current recipient.

Parnell genuinely tried to avoid harming others, which was not always easy given his military duties. Even when called upon to be deceptive, and sometimes even violent, he'd always been measured and careful how he dealt with adversaries. Personally, Parnell hated bullies and his natural inclination was to oppose anyone who sought to cheat, intimidate, rob, or harm innocent people, anywhere, whether for personal greed or in the name of religion, racial purity, political ideology or some other self-proclaimed right. Truth and justice had been drilled into him since birth. These were the qualities that had led to his rise through the ranks to Brigadier General.

The three-star General returned Parnell's salute then motioned him to be seated in front of the divisional commander's desk. The divisional commander was nowhere in sight, just his superior, III Corps Commander Lieutenant General Arnold Cromer.

"I'll come straight to the point, Parnell," the man said. "Your rank is reduced to Lieutenant-Colonel effective immediately." He did not pause or look up to note Parnell's reaction. "The army is offering you a choice of your future career. You can remain in the service, in which case, if you do, you will be court-marshaled on charges of 'conduct to the prejudice of good order and military discipline' and 'bringing the army into disrepute.'"

He paused then added: "… and anything else the Judge Advocate General's office can come up with, I suspect."

Now he looked up to read Parnell's reaction.

Parnell sat poker-faced, stunned. He stared back at the General.

Cromer continued: "Alternatively, you can resign your commission. I have an appropriate document available for you to sign right here." He swiveled a single piece of paper $180°$ on his desk and pushed it in front of Parnell.

"I'm in the middle of an exercise, sir. I've currently got 8,000 personnel under my command."

"You are relieved of that duty, effective immediately!"

Parnell glanced at the single piece of paper then looked the General straight in the eye.

"Without even a hearing?" he said.

"I'm not here to debate this matter with you, Colonel," he said, emphasizing Parnell's new rank. "This option is being offered to you by the Chief of the Army in recognition of your past long service and good conduct."

He paused again. "Before your recent mental illness," he added.

"Regulations state that military personnel should receive a written warning before disciplinary action is taken," said Parnell. "Am I not being given due process?"

"The army is trying to make this as painless as possible … for all concerned," said the General. "It's not your fault that you've fallen into this depressed and paranoid state with all this conspiracy theory nonsense, but it is clear that you are no longer fit for duty."

"It's not usual to demote someone before they are medically discharged," said Parnell.

"You're not being medically discharged. You're being offered retirement with dignity. You do realize that if you are court-marshaled and found guilty you will probably be dishonorably discharged without a pension?"

"Being demoted is hardly retiring with dignity," said Parnell.

"Your rank as Brigadier-General was never substantive," the general reminded him.

"My rank of Colonel is."

"Look, Parnell, you're being offered an easy way out. God knows what's got into your head with all the conspiracy stuff, but the army can't have people like you wandering around raving like that. The case against you is pretty strong. JAG has interviewed dozens of your subordinates, and other people you associate with. You're not going to be able to deny that you've been subverting your subordinates and spreading dissent. The army can't tolerate that sort of behavior. Take my advice and resign. It will be best for everyone, especially you."

"So, I'm being sacked for telling the truth?" said Parnell.

The General stiffened. The kind, fatherly countenance he'd assumed a few moments earlier disappeared from his face. "I'm not here to debate with you on that matter either," he said. "I'm here to offer you a choice … before matters take an irreversible course." He slid a pen across the desk towards Parnell.

Parnell sat silent, then he sighed. He was an experienced enough warrior to know he faced overwhelming odds. He picked up the pen and scrawled his signature at the foot of the page. Then he rose and raised a slow, almost insolent salute to the General. The General returned the salute.

"Dismissed," he said to Parnell with a slight touch of sympathy.

Parnell departed.

Parnell brooded the demise of his thirty-seven-year military career for the remainder of his army service – the three-week disengagement process which led to his entry into civilian life, and for several months thereafter. Slowly, painfully, he accepted the new reality of his life. He understood the army's position – it was to be expected really. His demotion was punishment for his persistent advocacy for a new investigation into the 9/11 event, despite his caution, diplomacy, and careful selection of interlocutors. Obviously, word had finally reached those upstairs. It was an irritation his superiors could not tolerate.

This jarring finale though was a surprise. But he was not naive: there'd been sufficient incidences in his long military career when the need to do his duty had required borderline ethical judgment to fulfill his mission. Any one of these occasions could have been portrayed as unauthorized, even treasonous, particularly if some embarrassing public revelation required a scapegoat to save the careers of the real culprits higher up the command chain.

Parnell was not, by nature, a duplicitous man. He had always known this particular fate could meet almost any senior military officer merely doing his duty. Resign or face a court-martial were not the only choices on offer if he did not refrain from his 9/11 advocacy but they were probably the most likely.

Despite those known hazards, he couldn't ignore the evidence before him, so his option to resign was his best choice. The double demotion, however, had not been expected and added deep insult to his now well-ensconced sense of betrayal. Luckily, he was not without friends.

If Jackson Parnell had an Achilles Heel it was in his social interaction with women. With them, he was nervous, awkward, and even shy. He was not a natural lover but when he met the bright, mischievous Canadian nurse, Elsie Chambers, he fell hopelessly in love with her, and she with him. Their match was inevitable given the skillful wiles of his drinking buddy, Father Andre LeMonte, whose calling had prepared him well for such intrigues.

Parnell had usually lived an orderly well-structured life: he rose early, focused on work tasks, ate regular meals, and retired relatively early. He lived a sober lifestyle. Even on weekends, and whilst on leave, his recreation was outdoorsy but quiet, fairly solitary and reflective. The exception was when he was on deployment when the operational situation dictated the tempo of his life. Beyond his morality, Parnell held no particular religious beliefs and indulged in no outlandish or wild activities.

Parnell had few personal friends, save perhaps LeMonte. The two engaged in long and robust debates about politics and religion whenever the opportunity arose, usually, and this was the exception to sobriety for both of them, fueled and stimulated by pure Scottish malt. In these more relaxed and intimate occasions, Parnell sensed the prelate had moved a considerable distance from the 'turn the other cheek' philosophy of his espoused religion.

"Another?" LeMonte waved the scotch bottle over Parnell's empty glass.

Parnell watched the amber liquid sparkle then slosh into his tumbler. "Steady on, old man." This would be his third for the evening and he was starting to feel a little light-headed. LeMonte moved the bottle in the direction of Chambers' glass but she placed her hand over the top of it. He smiled. The wily old priest had seen many a couple's love develop from polite courtesy to deep involvement during his forty-three-year ministry. He thoroughly approved of what he saw developing between the quiet-spoken early-fifties soldier and the energetic late-thirties nurse even if they did not quite perceive it themselves yet.

Parnell would not have survived this difficult period in his life without either of them. His anguish had intensified the more he thought about Toulemont's 9/11 revelations to him. The success of his career had rested on his dedication to duty but his pursuit of this new cause rested on a deep morality that went to the core of his being. The two had become irreconcilable and the outcome inevitable.

Parnell noticed Andre's tremors had grown noticeably worse since their first meeting. The strain of his calling was starting to take its toll on the older man. The thin pale hands placed the bottle gently on the table. Chambers' eyes met Parnell's across the table. Her face displayed the same concern for the old man's health.

Developments

Rising early, as usual, Fifth underwent his usual light workout. He had breakfast then settled down to four or five hours of focused work. He took a light lunch, an afternoon nap then worked another hour. At 4.00 pm he glanced at the wall clock, placed his personal compact computer on 'rest', leaned back in his great leather chair, and stared at the ceiling.

A minute later Charles James Hardigan, 8th Earl of Monvale, entered the room. The English aristocrat headed a long-established commercial empire almost as diverse as that of the Darcy family interests along with his British establishment colleagues, including the British royal family, especially the reigning monarch King George VII. He had that British upper-class habit of referring to everyone by their surname, except for Fifth, who he respectfully called 'Sir'. One does not address the Head Master by his surname, does one?

"And how was His Majesty today?" Fifth inquired.

"Oh, he was fine, or so he said," replied the supercilious Englishman. "Personally, I don't think he has much of a clue about his situation." Hardigan had little time for the 'King of Great Britain and Northern Ireland and his realms beyond the seas', so the royal waffle went, even though his earldom emanated from that same obsolete social structure. Neither did Fifth.

"And his reaction to our advice?"

Hardigan shuffled his feet; spread his hands in an exasperated fashion.

"Well, just as I said … he just said 'Of course' as though it was initially his idea. He certainly didn't question it or even ask for further details. He thinks issues like this are beneath him. You know, that's the Prime Minister's job, that's how he sees it."

"Oh well done, Charles," said Fifth, his smooth New England accent reflecting a more melodious tempo than the haughty twang of the English aristocratic. "If he really does think it's all his idea then we won't have any trouble from him or his coterie of fawning sycophants. I must say, Charles, your diplomatic skills are unmatched when it comes to selling ideas to people … even kings."

Fifth believed no such thing. He liked intelligent, sophisticated and cultured people. Since he only moved in elite circles, his closest associates were also rich and cultured, though few were close to him, save for his sons, John Darcy the Sixth and Hedley Darcy, and his closest friend, Prince Gerhardt. He detested stupid, vain, or rash people so he hadn't risen when Hardigan had entered. Hardigan was just as vain and moronic as his liege lord but Fifth also knew the aging peer reveled in flattery so he heaped it on in excavator loads whenever the opportunity arose.

Hardigan beamed. "Yes, I don't think we'll get any resistance from that quarter. The king will no doubt tell the Privy Council and they will spread the royal concurrence further afield. He'll also tell the PM at their next meeting – next Tuesday, I think – but I don't think we should rely on this approach to win over the whole cabinet. They haven't much time for the king anyway so we'll need to do the political persuading from another angle to win them over."

"There's no need to worry about that," said Fifth. "We've got several initiatives already on that front. It was the Royal Front I needed your unique talents to address at this point."

Fifth's put-down was subtle, perhaps too subtle for a plodder like Hardigan, but the message that this particular discussion was over seemed to have got through.

"Of course, sir, I'm sure you have," responded Hardigan. The 'Sir' was included in its acknowledgment of the seated man's superiority, but it was not something Hardigan usually did. In the privacy of the GSC, even the truly great and powerful used that title of deference to Fifth, and even Hardigan was not so stupid as to think he was one of those.

Fifth changed the subject. "I'm flying to Nice first thing tomorrow for a quick meeting with Gerhardt. Then I'm joining Faisal on his yacht for dinner while we cruise to Monte Carlo. I'll be back in Zurich the next morning.

'I've asked Henri and Biggy to meet me on Thursday for an update on their progress on *Operation Agro Lord*. Your confirmation from King George will clear the way for the land clearance program for the British Caribbean possessions. I want some clear recommendations to put to Council on the 25th. I don't need you to do anything more specific at this time, but do give some thought to the agenda items for the upcoming Council meeting, items that will need addressing in the short to near term. Is there anything else you need from me at this time?"

The dismissal was polite but clear and Hardigan could see no option other than to withdraw graciously. He did like a little social interaction with his meetings, and perhaps a small taste of Fifth's legendary stock of finest old malt, but it was clear that he was not going to get either on this visit.

"No, I have everything I need for the moment, thank you, sir. I'll see you on the 25th." He didn't wait for a response; simply turned and left the office in the most dignified manner he could muster.

Fifth nodded once and glanced back to the clean crisp piece of paper on the desk in front of him. He started to pen Item 5, adding to the list already on the page. 'Royal ascent obtained,' he wrote, after leaving a considerable space between this new item and the four already listed, enough for several further entries to be inserted.

Hardigan's contribution was useful but not crucial. He would use the newly noted item as a prompt at the next Council meeting to allow Hardigan to recount results of his efforts with the current, if somewhat tenuous king in his own words. Hardigan would, of course, drone on so Fifth would have to cut him off after a couple of minutes. But that would be enough for Hardigan. The English

Aristocracy was a useful resource to the Council so having both the king and his extended network of influence-peddlers strongly supportive of the Council's aims was still valuable even if their grip on political power within the British realms was waning – well, within the English realm anyway. The Scottish and Irish realms and the 'realms beyond the seas' were not so certain these days.

The GSC had largely been Fifth's brainchild from the outset but the idea for its formation had received instant support from the European aristocracy, particularly Gerhardt, and the then king of Spain, Juan Carlos III.

Fifth did not recognize weekends or periodic leave – he was too busy enjoying life doing as he pleased. He mixed business with pleasure seamlessly. Faisal's two-hundred-and-forty-foot luxury motor yacht *Saladin* presented an opportunity to do both. The vessel cleared the harbor mouth the following day just as the sun touched the horizon. Along with his host, Faisal bin Ali bin Saud, Fifth was joined by a small gathering of casually dressed, middle-aged men, two dressed in white flowing Arab robes, the rest in open-necked shirts and loose-fitting European-style slacks. A dozen stunning young women hovered and mingled amongst them, chatting, laughing and playfully flirting with the assemblage. Half an hour after the diesel-powered vessel turned due west, Faisal announced in a slightly raised voice: "Gentlemen …"

All conversation ceased. The women promptly withdrew. The men assembled respectfully in a semi-circle in front of Fifth and Faisal who sat side by side facing the stern of the vessel. And here, Fifth, the de facto Global Emperor, held court.

Structured on classical organizational lines, the GSC comprised nineteen individuals, an odd number to ensure no tied votes. All were appointed by invitation initially, and by two-thirds of existing councilors' votes to secure replacements. There were no set terms for membership. Each councilor served for as long as he, or she, considered they made a valuable contribution and enjoyed the support of the constituency he or she was expected to represent. The exceptions, of course, were the President and Vice President. Experience since the formation of the Council showed that councilors tended to serve for an average of eleven years, although that track record had ranged from seventeen years in one case to four and a half years for one councilor who, unfortunately, had incited considerable criticism from his constituency and had died from a mysterious accident while in office.

Beneath the Council was a salaried executive staff, of which the two most prominent positions were Chief Political Consultant and Chief Strategist. Henri occupied the former position, and Biggy the latter. The Chief Executive Officer (CEO) acted largely as Fifth's private secretary and rarely took initiative without consulting his master first.

Of the ten men standing in front of Fifth and Faisal, three had been participants in the teleconference with Fifth a few days earlier, along with Faisal. The two Arabs were Faisal's subordinates. The other five were subordinates to the three European executive committee members in attendance or delegates to the two remaining European ExCom members who'd been on the call but had been unable to attend this seaborne meeting. Collectively they comprised the Western Europe Regional Strategy Council (except for the Spanish King) and the Arab sub-section of the Further Domains Regional Strategy Council.

This meeting comprised mainly an update on the progress of *Operation Argo Lord*, the GSC global campaign to consolidate its control of global agriculture, and an introduction to the main topics to be covered in the upcoming GSC annual conference.

The briefing, and its attendant question and answer session, concluded at 8.00 pm when the dinner gong sounded. The female escorts re-emerged and the gathering headed to the dining room. After dinner, the guests retired to their leisure, with or without company, as their inclination dictated. Fifth retired unaccompanied at 09.30 pm.

Saladin cruised the Mediterranean Sea throughout the night, scheduled to arrive in Monti Carlo at dawn. Fifth breakfasted in his stateroom; he left the motor vessel at 8.00 am and traveled to the airport where Juan Carlos's private jet transported him to Madrid. There he met with the reigning Spanish monarch. From there, again at Juan Carlos's largesse, he jetted to Zurich for the meeting with Henri, Biggy, and three Swiss banks. Then he flew to New York on his *Learjet 85* which Henri and Biggy had used to arrive in the Swiss city – they would make their way home via commercial flights. From New York's La Guardia airport Fifth was chauffeured to his main residence in a walled two-hundred-acre estate in upstate New York – Fifth only travelled in private vehicles, chauffeured limousines, private jets or luxury yachts.

Once back in his home office he spent the remainder of the day planning a conference scheduled for three months hence, the venue for which was a luxury hotel on the shores of Lake Champlain in upstate New York. Delegates would include the economic potentates of what the Europeans quaintly referred to as the 'Far East' and 'Middle East'.

Fifth retired to a healthy dinner at 7.00 pm, relaxed for an hour and half reading Shakespeare's *Tempest* then made an early retreat. He had neither social functions to attend nor important calls to make, but even if he had, he would not have stayed out beyond midnight. First thing next morning, still in his dressing gown, he peered into the video phone on his study desk. "How many invitees have responded to date?" he asked.

On the other end of his call, Henri replied: "Two hundred and fifty-three, sir."

"Including all the VIPs?"

"Only the German Chancellor is wavering," said Henri.

"Fine. I'll get Ekherd Thyssen to give him a nudge. Is there anyone else I need to prod?"

"No, sir, I think we've got all of the other key players on board."

"Fine. Thank you, Henri." Fifth hung up.

Nominally, the GSC boasted a full membership of around 4,500 individuals, who one distinguished American author in the 21st century had referred to as the 'Superclass', although that particular commentator had put the number closer to 6,000. Not all the 'Superclass' had opted for membership or affiliation to the GSC but a large majority had, as it was in their best interests to do so. It was essential for the stratum of global society that stood at the apex of the global-power-and-wealth pyramid to have such an entity.

It was an ever apparent feature of the human condition on planet Earth that the 'one percent' of the 'one percent' of the 'one percent', or thereabouts – essentially the one in a million individuals on the planet that owned most of the world's wealth and wielded most of the world's economic, political and military power – have some mechanism for global control. These were the modern world's equivalent of the old Roman Patrician Class, and their influence and control were just as pronounced.

Both Henri and Biggy were familiar with this elite group. In the hallowed precincts of the elite colleges where they both had taught, where they had enlightened the privileged few of the student body who were members of the secret societies, that only the offspring of the elite, or the *really* talented recruits from the laity, like the Dutchman van Kleist, were invited to join. Most of the former were already acquainted with the ruling elite by virtue of their birth and upbringing.

"You have to understand," Henri was fond of saying to the newly initiated, "you have been granted a unique opportunity. This fraternity is not something mere money can buy. And you have no particular right to even be considered to become a member of it. This is an ancient order. If you violate its code of conduct, the consequences will be the severest you can imagine. The Order will not tolerate betrayal. Do you understand?"

The 'Superclass' was not a single entity. It would be too dangerous to risk such a structure. Rather, it was an interlinked network of entities operating largely beyond the constraints of governments, except within their respective local jurisdictions – in many cases, its members were the government. Even in those countries that professed to have democratic governments, the influence of their own 'Superclass' dictated much of the political discourse through more subtle yet still influential behind-the-scenes roles through 'think tanks', political patronage, elite schools, universities, and exclusive social clubs.

"Consider yourselves to be lords-in-waiting," Biggy would tell his charges. "Honor the code, maintain the confidences, support your compatriots, and in time you will become one of the overlords. But violate this sacred trust, and, well … let me just say: 'Don't!' and let's leave it at that."

The 'Superclass' had been diverse, disbursed and uncoordinated. Its influence, until recent decades, had largely been centered within national boundaries. Fifth and Gerhardt changed all that. Gerhardt had initiated the co-ordination by bringing together the old European aristocracies, and Fifth had brought the new 'Robber Baron' descendants of the American power elite into the union. The two then initiated the inclusion of the new Far East potentates and the ruling elites of the Middle East oil sheikdoms, plus the new potentates in the newly independent African states, and the old ruling families of Latin America. Not all had joined, of course, but enough to ensure that Fifth's new global organization was without peer in terms of economic power and political influence.

"Ja, Herr Darcy," reported Thyssen. "The Chancellor will be able to attend."

"Good," said Fifth. "Guten Abend." Fifth's German was fluent but not native sounding. But then, there was not much more that needed to be said.

Not much was asked of the bulk of the membership of the 'Superclass', this 'rich persons' union'. Although many members were 'self-made', often by other than strictly legal means, there was also a large number who'd inherited their wealth. Many of them were not sufficiently talented to contribute effectively to the rarely mentioned cause – and certainly never in public – of actually running the world. That last-mentioned task fell only to those considered most suitable for such a vital task.

Considered most suitable by whom? Why to Fifth, Gerhardt, and the GSC Council, of course. Why else does one found an organization if not to do what you want it to do? Both Fifth and Gerhardt were billionaires in their own right and they each wielded significant influence.

But both Henri and Biggy, as eminent educators, knew a pertinent fact they did not share with their youthful protégés: local power is far from being global power, and to get global power you needed to marshal the global power brokers into a coherent force. That meant you had to create a coterie of very talented individuals to work with you, not just rich people but truly talented people, people who had proven they could get really difficult things done in really difficult circumstances. Often those types of people did not have the time or the inclination to simply focus on making money. They had been focusing instead on running the world or an important part of it.

So the 'Superclass', or the 'Global Patrician Class', or 'the global elite' – call it what you will – did not just comprise billionaires. It also comprised others of significant influence, people who had proven they could get things done, really talented people. And that was the gene pool from which Fifth and Gerhardt drew the members of the GSC Council – well, those who saw things their way. Dissenters, do-gooders and idealists need not apply.

Fifth, Gerhardt and Hardigan were part of the 'Superclass' by virtue of their wealth. Henri, Biggy and van Kleist were part of this elite group by virtue of their talent. And also, because they were of like-mind to their overlords.

Political Campaign

General Frazer entered the ground floor lounge of the hunting lodge precisely at 20:30 hours Western Standard Time, exactly as Fifth had ordered him to do. Forty years of military service had taught him that being precisely on time was a good way to reduce the range of contingencies that could disrupt any military operation. Even his current exalted rank, with four stars on each shoulder, and as Chairman of the Joint Chiefs of Staff for the United States Armed Forces, his iron self-discipline did not permit him a more lax regime since the biggest critic of his traits was himself. It was important to set the best example possible if one expected his subordinates to aspire to the same high standards he encouraged.

Fifth, of course, would not have been so demanding. He would have referred to the encounter as an invitation rather than an order. He would have allowed a little latitude to a man of Frazer's rank, overtly at least. But he would have mentally noted any laxity. If it had occurred too frequently he would have subtly made sure such indiscretions were not appreciated by him. Frazer knew that, and he was determined not to afford Fifth any reason to detract from his view of him as a loyal and dependable servant.

That was important at this particular point in Frazer's career. He'd gone as far as he could go in his role as a military officer. The four stars on each shoulder attested that he could not be awarded a higher military rank than he currently held. The next promotion for Frazer had to be a political rank, not a military one.

But Fifth was not the President of the United States of America so he could not offer such an appointment, not directly anyway. All Fifth could do was to suggest to the President that he should appoint Frazer to such positions. And if Fifth should make such a suggestion, the President would agree. If he did not, Fifth would make sure the President did not stay the president for very much longer. Anyone who knew anything about the power structure of the United States of America knew that, even if the general public did not.

So Frazer was keen not to keep his host waiting even for a second. He was not sure what his next post would be although he was reasonably sure it would be some sort of promotion. He'd been a loyal and dependable servant up until now. He could not see any reason for him to have been summoned to be disciplined, admonished, or criticized.

"Ah, General," beamed Fifth as the medal-bedecked officer entered. "Thank you for coming."

"My pleasure, sir," said Frazer.

Like most military people, he referred to most senior civilians as "Sir" because often he did not know the person's actual rank. But in Fifth's case, the "Sir" really did denote deference because the latter practically held Frazer's life, his career anyway, in his hands.

"Take a seat."

Fifth motioned to a large, plush, padded armchair angled towards the glowing fireplace in the center of the room's stone feature wall; he waited politely for his guest to sit before seating himself. Fifth stared into the fire and spoke quietly.

"General, you may be aware that you are held in the highest regard by many of the leading citizens of this country, both for your unswerving loyalty and dedication to your military duties and to the inspiration you bring to your military subordinates. Many of us feel that you are a leader not only in the military but of the people as well."

Frazer remained silent but noted Fifth had not taken his gaze from the fire. He was well aware that the aristocrat didn't like to be interrupted and clamped his lips together. Fifth continued:

"You have been at your current post for almost three years which is the usual term of office for that particular appointment.

Retirement usually follows, often with a tour on the speaking circuit or a board appointment to one of the firms in the defense industries."

Fifth continued to stare at the fire as he spoke. Frazer continued his silence.

"But some of us think you have a great capacity to continue to serve your country and your relative youth and obvious health suggest you would be well capable of doing so."

Fifth shifted his gaze from the glowing embers and fixed them on Frazer.

"Would you like to continue serving your country after your current term of military service comes to an end?" he inquired.

Frazer's heart leaped but he summonsed his composure and tried to appear relaxed and non-assuming. He turned towards Fifth.

"Well, sir, it's always been my privilege to serve this great country in any way I can and I would want to enjoy that privilege as long as I can."

"I thought so," said Fifth. "General," he said, "I will not beat around the bush. We, that is the council of which I am a member, you know the one, would like to see you nominated as the next Republican candidate for the post of President of the United States of America. Do you think you would be interested in such a role?"

Frazer visibly gasped. He had not intended to, of course, but he had no idea that he might have been in the running for such a promotion. He had actually hoped for Director of the Central Intelligence Agency. This offer took his breath away.

"I'm sorry, General," crooned Fifth. "I should have appreciated that a modest man like yourself would not have aspired to such a sudden elevation. I must stress though, that many of us believe that is highly appropriate given your exemplary record to date. Please, let us not speak of it further for the moment. You will want some time to think about this and I'm sure you'll want to discuss the prospect with your wife at least. Although, I would ask you to be very discrete about it for the time being."

Frazer had recovered his composure by now. "Yes," he said, trying not to be too enthusiastic. "I would like to run it by Teresa first. A soldier's wife is a difficult duty. She may have been looking forward to us having more time together."

"Yes, of course," said Fifth and quickly changed the subject. "Have you tried Guido's Chateaux Burgonet before? It's excellent. He sends me a case every now and then. Can I tempt you?"

"Oh, thank you, sir," murmured the now preoccupied Frazer. His mind was racing, and there was no doubt what his answer would be. But he knew when he had been dismissed and he also knew that he would need to be patient until Fifth broached the subject again before he could convey his acceptance.

Four days later Fifth was in New York where he presided over a meeting of the Political Affairs Committee of the North American Regional Strategy Council. The only item on the agenda for the meeting was the Democrat nomination for the upcoming presidential election. The favored candidates had been narrowed down to Senator Harland K. Chadwick, the senior senator from Vermont, former Governor Alison R. Kermit from Iowa and long-standing Democrat public favorite, former Oregon governor Emmitt Vandenberg II. Henri favored Chadwick and normally his recommendation would have been enough for Fifth. But Fifth was keen to ensure it at least appeared as though there had been a serious consideration of all key potential contenders. He sought the view of the senior senator for New York, Rogan Kranz, who was also a senate majority leader. He recommended Chadwick.

"Why Chadwick?" said Fifth.

Henri was about to take the cue when Marcus Lowery, the House majority leader, beat him to it. "Because he owes us big time," he blurted out.

"You could say that for any one of them," said Fifth. "In fact, you could say that for most of the Senate and the vast majority of the House, and most of the State Governors. Most senior public office holders are significantly indebted to us. Few of them would have been elected without our support. I think we need something a little more definitive than that."

Fifth's soft-spoken reasoning silenced most of the remaining opinion around the table so Henri now stepped in with his justification.

"I think, sir," he said respectfully, "it's because Chadwick is the most credible of the group. He is well respected by most of the senior Democrats and by the leading lights of the Left generally. His stint as Chair of the Senate Foreign Relations Committee puts him in good stead with the 'thinking' classes and he also has good standing with business leaders which makes him a believable advocate in the business and economic portfolios where the Republicans have strength.

"Vandenberg has strong support from among the blue-collar voters and the unions but their support has been largely neutralized over recent decades. He's also seen as being somewhat of a buffoon by the mainstream and the swinging voters. I don't think he could survive the primaries even with our help.

"Kermit is seen as credible on the East coast but he's seen as a snob, an 'Intellectual Lefty' and as being totally remote from the day-to-day experiences of the Democratic base. If we choose him it will look as though the Democrats are actually trying to lose the election."

"Couldn't he be bolstered with a Southern or Western heavyweight as his vice-president?" asked Wendell Harriman, White House Chief of Staff.

Fifth noted the bemused expressions of the four other New England senior senators and twelve senior House representatives seated around the table. He sensed their thinking, being: 'No doubt he has himself in mind for that spot'.

"Better to go with a strong candidate from the get-go," said Henri. "We have to make this race look real."

Discussion ensued for a further half-hour or so before petering out into an awkward silence. Fifth sensed its finality.

"Any more thoughts?" he inquired rather needlessly. A few murmurs ensued, a few heads shook, but mostly it was just more silence.

"Fine," said Fifth. "Let's vote. Those for Chadwick?"

Nine hands immediately rose in support of the Senator's candidacy. Three more rose within seconds of the initial showing in support. That constituted a majority in favor of the Vermont plutocrat and stimulated the remaining uncommitted voters to join the acclamation to make the vote unanimous. Henri, as a mere consultant, did not vote. Neither did Fifth. As chair, such a gesture would have been demeaning. He liked to give the impression of being inclusive and tolerant and his polished meeting technique usually resulted in unanimous decisions. He was a natural leader.

"It looks like Chadwick then," affirmed Fifth. "Thank you for your time and consideration, Ladies and Gentlemen." And with that the meeting ended.

Back in his office two hours later Fifth reached into the side draw of his opulent desk and retrieved his leather-bound notebook. He turned to the page marked "GSC Agenda". Under the fifth item on the list, in the space he had left between it and the item which Hardigan would address, he wrote:

"2028 US Presidential Elections: Frazer vs Chadwick."

With such a well-organized and disciplined structure in place, Frazer's movement into the White House was not difficult to achieve given the wealth, power and influence that the GSC had wielded over both the congress and the presidency for most of the last hundred years. With his unblemished military record the four-star general was a natural choice as Republican candidate for the 2028 presidential elections. The sexual morality and unrestrained corruption of his carefully chosen Democrat opponent made for easy prey amongst scandalmongers and journalistic embellishers who feasted off the spectacle. This stymied any serious opposition from the outset.

"It is now my very great privilege to introduce to you a man of impeccable record of service to this great nation, a born leader, a courageous warrior, and the next president of the United States of America, General Thomas Bedford Frazer," the Republican Party leader spruced at the launch of the old soldier's campaign.

As it transpired, Frazer won in a landslide. He was the man Fifth wanted in the job so anyone who had known anything about how the American political system worked would have known that before the campaign even began. Fortunately, most Americans did not. What followed was twelve months of theater designed to entertain the masses.

The installation of Sixth as his Secretary of State was also a mere formality with the incoming president making vague claims about his chosen candidate's suitability for office given his long service to the Council on Foreign Relations. Anyone with any real knowledge of those relations knew this was nothing more than deputizing for his father.

The rapid advancement of Colonel Hedley Darcy to the rank of Lieutenant General, although apparently achieved in unseemly haste, was justified by a few imperial and presidential honors from grateful allies around the globe in recognition of his invaluable services to 'collective defense'. Some of the details of those activities had been divulged to the Senate Armed Services Committee to secure its recommendation to the full senate for approval of his promotion, but it had not been considered prudent to disclose 'further details' for 'national security' reasons.

That the new president had previously been a key member of the GSC's inner sanctum was seen by most GSC members as a plus for the institution, but those with a little deeper understanding of the ways of the organization really saw the hand of Fifth behind it. Having an American Secretary of State in the membership was also seen as a plus, although it smacked of nepotism. Lieutenant General Darcy's involvement did not affect the conduct of the council's affairs in any policy sense since he was officially a serving officer of the American Armed Forces and hence directly accountable to their Commander-in-Chief, President Frazer. But the family connection between Fifth, the Secretary of State, and the North American Theater Commander of the most powerful military force on the planet did not go unnoticed by those who really understood the real power structure of Western Civilization.

In terms of self-interest, the new arrangements were not entirely unwelcome, even by those who had effectively been bypassed. Gerhardt and George were both facing growing unrest from their domestic populations, with particular angst directed against the monarchy in their respective countries. There was heavy pressure within their respective countries to reduce defense spending to help relieve the burdens on their restless populations.

"Yes, I know it's American dominated," Prince Gerhardt confided in King George. "But your military forces are no longer up to enforcing global order any more than mine are."

"Britain is still a significant force in the world," protested George.

"Yes, yes, I know," soothed Gerhardt, "but not to the extent that it used to be. Only the Americans have the clout to sustain the global order and we both know it. Let's face it, George, we're lucky to have them. The day they stop running the world will be the day we can all take early retirement."

Van Kleist, and the global mining conglomerate he led, was also well aware of the realities of the situation. The two monarchs were large shareholders in his company. He was the public face of their investments. He was facing increased resistance from nationalistic reactionaries in its world-wide host constituencies, whose territories it had systematically plundered for centuries. Having the world's most powerful military force under the direct control of GSC powerbrokers was no bad thing for any of them, and he knew it.

"I can spare you a battalion," King George had told him, "but you'll have to get the host governments to approve their deployment on their sovereign territories. They're all independent now, you know. They don't take much notice of me these days."

"I can probably designate a Special Forces Company as a personal bodyguard to your senior managers if the host government will permit that," Gerhardt had said. 'They took even less notice of Dutch royalty 'these days' too.'

Van Kleist needed much more than that. His operations spanned the world.

American companies spanned the world also. They were not short of military protection in most areas where that operated. They were not short of diplomatic cover either, not with Sixth in charge of that portfolio. That was very useful to them.

"It's alright for you," George had complained to Frazer. "You can deploy whole armies almost anywhere you want."

"True," Frazer had mused. But even he knew he did not have the ultimate power at his command. Fifth held that. Fifth controlled the global money supply, or most of it anyway. And Frazer also knew 'The Golden Rule': "He who has the gold, rules."

Rule of Law

Gary Knight's self-adopted role was that of a coordinator of national gatherings, a producer of political literature and livery supporting dissident and protester activity, with a distinctive non-violent overtone to a whole suite of grassroots political movements including the 9/11 Truth Movement.

Knight was a busy man and a much-traveled one. He traversed the continent each month, darting from one small group meeting to another to espouse the cause and coordinate activities. He used electronic media profusely but always in a non-threatening, almost passive, way. What criticisms he did voice via those mediums were always subtle, suggestive, even comic, so as not to attract undue attention from regime's spooks and overseers. In private, he was much more animated and assertive, but never threatening or aggressive. He was a quiet-spoken but powerful orator. His arguments seemed to have a natural, common-sense quality to them. Knight would have been a natural and charismatic political leader in any society where free and fair elections were the order of the day. But at that particular time, neither the United States of America nor Canada was such a society.

The fifty-nine-year-old divorcee was a native of Oakland, California. At just over five feet nine inches tall, this brown-haired, tanned-faced, high-browed man of symmetric Caucasian features was rarely short of female companionship. Indeed, his charisma was the main reason for the failure of his seven-year-long marriage to his plain-looking spouse who simply could not compete with the competition for his attention.

He graduated from UC Berkley with a Bachelor degree majoring in Graphic Design. But graphic design was not the topic of his discussion with Jackson Parnell on this particular day. It was law.

"Plaintiffs thus lack standing to bring their claims and the proper disposition is dismissal under Rule 12(b)(1)." Knight paused and looked up at Parnell's perplexed face.

"What does that mean?" asked Parnell.

"It means that the court does not believe the plaintiffs have the legal standing to bring this case into this court."

"Why not?" queried Parnell again.

"Well," said Knight, "according to this ruling, the Government's Motion to Dismiss revolves around whether the plaintiffs have suffered an injury just because the defendants have not provided the information they wanted to be reported to the congress. Also, the judge says that the plaintiffs lack standing because they have not suffered any 'reputational' or 'financial' injury – either one was the other leg the plaintiffs were relying on in support of their Opposition to the Motion to Dismiss. See, it says so here under section II of the ruling: 'This case involves informational standing and organizational standing'. So the judge threw the whole case out of court."

"Can he do that?"

"He most certainly can, and what's more, that's exactly what he did."

"But is there no appeal to that ruling? I mean, this is just one judge. Can he really throw out a whole case without even considering the evidence that is presented to the court?"

"Well, you can appeal," said Knight, "and that's exactly what the plaintiffs did. But the appeal court dismissed the appeal, which effectively says that the judge was right in his judgment. You could go even higher in the appeals process, to the Supreme Court, but you can only do that if the Supreme Court agrees to hear the appeal. And, in this case, it declined to do so. So that was the end of the matter for this particular case."

"But the evidence is overwhelming," protested Parnell. "How can a court just ignore all that evidence?"

"Well, in every case, to prosecute your case in a court of law you have to follow the rules of the court. In this instance, it was the Rules of Civil Procedure that had to be followed. One of those rules is that, if you are the plaintiff, the one bringing to legal action, you have to prove that you have the legal right to sue in that court, that you have what the court calls 'standing'. In this case, the defendants, essentially the government, proved to the court's satisfaction that the plaintiffs did not have standing. So the judge threw the whole case out without even hearing the evidence."

"But the evidence is as clear as day," said Parnell. "A blind man could see how clear the case is. How can a court ignore it just because some minor rule or technicality has been overlooked?"

"The court only sees the evidence that is placed before it," explained Knight. "If the judge says you've got no right to be in his or her court you are not allowed to place any evidence before him or her. End of story."

"And they call this justice?"

"No," said Knight. "They call this 'Law'."

"It's just not fair," insisted Parnell. "Is there no room for fairness in the judicial system?"

"Well," said Knight, "I'm no lawyer, but most lawyers would say that it tries to be. As best as I can understand it, it's a very formal process. Failing on any procedural step can sink your whole case. And that's what lawyers try to do, particularly defense lawyers. Their job is to get the case against their clients thrown out of court as quickly as possible. In civil cases it's up to the plaintiff, the one suing, to show they have the right to even be in court. If they fail to do that to the judge's satisfaction, the case gets thrown out even before it's heard in court."

"But the evidence clearly shows the government's story is wrong," said Parnell, throwing his hands in the air. "And since we're talking about a mass murder here, isn't the court even interested in looking at that evidence?"

"I'm afraid not," said Knight. "It doesn't help you much if the case gets dismissed before the evidence is heard. You don't even get to present your evidence to the court. Besides, this was a civil case, not a criminal one, so the standard of proof required is much lower, 'on the balance of probabilities' rather than 'beyond reasonable doubt', which is the criminal standard of proof required. Basically, it comes down to … who does the judge believe?"

"So, it all comes down to the judge's opinion?" queried Parnell incredulously.

"Yep."

"But it's a mass murder!" Parnell protested again.

"Murder is a criminal offense. To get that into court you need an indictment from a Grand Jury; Fifth Amendment rights and all that stuff."

"Couldn't they get that?"

"Not in this case. But they did try that in another suit around the same time … in the District Court for the Southern District of New York. It got thrown out on a technicality as well. And its appeal failed too. The government just does not want this issue aired in a court of law."

"But that's not justice!"

"I didn't say it was," said Knight. "As I said, it's 'L-A-W, Law'. And if you're going to have the Rule of Law then you have to follow the rules of the courts that administer the law. The job of the defendants' lawyers is to use those rules to get the case thrown out even before it's heard. And the government of the United States of America effectively has an unlimited budget. It can hire the best lawyers available anywhere. And that's what they do. You're up against the best of the best. In any case, you can't sue the Government unless the government agrees to be sued. And if they don't, we're completely stymied."

"What?" Parnell's frown deepened.

"Yep," said Knight, "it's called 'Sovereign Immunity'. You can't sue the government unless it agrees to be sued."

"I thought they passed legislation to nullify that,' said Parnell.

"Jester, or something like that."

"JASTA," corrected Knight. "Justice Against Sponsors of Terrorism Act, 2016. But that only applies to foreign governments. It does not apply to the United States Government. To sue it you still need to get its permission to sue."

"So how do you go about actually getting justice in this country?"

"Well …" said Knight, spreading his hands, palms up, "… you just have to hope that you get an honest judge to hear your case initially, one that can see the big picture and doesn't just focus on the technicalities of law. Then you have to find another group of honest judges to hear the appeal if you do win your case – the government is bound to appeal the judgment if they don't agree with it! And you have to achieve that in a system in which the government, via the Department of Justice, appoints the judges to hear the case."

"That's one rigged system!" said Parnell, shaking his head.

"Hmmm," Knight shrugged and nodded subtly. "You're not the only person to come to that conclusion. And this is not the first time this has happened in the 9/11 saga. There was the case of Rodriguez vs Bush in the early 'noughties' and the case of Gallop vs Chaney in the late 'noughties' – they suffered the same fate. Then there were the 96 cases of victims' families that did not accept the Bush Administration's 'bribe', err, sorry, 'compensation', after 9/11 – they all got settled out of court with 'gag orders', err … sorry again … 'confidentiality clauses' in their settlements. And, of course, those families that did accept Bush's 'compensation' also had to sign 'confidentiality clauses' in their settlements.

"As I said, the government just does not want any of this evidence seeing the inside of a courtroom."

"What you're saying," Parnell clarified poignantly, "is there is no such thing as 'justice' in this country."

"Not as far as the government is concerned," Knight confirmed. "Why do you think I do what I do? It would be nice to believe we can rely on the Rule of Law to gain justice for the victims' families of the 9/11 murders but to date, our experience hasn't been too encouraging. We need to get much more proactive than just filing lawsuits that will fail. Oh, I do agree they have to try," he added quickly, "but I'm not optimistic on the legal front given past experience."

"You're not suggesting we resort to some sort of military-type action, are you?" Parnell sounded apprehensive.

"Hell no!" said Knight. "But we do have a vast array of non-violent actions we can take to put pressure on the government to do something about the 9/11 issue. Gene Sharp lists nearly two hundred of them in his book *The Politics of Non-Violent Action*; — actually, many of them are just variations on a theme, but there are at least twenty or thirty specific types of political action you can take."

"Like what?"

"Oh, you know … strikes, boycotts, name and shame campaigns, ridicule … that sort of thing. All of them need to be adapted to each particular situation, location, target audience, etc., but there are lots of things you can do if you can get enough people fired up about an issue."

"Political action?" confirmed Parnell.

"Yes," said Knight, nodding. "Not passive but definitely not violent."

Parnell stared intently at the peace activist, then past him to the wallpapered wall behind him. He was starting to get the slightest whiff of optimism after the scary sense of betrayal his encounter with Toulemont had stimulated a few years earlier. Perhaps there was hope after all?

Knight was not a lawyer, as he had clearly stated, but in the thirty years after the tragic events of that awful 2001 September day, he had dedicated most of his waking moments to the 9/11 Truth cause. Few people knew more about it than he did. Parnell knew that much about him.

American Gandhi

Elsie Chambers had always believed in non-violence. Her professional calling had always emphasized healing over harm and she had done her best over many decades to bring relief to the suffering and hope to the despairing. Her work with the United Nations had taken her to many foreign parts including many war zones like Afghanistan, Iraq, the Philippines, and Taiwan. There she had seen the results of war firsthand. She was therefore not about to embark on any activity likely to cause destruction and privation on the people of North America.

By the third decade of the 21st century, it had become apparent to her and her colleagues something had to be done about the increasingly corrupt regime ensconced in Washington, and its equally obnoxious puppet in Ottawa. Her stance and demeanor were for an active campaign involving a suite of non-violent civil disobedience activities. These would, she hoped, result in both regimes seeing the seriousness of their undemocratic tendencies. Her involvement with the Alberta tar sands protests had already sensitized her to the need for grassroots action to protect the environmental landscape of Western Canada. Her sympathy for the heritage of the indigenous First Nations people was genuine. She had supported their cause between bouts of service further afield in Asia and the Pacific, both with the Canadian Army and the United Nations. In many ways, she found their situation similar to those of the dispossessed peoples in Thailand, Afghanistan, Taiwan, and Australia. Her role with those communities had been as a healer and comforter trying to pick up the pieces after more powerful forces had steamrolled over their ancestral lands. But over those decades she had never had to assume the role of a political leader or a master strategist.

That was about to change. Now she could see that unless something was done to curb the rapacious President Frazer, his regime and its plutocratic backers, the majority of the peoples of her beloved Canada, and its southern neighbor, would become an impoverished peasantry like the poorer disenfranchised minorities she had encountered overseas.

If it's going to be, it's up to me. The quiet refrain played over and over in her mind. *What are you going to do about it?* her conscience nagged.

It's not your job to save Canada, nor America, her darker alter ego challenged. *You've got no experience in political leadership. You're not qualified to do the job. Who do you think you are, anyway?*

On the other hand: *If not you, then who?*

She had given much thought to that question in recent years. Despite her best efforts, however, she hadn't been able to come up with a suitable candidate for the savior of the North American people, no-one that seemed interested in the role anyway. And as she thought about it, another little refrain began to sneak into her consciousness. It said: *If you see the need, then you're elected.*

But she didn't want to be elected. She wasn't even running for office. She wasn't the right person!

Or was she?

Of course not; what a silly suggestion.

Or was it? If not her, then who? *Yes, who?*

The voices wouldn't go away. They persisted. They wore her down. Until she finally realized the truth of their message: *No-one else is going to, so, if you don't, nothing will happen.*

Then she remembered LeMonte and the wisdom of his council over the years. She tracked him down and, in Vancouver in the spring of 2032, they caught up with one another, 'for a cup of coffee'. LeMonte reminded her of Parnell, who, he said, was in need of a little moral support over his unjust treatment at the hands of the Army. LeMonte suggested they get reacquainted, 'for old times' sake'. The wily old fox did not tell her what he really thought, that this was a match made in heaven if ever there was one.

Chambers and Parnell met in Seattle a month later. The encounter kindled a spark in both of them and their courtship began in earnest.

To Chamber's surprise, she was not as incompetent as a revolutionary as she had first believed. She had not studied the subject of revolutionary change in any formal way, but her experience in North America and throughout the world had brought her into contact with a wide range of cultures, each with their own myths, legends, stories, and histories. Many of those narratives recounted the feats of seemingly insignificant people who had seen the need for change and had found no-one in their time or location willing or able to bring about that change. So they had taken it upon themselves to assume the role of change agent, some consciously, some unconsciously, some willingly but most unwillingly, some by design but most by default or act of circumstance. She recalled Spartacus, Robin Hood, William Tell, George Washington, Ernesto 'Ché' Guevara, Mao Tse Tung, and Hồ Chí Minh. And there were more, all people from humble beginnings who had risen to lead their peoples, or, at least they had tried. And not just men, Boudicca, queen of the Britons, led the revolt against the Roman invaders of her native Britain; Joan of Arc, the French peasant had led her country-folk against the English; Margaret Thatcher, the grocer's daughter, had pulled Britain out of its downward spiral; and Golda Meir of Israel who led her people through perilous times. No, you didn't need to be a man to be a leader.

But of all of the world-wide historical figures that could be a source of inspiration Chambers all-time favorite was Mohandas K. Gandhi of India. The little man, dressed only in a loincloth, quiet-spoken, humble, modest, and defiant, was the man who had taken on the might of the British Empire and had won freedom for his people. That's who Chambers *really* admired.

What a man? she marveled. She particularly liked his statement: "There are many causes for which I am prepared to die but there is no cause for which I am prepared to kill."

Gandhi had achieved his political aims without violence. He had achieved them mainly by inspiring his people, all two hundred and seventy-seven million of them, to just say "No". And when they did that, the 100,000 Englishmen who had ruled their country for centuries became impotent. Despite their enormous military power, they had been unable to coerce the masses into obeying them. And when they realized their impotence, they also realized they had no alternative than to just pack up and leave.

Could Chamber's inspire the Canadian people to do that; to just say "No"? Like Parnell had said "No" to his military superiors? Like she was now saying "No" to her government in Ottawa? If they did, would Frazer and his gang of fascists also just pack up and leave? Or would they dig in and fight? Would they get brutal? Would they behave like an Adolf Hitler or a Joseph Stalin? Would they round up dissenters and send them off to concentration camps? Would they murder people, her people, by the wagonload? And if they did, what would that make Chambers if she had inspired the uprising in the first place – a hero, or the instigator of a holocaust?

Never mind *could* she do it? What about *should* she do it?

The quiet-spoken former American soldier who increasingly occupied her thoughts helped her decide even if he had not been aware of it. The way he spoke, the way he reasoned, the way he agonized and grappled with his inner demons, his quiet courage, and unassuming manner, they had all influenced her decision even though they had never actually reached finality in their discussions on the subject. So, in the end, she just decided: *I'd better just get on and do it.*

Chambers was not a scholar in the classical sense, but she was well-read as a result of long hours spent in obscure locations in lands where television was rare. She had habitually worked from dawn till dusk while on deployment but there were also moments of rest and retreat when a good book was as good a respite as any. She hadn't formally studied philosophy, politics, religion, or the classics. She had not even formally studied Gandhi's writings on nonviolent resistance, although she had become aware of his main philosophies through her casual reading. What she had read only increased her admiration of the man.

She had also become aware of throughout her life the popular accounts of some of the protest movements that had been influential in North America over the past several hundred years – movements like the Populists and the "Wobblies" in the nineteenth century, the Vietnam War protesters, the civil rights movement and the feminist movements in the twentieth, and the gay rights movement and the Occupy Movement of the early twenty-first century. So, when she sat down and thought about it, several of the non-violent options seemed to offer promise.

Chambers felt that civil disobedience and similar disruptive types of activities were a good start. They could render the process of government sufficiently ineffective to force the government to sit down with the people's representatives and discuss the re-introduction of normal democratic processes. They were all active measures but they should, if carried out calmly and deliberately, not incur any physical damage to property or physical injury to anyone.

"What do you think about Sharp's tactics?" she asked Parnell.

"I think there are a few things there we could use," said Parnell. "I think we need to take some action and soon, because if we don't take the initiative, some radical will, and you never know where that might lead."

Parnell waved his hand in the direction of the informal library he had accumulated over recent years. It contained Sharp's classic but it also featured his other more *kinetic* type texts, Ché, Mao and the other revolutionary writers. "We don't want anyone running around shooting people or throwing bombs, do we? I mean, God knows, we've got enough crazy people who are armed to the teeth now. We have to show the people they are not powerless, that they can do something without resorting to violence."

Chambers also discovered the writings of Saul Alinsky who had espoused a series of *Rules for Radicals* in a book of the same name. The early nineteenth-century American activist had set down a dozen or so of them and Chambers noted them down in bullet point form as best she could remember them:

1. Persuade the opponent that you were stronger than was really the case.
2. Stay close to the comfort zone of your own people.
3. Go outside the comfort zone of your opponent to "cause confusion, fear, and retreat."
4. Use your opponents' own rulebook against them.
5. Use ridicule – "man's most potent weapon" – because it is hard to counterattack and infuriates the opposition.
6. A good tactic is one your people enjoy.
7. A bad tactic is one that is not fun because it drags on and becomes hard to sustain.
8. Keep the pressure on your opponent.
9. Threats can be more terrifying than reality.
10. Pick the target, freeze it, personalize it, and polarize it
11. Have a constructive alternative – an answer to the question, "Okay, what would you do?"
12. Maybe a couple more, she could not remember.

Chambers liked the look of these. They did not involve any violent actions but could prove devastating if applied sensibly. Parnell agreed. She then set about planning their implementation.

"You could try a Gandhi-type 'salt march'," Parnell suggested.

"Marching from where to where?" said Chambers.

"Oh, I don't know," said Parnell. "Ottawa to the Saint Lawrence River?"

"In what cause?" said Chambers. "In support of what specific issue?"

"Hmm," said Parnell. "What about something else, a rent strike maybe?"

"Possibly," said Chambers.

"Alternatively, what about a protest against American intellectual property laws being applied to favor established industries and stymying new innovative Canadian start-ups? Or, perhaps, create a 'sit-in' of parliament calling for an investigation into any alleged Canadian State Crimes against Democracy?"

And so their deliberations went. There was a lot to think about.

Protest

Initially, Chamber's non-violent protest campaign was targeted at the Canadian Government but American sympathizers quickly took up the idea and, within a few months of the Canadian launch, dozens of similar dissident cells had sprung up all around the southern republic. So too did like-minded activist in other Western countries, particularly those that took their lead in social trends from American trends. Within six months a handful of sympathizers across the Atlantic were emulating their North American counterparts and, within a further few months, campuses, unions and activist groups were popping up across the South American continent, East and South East Asia, Southern Africa and Australasia. Within two years after the initial Montreal rent strike, enthusiastically initiated by the students of McGill University, the dissident non-violent movement, in all its diversity, had spread to upwards of fifteen countries with a hundred different variations.

The non-violent protests, however, met with mixed results. On the one hand, Chambers certainly brought to the attention of the Frazer regime and its Canadian puppet that a large minority of the American and Canadian people were not happy with the status quo. On the other hand, her program highlighted, in stark relief, just how much the North American elite cared about what they called 'the great unwashed' – practically nothing at all. To them, the protests were a mild inconvenience, and, in truth, not much of one.

"Better go to the service entrance," said the secretary. "Security will meet you there and escort you to the VIP lounge."

"Right," said van Kleist and terminated the call. "Service entrance," van Kleist said to his driver.

"Si, Senor," said the driver.

"Damn protesters," muttered van Kleist as the limousine exited the freeway and headed for Sao Paulo airport. This was the very thing that his export managers had been complaining about for months now. "What is the matter with these people?" he muttered.

"Senor?" queried the driver.

"Oh nothing," said van Kleist, but finished his thought anyway: *Don't they know that their iron ore exports are what keeps this country afloat?* Apparently, they did not. Or if they did, they were not happy with their share of the profits it brought to the country. But that was not van Kleist's problem, so he ignored that point of view.

Van Kleist was not atypical. The elite did not use public transport, certainly not the urban commuter type anyway. When it came to interstate and international air travel they entered and exited via privileged-access first-class lounges and were driven by chauffeur-driven, darkened windowed, bullet-proofed limousines. That is, of course, when they were not airlifted from rooftop or private estate-maintained heliports. And when they were ensconced inside public buildings they invariably entered and exited via private lift systems to and from fortress-like private suites, offices, and boardrooms. Their private homes were highly secured fortresses complete with walls, gates, private guards, and the very latest in electronic security. In short, they did not even inhabit the same world as the masses.

The non-violent protest movement mostly inconvenienced the middle class, or what was left of it. The uppermost segment of this cohort comprised mostly the professional servant class, like van Kleist, that lived a relatively affluent lifestyle as a reward for catering to every whim of the elite. They were the lawyers, accountants, stockbrokers, executives, medical doctors, engineers, architects, university professors, advisers, therapists, and their ilk that made being affluent worthwhile.

This was the class that ran the 'empire'. It included the generals, admirals, magistrates, senators, House representatives, cabinet ministers, directors, departmental managers and others of their rank, the trusted servants, those who shared in the spoils sufficiently to justify their loyalty, devotion, and perpetuation of a system that had long ceased to resemble anything like an egalitarian participatory democracy. Beneath them were the 'upper' middle-class managers, both military and civilian, who oversaw the various institutions that made up the complex structure of an advanced technological society. As a brigadier general Parnell had almost been one of those, but not anymore.

Then there were technical specialists who managed the affairs of society at the operational level rather than at the strategic or policy level, and who performed the highest skills jobs of their respective vocations. They too needed to be looked after and were handsomely rewarded because they were the ones who really did the high-level work – in some cases the lifesaving work, upon which their superiors relied and depended. The skipper of the *Saladin*, who had guided Faisal's yacht safely through the busy shipping lanes off the Riviera, was one of those.

Beneath the middle-class was the 'lower' middle class. These were the sergeants, warrant officers, the forepersons, the section heads, local branch and section managers of the vast plethora of contractor and sub-contractor organizations, plus the mostly overworked and underpaid small business proprietors, who saw themselves as free enterprise and self-directing, but who were, in reality, little more than labor slaves destined to strive but rarely to prosper due to the market power of the large corporations controlled by the elite. The personal assistant who had just warned van Kleist to go to the service entrance was one of these. So was his Saville Row tailor.

Then there was the working class, those who actually did the work, the bottom sixty to seventy percent – the 'masses'. They struggled along with ever-diminishing wages and deteriorating social benefits. The chauffeur currently driving van Kleist was one of these, one of the lucky ones: at least he had a job.

And beneath them were the unemployed; the dispossessed; the displaced; the disenfranchised; the bottom twenty to twenty-five percent of the people who really lived in a different world to mainstream society. Several of the chauffeur's immediate family was amongst this less lucky class – they were 'the invisible people'.

It was the lower middle and working-class lower groups – sixty to seventy-five percent of the population – that Chambers and her fellow dissidents mostly inconvenienced. As for the 'invisible' people, well, they weren't really in this world, so nobody of any importance knew how they fared, and no-one cared.

Some protest activities went reasonably according to plan. At LAX, Antoine Struber emptied the contents of his pockets onto the counter of the security barrier immediately in front of the hand baggage security screen. They cascaded all over the counter, some fell to the floor and a roll of coins rolled into the screen tunnel and dropped down into its scanning mechanism below. The conveyer belt jerked to a halt and made a sickening grinding noise. Antoine stooped to pick up the fallen items from the floor then reached into the tunnel and groped for the offending coin roll.

"Leave it," yelled the security guard. "Come over here, you smart-assed little punk."

Antoine did as he was ordered.

"There'll be consequences over this," said the guard. "That's sabotaging official government property."

"It was an accident," said Antoine with an insolent smirk on his face.

"Like hell it was," said the guard. He turned to the rear, addressing no-one in particular: "Call maintenance," he yelled.

The crowd queued up behind Antoine groaned and glanced apprehensively at their watches. Antoine was not alone. Many Los Angeles passengers missed their flight that day.

Similar scenes played out at JFK, O'Hare, Heathrow, Olay, and other leading airports around the world. Students and holidaymakers secreted coins and other metallic objects about their persons to disrupt the aircraft boarding procedures. Metal detectors worked overtime. Similar items in travelers' checked baggage cause equal confusion. The campaign snarled up airports for days and drove transit authorities crazy, but only for a few weeks. All the ploy really did was extend the length of check-in queues. Airport security personnel grew irritable and a little 'pushy' at times but nothing of any significance emerged from these protest tactics.

Throughout the entire Western world, plus Japan and South Korea, activists, as usual, followed American social and political trends as they had done since the end of the Second World War. A public campaign encouraging taxpayers to delay lodging their tax returns was mildly disruptive in France, Spain, and Italy, in particular, where the cash strapped government had to apply to the International Monetary Fund for short term loan relief.

Surprisingly this was one occasion when Hardigan did not get upset. As a board member of the Bank of England, he merely waved the problem away, confident the Governor of the bank would 'do the right thing'. 'Across the pond', elites were similarly unconcerned despite the significant level of participation which was encouraging from the protesters' point of view. The tax return strike had little effect on US and UK governments because they just reverted to their earlier tactics of increasing the money supply. The banks created money out of thin air and increased their government deficits and national debt to cover the temporary shortfall in revenue inflows.

"Quantitative Easing," crooned the English aristocrat. "No problem." All the tactic did was diminish the purchasing power of the retirement savings of the middle class. That didn't bother Hardigan.

Japan did the same, although the remedy did have a negative impact on bond rates because Japanese debt was now almost at national suicide levels.

So that particular financial tactic was only tried once and then abandoned as being largely ineffective.

In Spain, the sons and daughters of the 'Indignants' and '15-M' movements saw it almost as a patriotic duty to disrupt their government and participated enthusiastically in all manner of creative protests. And in France, the Yellow Vests voiced their dissent with traffic flow disruptions. The Germans, however, were more subdued, as were the Dutch and Belgians. They, like the British, were still mainly focused on immigration issues.

Numerous forms of strike action were tried. "What do we want? [Whatever it was the protesters were demanding on this particular occasion]. When do we want it? Now!"

It was a familiar refrain. Street marches, underground press, and other classical non-violent tactics were also stepped up but yielded the same result. In the United States the AFL-CIO called for a national strike.

"Everybody out!" was the cry. And many did strike. But by this time union membership was down to single-digit percentages in the United States and not much better in Western Europe where union membership had been traditionally quite strong. After one attempt in each of Canada and the United States, two in Germany and the Netherlands and three in France and Great Britain, the tactic was also largely abandoned. It had become quite clear by then that rebuilding union power within Western Civilization would be a decades-long affair.

And these were the 'successful' non-violent tactics.

Some campaigns had been a disaster. In the summer of 2034 a reoccupation of Wall Street, reminiscent of the 2011/12 event, was met with a swift and brutal response by the New York City major. No further attempt at public occupations was attempted in that city thereafter.

Popular local agitator Gary Knight led a similar event in Los Angeles and was met with a similar response but with no casualties save a few sore heads. So no further attempt was tried there either.

In Montreal and Ottawa on consecutive weekends, firebrand dissident Canadian Piers Rouleau fared similarly but with persuaders who had discarded their famous scarlet coats for the more intimidating riot control black, again, without casualty except for a pensioner in the Canadian capital who had a heart attack during the frenzy.

Around the world, authorities made it very clear that mass occupations of government buildings and public spaces would be met with a strong police response. In London, dome-helmeted "Bobbies" proved as effective as their North American counterparts, so were the Gendarmes of Paris and as were the various local, provincial and national law enforcement agencies elsewhere in their respective jurisdictions. So the three-month campaign was quickly abandoned despite events taking place in 132 locations across seventeen countries.

But not before blood was seriously drawn. Student protests in American universities were more frequent and enduring and drew a more robust response. Like their forebears in the 1960s, some American Governors called out the National Guard. The part-time soldiers had received little or no training in crowd control or civil disobedience confrontation. In Alabama, a frightened National Guard unit, comprised of mostly white middle-class kids trying to make a few extra bucks, found themselves surrounded by a sea of angry students. The students were protesting the level of college fees and student loan debts. The soldiers panicked and opened fire with live ammunition. Eleven students were killed, three more died later in hospital, and forty-seven were treated for gunshot wounds.

In Miami, the outcome was worse. Coming a week after the Alabama sit-in, some of the students had come to the protest armed and prepared to defend themselves. No-one knew who fired the first shots but whoever did started a firefight that took the lives of fifty-eight students, seven National Guardsmen, and three police officers.

Most gruesome of all was the fate of two police patrol personnel, a mother of three, and a father of two. Neither had been confronting students on campus but had been parked in a side street nearby. Students from the Chemistry faculty, unarmed but enraged by the violence they had just experienced, retreated to their labs and produced a lethal cocktail of volatile substances –alcohol, phosphorus, gasoline – in boiling flasks that would mix and ignite when shattered.

Four of these devices impacted the stationary police car one after another. One of the officers did not make it out of the car before being engulfed in flames. The other did get out but provided the horrible spectacle of a screaming, flaming, human torch racing desperately down the street until she collapsed thirty yards away in a writhing smoldering mess.

Chambers and Parnell watched the nightly news in horror as these tragedies unfolded.

"End it. For God's sake, Elsie, end it!" pleaded Parnell.

"Yes," said Chambers. She spent the next three full days calling dissidents across the world. The network she had so carefully built up to conduct her non-violent campaign she now tried desperately to shut down. She begged them, pleaded with them, and even ordered them to stop.

No more occupations were staged anywhere after that. The Atlanta and Miami scenes had both been filmed on mobile phones, the videos beamed around the world. The effect was numbing on protesters near and far. No-one had wanted this.

A Stella Career

'I wonder if Ike did this,' thought Frazer as he leaned back in the great leather chair behind the huge desk in the Oval Office. He stretched out his legs so his heels rested firmly on the front of its surface. He stared at the ceiling. 'No', he thought. He couldn't see Ike doing such an ill-disciplined thing. But then, he had never expected he would have been so fortunate as to be in this position: *Commander-in-Chief.* He smiled at the thought. It had a nice ring to it.

Frazer had not always been a star performer. In his early career, he had been modestly competent at most things he tried but had never really excelled in anything. But he could be relied upon to perform whatever role was assigned to him to an adequate level of satisfaction. He had played football and basketball at high school and had participated in them in junior college but not in his senior years at Iowa State University. Such roles then were largely reserved for those with sporting scholarships.

Academically his performance was also adequate, usually resulting in grade point averages somewhere near the middle of his year at both high school and college, so he was not sought after for recruitment to any Ivy League College nor by any major corporation upon graduation. He majored in Chemical Engineering with a minor in Project Management. And as a Mid-West kid from a rather run-of-the-mill middle-class family, there were also no strings his relatives might pull, nor network of valuable contacts that might be tapped to ensure privileged access to some desirable profession or vocation.

There was however one available opening. As always, a war was going on so the United States military was on the lookout for competent individuals to join the officer corps of each of its four services engaged in this mostly-foreign adventure.

Frazer smiled inwardly as he rocked backward in the great chair. He could still see the scene in his head.

"How do you feel about travel," the young lieutenant had asked?

"Yes. Yes, I'd love to travel," he'd said.

"Some of the places we go are pretty primitive."

"The wilder the better," he'd responded keenly.

Frazer had left the joint services recruiting office feeling pretty confident.

The Army made the first offer, and Frazer, being the somewhat apprehensive individual he was, snapped up the offer as soon as it was made, particularly since the invitation involved attending the prestigious West Point Military Academy. He graduated twenty-seventh in the class of 1995 and was assigned to the United States Army Corps of Engineers where his chemical engineering skills were honed further through specialist courses in the daring arts of explosives handling, demolition, bomb disposal, and infrastructure removal. Then he was shipped off to Kuwait to support the allied efforts to remove the mess created by that conflict.

Frazer didn't like the duty very much. It involved removing piles of mangled scrap metal after the exceedingly generously paid private contractors had put out all of the fires that had lit the place up like a giant birthday candle. Adding insult to injury, he had to deliver that scrap metal to other 'private contractors', most of who appeared to be American. These contractors then made obscene profits selling it to ..., well, Frazer was never really sure who.

There were also other rather mysterious aspects to the 'scorched-Earth' devastation visited upon the small sheikdom, but Frazer had learned by this time in his career it was best not to ask too many probing questions into what he observed, and even less wise to challenge or contradict what he was being told by his superiors.

Unknown to Frazer, however, his discretion had not gone

unnoticed. Although his performance reviews were not particularly spectacular, he was marked highly on such subjective qualities as 'soundness of judgment', 'reliability' and 'team participation'. So he was somewhat surprised after his Kuwait tour of duty and a further tour in the small African nation of Djibouti, where he trained special forces teams in explosives handling, demolition skills, and sabotage techniques, to be posted for specialist training at the School of the America's at Fort Bragg. This exposed him to even more intense and esoteric training in the 'black arts' of military operations. From there he was posted to a rather obscure unit known only as 'Delta Special Task Force 5' located in a wooded campsite on the edge of Fort Drum in upstate New York, nominally attached to the 7th Engineering Battalion – although no-one at the battalion headquarters seemed to know much about the unit.

Frazer's career *really* took off on 11th September 2001. It was then that his engineering expertise and his proven discretion were fully put to the test. He shone in the role he was assigned on that date to near perfection. 'Near' that is, in the sense that everything had gone to plan but there had been a small hiccup along the way, which had caused his superiors some embarrassment … but not so much that it could not be covered up with a little judicious lying.

Frazer's role in the three months leading up to that momentous day was to supervise the installation of the demolition charges on the central elevator shafts and the peripheral columns from the 78th Floor to the top of the South Tower of the World Trade Center, under the guise of effecting repairs and replacing the fire-proofing on the supporting columns of the building. He had supervised the installation of the high technology explosive charges exactly as instructed and had done so without anyone outside his dedicated team noticing anything unusual about this 'remedial repair work'.

"All charges now in place," he'd reported back to his immediate operational commander, a certain General Sheldon, who Frazer had never heard of before being deployed to this clandestine operation.

"Good," said Sheldon. "Stand down, Captain. Report back to Fort Drum and await further orders."

"Yes, sir!" said Frazer and did as he was ordered.

It was on the fateful day of September 11th when the hiccup occurred. At 1700 hours the previous day, the telephone had rung in his billet room at Fort Drum. He'd been ordered to report back at exactly 0730 hours the following morning to the Control Center where his demolition charge firing trigger was located. He arrived there and took up position exactly on time and exactly as ordered. Then he waited, as ordered.

At 0903 hours a large Boeing aircraft slammed into the building between the 78th and 84th floors of the South Tower of the World Trade Center, slightly to the right of where it was supposed to hit. The ensuing fire from its burning jet fuel engulfed the building right across that floor, also as it was supposed to do. After the initial burn, comprised mostly of jet fuel, had exhausted itself, multiple office fires broke out right across the floor and burned exactly as expected for the next forty-odd minutes. The whole process was going perfectly, according to plan, as were the fires in the neighboring North Tower that had been struck by an earlier plane.

Frazer peered out of his mobile command vehicle and observed the panic of the crowds surrounding the building. But he remained at his post, calmly waiting for the scheduled time when he had been ordered to fire his charges.

Then something went wrong. Instead of the fires burning for the full specified time in the demolition plan before he was due to fire the charges to bring his section of the building down, the nano-thermite charges at the impact point of the South Tower began to burn. They burned so brightly, and so hot, that some of the melted steel started gushing from the building in a bright yellow river of molten metal that could be clearly seen by observers on the ground below. Then the supporting columns on the periphery of the building started to buckle causing the uppermost thirty-odd stories of the building to topple a full 23 degrees from the vertical at its hinge point on the 78th Floor. Frazer watched in horror as the slow-motion spectacle unfolded before his vantage point half a mile away. Suddenly his handheld radio squawked into life:

"Blow it!" it screamed. "For God's sake, blow it!"

Frazer jerked into life. He raised the manual detonation override switch to eye level, flicked up the safety cover, and pressed the red button. Instantly the building around the 78th Floor of the South Tower exploded into a pyroclastic cloud of dust and debris that shot laterally outwards from the stricken floor on all sides. Then the rest of the charges fired in sequence with the explosion front moving steadily up the building towards the top. Simultaneously the floors below the stricken area began to explode also, the demolition front moving steadily downwards just ahead of the now collapsing building. It fell to the ground in less than twenty seconds. In its place arose a huge cloud of grey dust that engulfed everything around where the South Tower had stood, hiding even the still standing North Tower.

The building had come down exactly as intended. Frazer had done his job. But the clearly visible stream of molten steel and the discernible tilting of the upper section of the building now posed serious embarrassments to what otherwise had been a perfect job.

Frazer's hiccup might have been more detrimental to his future had it not been for the even greater failings of his counterpart over on World Trade Center building number seven – he and his team had been responsible for laying the charges throughout that 47-story buildings and bringing it down shortly after the collapse of the Twin Towers. It was not scheduled to receive any airplane impacts but it was expected to be completely obscured from view to all by the dust that was expected to arise from the demolition of the two larger towers. As a consequence, it was not expected onlookers would even know it had gone until the dust had settled hours later. Then it was planned that the falling debris from its looming neighbor, the North Tower, could be used to explain why the integrity of the building's structure had been compromised and caused it to collapse also.

The demolition of this third building was to destroy incriminating evidence about insider trading on the New York Stock Exchange accumulated by the Securities and Exchange Commission, some embarrassing evidence of the Central Intelligence Agency's spying on the United Nations, and the back-up copies of Department of Defense financial records currently being audited by investigators at the Pentagon, all of which were housed in the building. All this dangerous information had to be disposed of for they might have embarrassed many senior military and political leaders if it ever saw the light of day.

But WTC7 did not go down on cue even though some of the initial charges did ignite at their designated time. The hapless demolition teams tried a couple of times throughout the day to bring the building down, even starting a series of fires to support the explanation that it was office fires that had caused its collapse. They finally succeeded at 1720 hours, but by then the dust had largely cleared giving an unimpeded view of the fall. The building came down symmetrically, and at near free-fall speed for much of its descent, leaving those who knew about controlled demolitions in no doubt that the structure had been brought down by experts in that esoteric art. And *that* really proved embarrassing to Frazer superiors, far more than his minor South Tower hiccup.

Frazer had not been briefed on the WTC7 demolition before the destruction of the Twin Towers of the World Trade Center. All he'd been told was to exit his control vehicle immediately after he'd fired his charges via Vestey Street West and proceed to the New York Public Library where he would be met and given further orders. He did not need to know any more than that at that time.

He obeyed his orders diligently as was his want.

Frazer had attained the rank of captain by the time of his New York assignment. Within two weeks he'd been promoted to Major and within a further two months had been whisked off to

Afghanistan to train the rebel fighters of the Northern Alliance in demolition and sabotage tactics. Sixteen months later he was promoted to Lieutenant Colonel and after serving two tours of duty in Iraq and a further short tour of duty again in Afghanistan, by the end of the second decade of the 21st century, his career and his reputation as a reliable, dependable and discrete officer who could be trusted with important secrets had been well established and a single star had settled on each of his shoulders. He had also accumulated both friends and valuable contacts amongst the more covert powerbrokers within America's global power structure who appreciated his discretion and his diplomacy. He recalled one specific meeting that started the ball rolling.

"May I present Brigadier-General Frazer," crooned the diamond-bejeweled Washington socialite who was hosting the particular soirée to which he'd been invited.

"Delighted to meet you, General," said Fifth. "I've been hearing good things about you."

"Oh," said Frazer. "I can't imagine what they might be."

"Oh, come, come, General," said Fifth, "you are being far too modest."

By the latter part of the second decade of the new century, the de facto Global Emperor's particular interest was in gaining access to Central Asia's vast oil and gas reserves. Russians, Chinese, and Europeans had similar ideas. Fifth hoped to beat them to it, or, at least, to share in them to a significant degree. So he was keen to talk to anyone who knew the Central Asian region well. A trusted star-ranking army officer with experience in both Iraq and Afghanistan was such a man. Fifth was not so much impressed by Frazer's talent, experience, or specific skills. What Fifth liked was Frazer's capacity for keeping his mouth shut.

Purr, purr. The sound interrupted Frazer's daydream. *Oh,* he thought: *incoming.* He quickly withdrew his feet from the desk. Placing them on the floor, he dragged the chair forward until his stomach almost touched the desk and pressed the green intercom button:

"Frazer," he said in his customary commanding voice.

"Mr. Darcy, Mr. President," the mature-aged woman's voice announced.

"Please ask him to come in," said Frazer. He quickly adjusted his tie and ran his right hand over his hair.

Fifth entered the room extending his right hand as he did so, "Mr. President," he said.

Frazer rose from his chair, quickly skirted the leather-topped desk and extended his hand in greeting. "Sir," he said.

Fifth and Frazer settled down facing each other across the coffee table in the Oval Office. Frazer had spent the morning being briefed in the Situation Room at the White House and Fifth had been similarly briefed before his arrival.

"Marshall Law? Do you really think it's that bad?" asked the surprised Frazer.

"I do," said Fifth.

Frazer nodded slowly. He glanced at his master. He could see the resolve in Fifth's eyes.

"Yes, sir," said Frazer. "Marshall Law it is."

Planning the Campaign

"Fifteen minutes, General," called the skipper down into the bucking cabin as Parnell gathered the remaining maps and papers from the neatly stowed bunk table and stuffed them into his backpack. His pilot had still not adjusted to using the 'Colonel' title to Parnell's name or he stubbornly refused to use it in sympathy with his former boss.

"Right," said Parnell. He swung the backpack onto his back and mounted the stairs to the pitching quarterdeck. The battered old trawler had taken a long circuitous trip back to the United States but Parnell had put the time to good use planning the upcoming campaign.

His round trip to Juneau had been largely futile. The Alaska dissidents he'd met with seemed hell-bent on some kind of quasi-military operation. They had called for his advice at the insistence of the captain of the little vessel which now brought him home, the skipper formerly a US Army warrant officer who'd served with Parnell in Afghanistan and the Philippines. He knew what they were planning was folly and had hoped Parnell could dissuade them. But most of them were young and had no real experience of war and seemed uninclined to listen.

"Military operations, no matter how well planned and executed, often result in casualties, both military and civilian, and it's usually the civilians who suffer most," Parnell had told them. "That is something we have to avoid at all costs."

"You can't make an omelet without breaking a few eggs," had said some fuzz-faced kid who'd obviously never been in a combat zone.

"I've dedicated most of my adult life to protecting the American people and I have no intention of abandoning them now," said Parnell, slightly irritated.

"What do you suggest, General?" interceded the veteran Warrant Officer.

"Hold tight for the moment," said Parnell. "We're working on several initiatives at the moment. I'll get back to you in a few weeks. Trust me. We will be doing something, but not this."

The small group of young radicals had acquiesced but not convincingly. Parnell urged the veterans among them to keep the youngsters in check but he was not sure they could do so. He knew he had to act, and soon. He had to topple what currently claimed to be the legitimate government of the United States of America, a claim Parnell was now totally convinced was a false claim, but he had to do it in a way that did not hurt the American people. A new comprehensive and sensible plan was desperately needed to avoid disaster.

Parnell was not unfamiliar with the development of a grand military strategy. In his former more exulted role, he had planned military deployments of brigade-level operations on numerous occasions. He had also attended many strategic briefings throughout the two decades of battalion-level command. Many of those deployments were undertaken with units from the other armed services of the United States and with America's many allies around the world. As a result, Parnell was equally at ease with combined arms operations with both military and civilian forces and with joint operations with multi-national forces.

But this time it was different. This time the planned campaign was to be on American soil and directed against his former superiors. His new enemy claimed they were acting on behalf of, and for the benefit of, the American people. They even claimed to be the legitimate Government of the United States of America. But Parnell didn't think so. Some of them were not American and Parnell doubted they were acting for the benefit of all, nor even for the majority of Americans. If he had thought so the planning for this campaign would not have been necessary. No, Frazer and his regime were alien to the American nation, an obscene and malignant tumor that had invaded the body politic and usurped its legitimate governance. They had to go and go they would if Parnell had anything to do with it.

Parnell, like most of his professional contemporaries who knew armed conflict, regarded war as being so terrible that the sooner it was over the better, that the least suffering for all concerned would be achieved by the speediest accomplishment of the mission, even if the initial devastation visited on the enemy was as violent and effective as could be. Do it quick, do it clean, get it over with.

The small ship heaved to about fifty yards offshore. The forward deckhand lowered the rubber raft into the churning surf in the lee of the mid-ship. The skipper motioned the mate to take the wheel and moved quickly to lower himself into the fragile tender. As soon as he was set, Parnell mounted the craft and seated himself on the wooden bench directly in front of the skipper, facing the front. The skipper gunned the outboard and the craft moved away from the trawler and headed shoreward.

The bouncing trip gave Parnell a respite from his weighty thoughts. He'd begun his planning months before he headed back to the lower forty-eight states. He would have liked a speedy outcome in the upcoming campaign – all he wanted was for Frazer's puppet government to submit themselves to the will of the people by holding democratic elections for the Presidency, the Senate and the House of Representatives. They were welcome to stand as candidates if they wished and if they won a popular mandate from the people then Parnell would have been satisfied. But Frazer and his regime were showing no signs of doing that since they had declared the State of Emergency and suspended the constitution. So Parnell had no choice but to compel them to.

Parnell had been deadly serious about his concern over civilian casualties. As an ex-military man, he was equally concerned about military casualties too. He was also still haunted by the scene of the burning police officer and other scenes of useless violence the world had witnessed since the non-violent struggle commenced. The fight had to be fought, but it might take some time if he was going to keep casualties, both civil and military, to a minimum. Would the young radicals be that patient? Probably some of them, not, he thought.

By the time Parnell had scaled the windy bluff overlooking the small sandy cove two miles south of Cape Alava on America's northwest coastline his briefcase already held a thin file of papers, maps, reference texts, half a dozen books, and the notes he'd scribbled down as he'd scrutinized the classic texts on irregular warfare from electronic databases and the internet. They were, for the most part, short, cryptic and incomplete, scribblings for further consideration, memory joggers, and not-so-idle musings. But they were not incoherent, random, or unfocussed either. They revolved around his central dilemma: how to wage a war without actually hurting anyone.

To gain greater insight into that dilemma, Parnell had gone back to the mostly underground press of the numerous guerrilla and dissident movements that had flourished in various parts of the world throughout the twentieth century and the early decades of the twenty-first. He was surprised about how much open-source information was in the public domain. He was however hampered by the fact that any classified material he might still have access to now his security clearance had been revoked, would also be monitored by the Central Intelligence Agency, the National Security Agency, Department of Homeland Security, and a dozen other intelligence agencies. Parnell was not sure if he could access those resources without being detected and he was not prepared to take the chance.

Nevertheless, he'd been able to access some more innocuous sites, like the Wikipedia open-source encyclopedia, to which any schoolboy had access. He had also downloaded an electronic copy of Carlos Marighella's 1969 text *Minimanual of the Urban Guerrilla* but he did not find it particularly useful as a resource. Mao Tse Tung's book *On Guerrilla Warfare* was useful as was Ernesto 'Ché' Guevara book *Guerrilla Warfare*. *The U.S. Army Guerrilla Warfare Handbook* was a useful reminder of things he already knew as was its companion work on irregular ordinance. And his downloaded copy of the PowerPoint presentation of the British GCHQ training course on *Offensive Cyberwarfare Operations*, acquired courtesy of *WikiLeaks*, was also a helpful reminder of that latter-day battlespace tactics.

"That's quite a library you've got there, General," had said the skipper when he'd demounted the trawler's cabin steps to brew up some coffee.

"I'm hoping not to have to use any of them," Parnell had said. And he'd meant it. These were all general level, higher-order planning guides for commanding a guerilla army. Parnell was conscious that the lower level operational and tactical planning for smaller diverse units would need to be undertaken by subordinate commanders and tailored to local conditions. He still held out hope that non-kinetic tactics might suffice to win the struggle. But he had to be prepared for the worst if they failed. His research had at least provided him with a list of ideas that might be useful in developing his strategy further.

By the time he stretched out his hand to clasp that of the waiting LeMonte, Parnell's briefcase also featured a two-page document comprised mostly of subject headings, a grand overview of the upcoming campaign. It wasn't much but it was a start.

Not a lot was said after the initial meeting of the two rebels on the windy bluff. After exchanging brief salutations, the two sat and stared dumbly ahead as the dilapidated Ford *Tundra* bounced and jerked along the winding track through the temperate rain forest of the Olympic National Park, a route chosen especially by LeMonte to avoid detection by park rangers.

As the *Tundra* completed its transit of the trail and swung onto the Ozette campsite access road both men breathed a sigh of relief. If challenged now they could at least claim to be legitimate park visitors rather than unauthorized motorists driving along a prohibited road. Not that they were keen for that to happen even now. The FBI had been monitoring militants since the end of the second decade of the 21st century and LeMonte was already on the watch lists of both State and Federal authorities. Parnell was also, and had been since his discharge.

They sped on in silence down the park entranceway with the picturesque vista of Lake Ozette now coming into view to their left as the morning sun began to illuminate the tranquil wilderness. Parnell lowered the tattered sun shield. LeMonte did likewise. Then they turned northeast and headed at an unobtrusive pace out along Hoko-Ozette Road through Salku and Callam Bay, then south to Interstate 101, where they turned east and headed off towards their ultimate destination in the Clearwater Mountains. It was from there that Parnell would continue developing his strategy. It was only when they had completely cleared the Olympic National Park precinct that Parnell broke the silence and asked LeMonte:

"Have you seen Elsie?"

"She was down last week," LeMonte said. "She wanted to stay but something rather big is developing up north sometime soon so she had to get back. She wouldn't tell me what it was. She thought it was best I didn't know. She said she'd be in touch though when things get settled a bit more with her northern group."

A frown creased Parnell's brow. He hoped she was not involved in the Alaska operation; although he mused, if she was, it was more likely she would have been discouraging it even more vigorously than he had.

"How is she?" asked Parnell. He longed to see her and hoped she wanted to see him. He had hoped she would have met him along with LeMonte.

LeMonte suppressed a grin. "Oh, she's fine," he said.

"Oh," said Parnell and fell silent again. He was familiar with

LeMonte's mischievous brevity. He knew the old man knew he wanted more, much more, but he also knew it would not be forthcoming until LeMonte deemed it appropriate. There would be time enough for that in the weeks ahead so he did not press the inquiry.

Parnell also knew that LeMonte's priority at this point was to avoid getting intercepted by the US or Canadian authorities. And he also accepted that was why Elsie had not been there to meet him. She was on a watch list too, in both countries. And that was both of their key concerns at this time, to make sure that did not happen to any of them.

Coulterville

Janelle wandered back to the bar, coffee pot in hand, having just delivered Parnell's breakfast – hash browns, two eggs sunny side up, four rashers of bacon a tad overdone, and two slices of slightly underdone toast.

"More coffee?" she inquired.

"A bit later if that's okay?" responded Parnell.

"Sure," she replied with a slight smile.

She was an attractive woman Parnell observed; about mid-forties with a slim build, dark hair, and a pretty face despite her increased seniority. She was the kind of woman Parnell loved to meet, just like his late Aunt Jane. Aunt Jane had been just like Janelle when he was a boy and it was she who would give him a wink indicating that it was okay to take another cookie when Mom had said that he'd already had enough.

Off to Parnell's left sat an elderly couple, the man facing Parnell. They were the only other patrons of the diner that morning.

Parnell picked up his knife and fork and attacked his bacon. It cracked at the touch of this knife and a piece flew off and catapulted across the plate. It skidded across the pine tabletop and came to rest on Parnell's blue polo shirt.

"Damn," he muttered, gingerly picking it off and placing it back on the plate. He peered down at the small grease stain and grunted. *Not too bad. Maybe no-one will notice.*

Parnell turned back to his breakfast. He picked up a slice of toast and dunked its corner into the shining yellow yoke of his egg. It burst and showered yellow fluid over the white and the hash browns lying beside it. He mopped up the overflow with the remainder of the slice, wolfed it down and reached for the next slice to repeat the ritual.

He cast his gaze around the room.

In this early Spring of 2036, the whole scene was unchanged from when he'd last seen it nearly forty years ago.

Parnell ate on, his gaze wandering from his plate to his surroundings in short intermittent actions. They were not necessarily apprehensive glances but his quarry was running late and he was starting to feel the first pangs of concern.

When the eggs and hash browns were gone Parnell turned his attention to the remaining bacon and carefully consumed it, avoiding another grease stain. He continued to scrutinize his surroundings. They were so quintessentially American, a scene that had almost disappeared from the plastic-coated contemporary world in which most Americans now dwelt.

Janelle reappeared as Parnell downed the last of the bacon.

"More coffee?" she inquired again. Parnell nodded and smiled. Her timing was right, her attentiveness motherly. Perhaps she was Aunt Jane reincarnated. Parnell hoped so. He missed Aunt Jane.

But where the hell was Rouleau? Maybe he got lost. It was possible. He was a stranger to the American South West, his stomping ground being Quebec.

They had chosen Coulterville for the meeting because it was inconspicuous. It was quite credible for the Canadian to visit Las Vegas – the whole world wanted to go there at least once in their lives. And Coulterville was almost midway between San Francisco and Glitter City, easy for both parties to meet discreetly. Parnell was down from his headquarters on the banks of the central fork of the Clearwater River, apparently visiting friends in the bay-side city, and Rouleau was on an ostensive visit to the gambling capital of North America. It was a credible detour through Yosemite National Park by two apparent strangers each making sightseeing trips to two of America's tourist icons. Coulterville town's folk had made strenuous efforts to maintain the authenticity of the town's historic past, so a stopover en route was an ideal cover for the meet.

And there was a nostalgic reason to meet at Coulterville. Aunt Jane had lived here and Parnell had spent many happy days there on school holidays. The town was a living symbol of the indomitable spirit of the American pioneers. Parnell knew these people; knew they were the beating heart of American patriotism and the staunchest guardians of the Republic.

It was a fitting place for the meeting – an American patriot who refused to see the legacy of his forebears die in the face of tyranny, and a savagely loyal and proud French Canadian who refused to see his Gaelic heritage subsumed into Anglo-Saxon majority culture. They were natural allies if only each could meet and seal a bond that suspicion and doubt would seek to jeopardize.

Parnell glanced at his watch: 1015 hours. Rouleau was now fifteen minutes late.

Parnell genuinely liked most people, especially those he considered honest and straight forward, but he harbored a strong dislike for those he judged as devious, manipulative, or scheming. Given his humble beginnings as the son of Germanic ancestors from a small rural community just like Coulterville, his selection to attend West Point Military Academy was based purely on merit and his subsequent promotion was based mainly on loyalty to immediate superiors, dedication to duty and hard work. He disliked chaos, untidiness, and laziness. And he disliked tardiness too.

The elderly couple finished their breakfast and quietly left the diner, leaving their money on the table.

A few minutes later a red flash invaded Parnell's peripheral vision, right-hand side. He turned his head to address the interruption. A red compact, now almost stopped, crept slowly forward, the driver studying his surroundings. As he peered curiously over his right shoulder at the Western facade of the weathered diner Parnell recognized the bearded scraggy face of the big French Canadian from his internet website photograph. The car eased forward and disappeared beyond the window.

Parnell released a soft sigh. At last, the meet was on. But, he wondered, had Rouleau brought what he needed? More importantly, was he here on his own behalf, or was he here to represent Les Quebecois? Was he here to do a simple deal, the exchange of a few artifacts that would make little difference to the overall struggle in which each was engaged or was he here to lend the weight of the Canadian East to the strength of the American West and receive from the later the commitment to support his homeland's independence in their beloved Quebec?

Only one way to find out, Parnell concluded. He gulped down the last few mouthfuls of his third cup of coffee, placed the cup back on the cleanly wiped pine tabletop, and gently pushed back on his chair. He dropped a fifty on the table and maneuvered the coffee cup so it pinned the note to the table. It was a generous tip but the food had been good, the service warm and friendly and his loving memories of Aunt Jane refreshed in his memory. He rose and walked as casually as he could out of the diner.

Outside, he glanced across Main Street to the car park adjacent to E E Warne's old store and Bruschi Brothers' old warehouse where Rouleau straightened and stretched to restore the circulation to his body, his long drive over the mountains from the Nevada desert taking its toll. Parnell glanced in both directions then strode across the street, aimed for the front passenger's door of the red compact. As he neared it, he called softly but in a projected voice:

"Rouleau?"

The big man with the bearded scraggy face nodded and responded: "Parnell?"

Parnell nodded and reached for the door handle. "Let's go for a drive," he said, quickly opening the door. He slid into the passenger's seat and Rouleau slid back into the driver's seat.

"Have you got the stuff?" queried Parnell as Rouleau reached for the ignition key.

"It's in the trunk," said Rouleau. "Have you got the maps?"

"Yes."

The red compact backed from its parking bay and swung

towards Highway 49. They drove north in silence until about half a mile from the intersection of Main Street and Highway 132.

Then Parnell said: "Turn left here."

Rouleau did as told and drove the short way up the hill and around to the left bringing the car into the parking lot of the old battered motel.

"Number 9," said Parnell, and Rouleau maneuvered the car and parked in front of the door of the unit. They alighted and moved to the door which Parnell unlocked and motioned the Canadian forward. Inside he gestured toward one of the dilapidated chairs next to a small round faded table and sat down opposite the fierce-looking lumberjack. They both paused, blinking slightly to adjust their eyes in the diminished light inside the cabin. When Parnell spoke next his voice was firm but with the slightest touch of apprehension.

"And the word from your council?"

"The word is 'oui'," said Rouleau, but he added quickly: "but you will need to be modest in your demands. The French government has declined to give us any material support. They are afraid of incurring the wrath of the American government. Naturally, the British will not support us because they consider us to be terrorists, along with the Canadian government. None of the rest of the European powers wants to know us either because they say that North America holds no particular interest to them. The Russians make promising noises but, so far, they have done little for us. The Chinese likewise.

"In truth, none think we have much of a chance of achieving anything. As of this moment, we have a few thousand dedicated and loyal fighters but we lack arms, equipment, supplies, or anything resembling modern military logistics. We are very much a small guerrilla army fighting for independence, with much hope and no shortage of courage, but very little else. The one thing we do have, however, is the overwhelming support and sympathy of the French Canadian population of both Quebec and much of

Ontario as well."

"Arms are not a problem," said Parnell. "We have plenty of weapons. We too have the support of the great bulk of the population, particularly in Montana, Utah, Nevada, and Arizona. But they will only fight locally, and only against the Federal Government in Washington. Of course, we have the support of the Hispanic population of the American southwest generally, but many of them are thinking more of a Hispanic state after this is all over, possibly reunification with Mexico. The politics, as you can see, is quite messy. We have to tread carefully with what we promise and how we balance all these conflicting interests."

He looked directly at Rouleau, wondering if the big Canadian appreciated the delicacy of the political situation.

Rouleau offered no insight into his thinking.

So Parnell continued. "But for now," he said, "we need a front in the North East, particularly across the territory that carries the Greenland and Eastern Canadian oil and gas pipelines. That's your territory. A new front there would be of tremendous help to us even if it is a low-level insurgency operation that can tie down large swathes of the American and Canadian armies. It could just be the extra strain that brings the Washington regime to realize they cannot prevail against us, not with a three-front war to fight. So, are you with us?"

"What about Quebec independence?" asked Rouleau.

"Our policy is that no state or province should be forced to be a part of any union that does not want to be," said Parnell.

"It will depend on the details," responded Rouleau, "but, in view of your last statement, as a general policy I am authorized to tell you 'oui'."

Parnell flopped back in his chair and mentally sighed. For the first time since this great campaign began, he saw hope that it could succeed. He grinned; leant forward slowly and extended his right hand to the other man.

"Welcome, mon amie," he said.

"Et tu," said the other and extended his right hand also. The alliance had been formed.

All Parnell had to do now was to get the American Patriotic Association, the organization which he purported to represent in this encounter, to authorize him to enter into this treaty.

The Rebels

The American Patriotic Association, the APA, was founded in the spring of 2033 headed by the California political activist Gary Knight. It was a loose collaboration of a dozen organizations, mainly western and mountain states, with similar goals and objectives. Parnell had joined in July 2035. Three years later the confederation had grown close to 300,000 individuals across the United States. Canadian groups had joined in February 2036, Rouleau's group being the first.

The main bone of contention amongst them all was the increasingly autocratic governance style of the Frazer administration, particularly his invocation of martial law in the United States, even amongst the Canadians, who believed their own national government had become little more than a puppet to its southern neighbor.

The organization – if it could be called that – was a network of patriotic and social welfare groups each with its unique organizational structure and mission. The key common objectives were to achieve social and political change through peaceful and legal means.

But Parnell was also aware that some militant groups within the network thought armed conflict would become inevitable in the struggle to restore freedom and democracy to the continent, especially Rouleau's Quebec separatists and some Hispanic groups. Parnell did not agree but understood their viewpoint. After all, the United States of America had not come into being by non-violent action. It had required armed struggle.

The council was silent as it studiously perused Parnell's latest draft of his APA Grand Strategy document. In all, thirteen councilors were physically present plus Gary Knight who sat quietly at the head of the meeting room table. He'd already read the document. Five other council members had offered their apologies and two more were in transit and hoped to make an appearance before the meeting ended.

The largest affiliate in terms of numbers and resources was the Peoples' Alliance of the American South West. It boasted an informal membership of over 80,000 made up mostly of Hispanic-descended itinerant agricultural workers and a raft of inner-city urban gangs. It varied in ferocity from the virulent Sons of Atzlan, whose agenda was nothing less than the return of Mayan and Aztec glory to the milder, more social justice-orientated Southern Californian Workers Union, who just wanted decent wages for its members.

Gillian McCloud, a fiery redhead, currently represented the Alliance.

Sitting across the table from Parnell, the diminutive redhead's face grew redder as she scanned the document, her head shaking intermittently. At the end of each page, she furiously licked her right forefinger to facilitate her speedy leafing to the next. Occasionally, she paused and glanced up, scowling as she scanned the rest of the panel as they also leafed through the document.

The second-largest group of the APA was the Canadians headed by Elsie Chambers' Western Canadian Patriots. Numbering close to 26,000, about ten percent of the membership had borrowed from the mantra of their southern neighbors in believing that every person had the right to bear arms even if Canadian law did not see it that way.

Piers Rouleau's Quebec Separatists boasted 17,000 activists including a small army of around 2,000 front-line guerilla fighters who were armed with whatever weapons they could find. The former was headquartered in a network of rotating mountain hideouts in the Canadian Rockies in northern British Columbia, the latter in forest and lakeside retreats in and around Trois Riviers in Quebec while the significant city-based chapters gathered in Quebec City and Montreal. A further 10,000 to 15,000 activists were spread across the other major cities and towns of Canada bringing the total Canadian affiliates to over 50,000. About ten percent of these were armed, trained, and available at short notice for military service if required.

Chambers was absent on this occasion but Rouleau was present. He showed a disinterested nonchalance as the council read the strategy document. He already knew its contents having reviewed it for Parnell before they'd convened the meeting.

The third largest of the APA's regional groups was headquartered in Atlanta, Georgia. It totaled around 43,000 hardcore activists but its extended network was indeterminate and numbered many tens of thousands more because APA militancy effectively revised the separatist sentiments of the old Confederacy. Glen Moira from the Florida Civic Council represented this group. He scanned the document intensely with an occasional smile briefly crossing his face as he read items that met with his approval.

No-one among the Southerners wanted a return to the old segregation days, not even Moira, despite the suspicions of some of his compatriots that he was sympathetic to 'The Klan'. But southern patriots had felt the heroic struggle of their ancestors had been a noble one since they still felt that any state, not only the South, should have the right to leave the union if it chose to. For them, states' rights prevailed over federal rights. This is what their great-great-great grandfathers had fought for in the Civil War.

The Southerners generally, and Moira in particular, sympathized with Les Québécois and the thought of seeing Ottawa, in the Canadian case, and, in their case, Washington, humbled by people of like mind to them was a vision the 'Rebs' had long cherished. It now looked like a real possibility so they responded enthusiastically to the new rebel cause.

New England Region held a similar mystique for its rebellious citizens. They too harked back to the days of Washington, Jefferson, Adams, Franklin, and the other fathers of the nation. Freedom, democracy, no taxation without representation, and all the other symbols of the American dream was invoked by the failure of the national government to submit to the will of the people. King George (the III, not the current British monarch George VII) had not believed he needed to but his American subjects had disagreed and had fought a long and bitter war to make their point. Even Lincoln had gone to an election in the middle of a national emergency. So too had Roosevelt. They saw no reason why Frazer and his government should not do the same. Over 40,000 New England activists took up the cause and cherished their right to bear arms like their forefathers. Former marine sergeant Charlie Chivers represented this group. Now a garage proprietor in Albany in upstate New York, he read quietly and nodded approvingly from time to time, occasionally shaking his head at others.

Central Region was headquartered in Chicago. It covered eighteen states comprising the American heartland west of the Appalachians, east of the Rockies and north of Texas and Alabama. It comprised just fewer than 40,000 activists and had roughly 5,000 armed potential fighters. The core of this region was situated in the industrially decimated cities of Michigan, Illinois, and Ohio and its mix of ethnically diversified groups was as widespread as its southwestern counterpart, although the African Heritage component and those of the other African American associated groups outnumbered those of the Hispanic's.

The mid-westerners were at war with the East Coast as much as anything else, and their targets were just as much Wall Street as they were the White House, Capitol Hill, and the Pentagon. Former United Automobile Workers local organizer and ex-General Motors Bay City assembly line foreman Alex Gerenco represented this group. He read slowly and deliberately displaying little emotion as he scanned the document.

Faith-based groups, mostly Christian, made up around 27,000 members of a second West Coast network of affiliates, the United Faiths Convention. These ranged in virulence from the 6,500 strong God's Army to an array of milder-orientated devotees from an assortment of mostly protestant church groups, each numbering a few thousand. All of these activists believed they were doing divine work but they ranged from those who believed they were in God's hands to those who believed the Lord helps those who help themselves. They included such mild-mannered groups as the Single Mothers' Association and the more vocal but kinetically restrained American Lawyers for Social Justice to a handful of far-right fanatics such as the American Nationalist-San Francisco Branch and the Black Messiah group of radical African American hotheads. Pastor Allan Trench represented this group on the APA Council on this occasion. He read quietly and showed little emotion as he scanned the document before him.

Parnell headed the North West Region, the smallest of the regions, and was centered on Washington State, Oregon, Idaho, and Montana but it also had a close liaison role with the Western Canadians across the border in British Columbia. Its effective activist base was just under 19,000 local affiliates whose ranks had been swollen by a further 3,000 drawn from the other regions as specialist militant units – it was through two of these northwestern states that the Alaska and Alberta energy pipelines passed on their way south and east.

Parnell acted essentially as a Chief-of-Staff to the APA. He had made his regional operational headquarters in the eastern foothills of the Bitterroot Mountains of North Western Montana where the Lolo trailer park provided a useful barracks for the occasional assembly of his specialist forces. His personal retreat was on the other side of the range, just east of Kooskia, Idaho, on the Banks of the Central Fork of the Clearwater River. The former farming property doubled as the unspoken 'APA Military Wing' headquarters, a formation that existed mostly in Parnell's head and one he hoped he would never have to activate. The eastern trailer park hosted Parnell's small 200 strong volunteer intelligence analysis and strategic planning staff. Most were part-time and were disbursed amongst the general populations in Missoula, Hamilton, and throughout the Bitterroot Valley but close to the operations center to facilitate quick assembly for planning and coordination tasks. It also housed the 150 strong National Communications Unit whose role was to locate, prepare, transport, and reestablish the central command's headquarters facilities. These facilities were constantly on the move to avoid detection by federal, state, and local government authorities which formed the bulk of the American and Canadian governments' field units. The distance between the two, the Lolo HQ and the Kooskia retreat, with a mountain range between, afforded Parnell a reaction time should the operational headquarters ever be raided and also a small personal private space where he could truly relax when not on duty.

The Cauldron Bubbles

"I don't know, Jackson," said Elsie. "I tried to dissuade them from doing anything rash but some of the younger ones are really chafing at the bit to do something 'heroic'." She simulated quotation marks with her fingers as she spoke. "I'm not sure I can hold them."

"You have to, Elsie," said Parnell. "If these hotheads let loose it will give Frazer a propaganda coup irrespective of how successful their on-the-ground operations are." He turned to Rouleau. "Piers, these are your people. Can't you hold them?"

"That's the problem," said Rouleau. "They're not my people. My people are in the east. In the west, they don't really take much notice of French Canadians. They identify more with you Americans than with us."

"Military options have to be our last resort," said Parnell. "Once you start shooting things tend to get out of hand very quickly. We still have plenty of non-violent tactics to use before resorting to military action. "No," he shook his head, "it's just a matter of putting enough pressure on the regime to make it call for new elections. Once we start any sort of physical confrontation, they will crack down hard on everyone. They'll say: 'See, we told you that we had to impose martial law'. They really believe that they have the military might to crush anyone. They'll apply that power too if we give them an excuse to do so."

And Parnell did firmly believe that neither Frazer nor Fifth intended to slacken their iron grip on North America. Having command of the most powerful military force in the world was not something they would surrender just because a few North American citizens wanted to have a say in how it was used. It was too valuable in maintaining their control of the wealth of North

America. It was also the key instrument by which it kept the rest of the world in line. Relinquishing command of that mighty force was unthinkable to them. It would lead to the ruin of practically all GSC members and their vital interests. It would also largely spell the loss for many of them of their personal liberty.

Though faced with a mighty adversary, Parnell's main concern was not how to defeat the United States armed forces but how to do so without harming the North American people. He had more than enough resources within his potential guerrilla army to create mayhem even though the United States Army, Navy, Air Force, Strategic Force, Space Force, and Marine Corps numbered over one and a half million regular service personnel. Such a force was adequate to defeat any peer competitor in a conventional war anywhere in the world … well, almost anyway. History in recent decades had shown it could not prevail everywhere.

But it was still an insufficiently sized and equipped force to decisively defeat a well-trained and dedicated guerrilla force that enjoyed the popular support of its North American people. History had shown that governments needed ratios of twenty to one and even higher to defeat well trained and led guerilla forces when they were supported by local populations. Even with the quasi-military forces of police, coast guard, border patrol, customs service, fire services, parks rangers, and many civilian agencies, the combined forces at the disposal of the formal governments of the two northernmost countries on the North American continent were insufficient to control the wider civilian population … if that population saw the rebels as the champions of their freedom and the governments as their oppressors.

And, for the most part, they did. By this time in its history, the late 2030s, most Americans and Canadians saw the governments in both Washington and Ottawa as alien authorities, ones that had installed themselves into power without their approval and which ran their respective countries for the benefit of a small, largely faceless, elite rather than for the benefit of the people as a whole.

So, provided the rebels did not do anything to seriously disrupt their lives, or cause them more pain and suffering, the general populous took considerable delight in seeing their government overlords humiliated and frustrated.

Although Parnell and his high command were perfectly capable of developing a devastating military strategy, and although he had the resources to carry out such operations, he knew if he did so too aggressively he would only end up alienating the American and Canadian public, the very people he was trying to save. So his strategy had to encompass a large component of non-violent civil action and only a small, subtle, but disruptive, sabotage program, and only a very small segment of either overt or covert traditional military activity. He even hoped he would not have to resort to that last-mentioned kinetic option at all.

Should it come to that though, Parnell believed he had at his disposal several elements of hard military power. Within the Canadian commands, both eastern and western, were several tough, well-trained, and fiercely patriotic units, many with battlefield experience in distant war theaters. The Quebec Separatists, in particular, were not particularly squeamish about robustly confronting the government forces of either Canada or the United States. In the American South East, the great-grandchildren of the old Confederacy were equally dedicated, particularly the ultra-military cadres of the Robert E Lee Brigade and the Nathan Bedford Forrest mobile brigade. And in the South West, the Sons of Atzlan were as ruthless a group as any division of World War II storm troopers. The Special Forces under Parnell's direct control comprised mostly former US and Canadian Army, Navy, and Marine Corps veterans, including several hundred commissioned and non-commissioned officers of the United States Special Operations Command. He also had several hundred former agents and operatives of the United States and Canadian security services including the CIA, FBI, and Department of Homeland Security.

There were a few worrying groups too. Some of the rabid

nationalists definitely needed watching, and the Confederate command also included a few hotheads with Klu Klux Klan sympathies. Some of the Hispanic groups had a wider agenda than the current struggle, as did Les Quebecois generally, and in the South East a couple of the Cuban-American groups had more criminal intent than political objectives, as did several of the cross-border groups of Mexican ancestry.

Parnell was not a great fan of centralized intelligence dossiers. He did not want to foster a police state as a result of this struggle, but he did make sure that his security service did keep some files and a close eye on some segments of his potential rebel army.

The APA's hard power, particularly the well-trained veterans who knew how to plan well, resource, and execute professional military operations, only comprised about ten percent of its total activist base. The bulk of Parnell's forces were mostly well-meaning, although dedicated, amateurs, people who took up the cause because they believed that something had to be done to save their respective countries from their insatiable overlords. And in many cases, their skills were valuable, particularly the medical professionals; electronics technicians; civil, mechanical, electronic and electrical engineers; computer experts, cryptographers, and media specialists. Even mild-mannered accountants could be useful in disrupting government financial flows and raiding government financial resources to generate the funds all organizations, even a rebel army, needed to pay for its resources.

All participants, from the most highly dedicated to the occasional contributor, were valuable to Parnell's battle plan. But to avoid alienating the very people they were trying to rescue, the rebels had to concentrate on operations that did not involve the death or physical injury of the civilian population, nor significant damage to the civil infrastructure the mainstream population needed for its daily life. Even physical harm to government military and quasi-military personnel had to be kept to a minimum to avoid alienating the former military and government veterans within the rebel ranks – they too agonized over their loyalty to their former comrades-in-arms and their now newly perceived duty to their respective countries and peoples.

As a result, if Parnell had a role model in mind for his rebellion, and it is not clear that he actually did, it would have been more of a Mahatma Gandhi figure than a Ché Guevara, or a Mao Tse Tung. Parnell's objective was to make the United States and Canada essentially ungovernable. He did not want to destroy these states, or their unions, or even their key instruments of state power. What he wanted was to force the incumbent federal governments to hold elections for the head of state, in the case of the USA, and the upper houses and lower houses of their respective legislatures, just like they had in his youth, just like their respective constitutions stipulated. He had no doubt that, if he could do that, the American people would do the rest in the United States. And as for the Canadians within his ranks, all they wanted was the sovereignty of their country returned to them. Except for Quebecois Separatists, of course, who wanted independence from the rest of Canada and who, at this particular point, with Parnell's reassurance of American non-intervention, felt confident they could work that out with their English-speaking country folk.

"And you think you can do that?" LeMonte had asked him as he'd sat and waited for Chambers and Rouleau to arrive. "I mean, you're trained to kill, aren't you? Isn't that your profession? What credentials do you have as a peacemaker?"

"Well, yes and no," said Parnell. "Certainly, as a soldier, you're trained to kill, but you're also trained to avoid conflict if possible. Violence begets violence. Once you start applying violent solutions to solve problems you invariably create more problems than you solve. Physical destruction alone is costly, let alone the cost in human lives. And, even if you do prevail, you often create so much resentment that subsequent peaceful resolutions become extremely difficult."

LeMonte took another gulp of his pure malt scotch, the amber fluid sliding smoothly down his gullet and warming his stomach and inner spirits. Parnell and he did not often get a chance to indulge in this mutually gratifying pursuit, perhaps no more than a couple of dozen times since they had met in the Philippines two decades ago.

Father Andre LeMonte was the solitary sibling of a Canadian couple of Irish and Métis ancestry who had settled in Saskatoon, Canada in the 1950s. He was a surprise baby who arrived rather noisily in the late summer of 1976. He was an only child so he filled his childhood years as an altar boy at his local Catholic Church in the company of a kindly priest. The priest encouraged his interest in the faith and facilitated his entry into St. Augustine's Catholic seminary in Toronto from where he graduated with the degree of Master of Theology in 2001. By this time his muscular five-feet-eleven-inch frame topped by reddish-brown hair and his piercing emerald green eyes made him an imposing figure. His fiery temper and brusque manner made him appear even more formidable as Parnell had discovered at their first encounter.

LeMonte was a human dynamo. He rose at dawn, ate sparingly but adequately, and worked diligently at whatever task needed to be done. He worked seven days a week, preserving Sundays for his formal, pastoral duties but was otherwise dedicated to administering to his flock where ever that might be at any given time. Mostly, since being ordained, that somewhere was far from the shores of his North American homeland, initially in Fiji, then in Nigeria and then in the Philippines. Now he was back in North America.

A natural leader, mainly because he genuinely cared about people, especially the weak and vulnerable, LeMonte liked honest, direct, kind, and considerate people; he detested liars and thieves and those who were stupid, greedy, aggressive, or cruel. LeMonte had little time for military people who he assumed naturally embodied the last-mentioned qualities. So his first encounter with Parnell had been somewhat confrontational. He also disliked unpunctuality. So, it turned out, did Parnell and that was probably the first thing each came to appreciate about each other. After several months, however, they discovered they had something else in common. They both had more than a passing appreciation of fine old malt whiskey, the real stuff, from Scotland. LeMonte's favorite was Ardbeg Corryvreckan. Parnell preferred Bunnahabhain 18 Year Old. They did not drink often but when they did, they made sure it was the good oil they imbibed. During these rare occasions they also both discovered they enjoyed robust debate about almost anything.

While dedicated to his calling, by the third decade of his ministry Le Monte was beginning to have increasing doubts about religion. He wondered 'How could God be all-knowing, all-powerful, benevolent, and good yet permit such evils as he had witnessed in so many parts of the world?' He hoped for a better world where humanity, not barbarism, would prevail. But uncertainty and self-doubt were increasingly weighing on his mind. He was slowly losing his faith. He tried to hide his uncertainties but Parnell, his drinking buddy, had noticed. So had Chambers, who he had first taken under his wing when she'd gone to the Philippines.

Parnell, LeMonte, the newly arrived Rouleau, and Chambers paused and looked at each other, then past each other, into the distant recesses of their thoughts. The three men each took a further generous sip of the old malt. Chambers took a wee sip of hers.

Elsie Chambers was born the only child of Canadian parents in Pierson, Manitoba in 1976. Now, 60 years later the brown-haired, blue-eyed woman stood five feet seven inches in stockinged feet. Her slender, small-breasted physique belied the energetic, tenacious, hard-working dynamo contained within. It also hid her professional expertise and her competent management expertise whenever she was placed in command of challenging situations. She typically rose at dawn, worked diligently, retired early, and ate sensibly.

When she was not on duty, she was a different person. She was mostly solitary, often in retreat, enjoying nature. If she was in the company of others, they were usually kind, quiet, modest, moral, and strong. At work, she defended the weak and vulnerable tenaciously but in her private life, she shunned loud, aggressive, and cruel people. She craved peace. Her only real weakness was in insoluble situations when her skills could not heal, when her efforts were frustrated by suffering and failure.

LeMonte had come to know her well. He admired her, mentored her and was inspired by her humanity. She was a prop to his failing certainty even if he dared not show it, although she was also astute enough to see through his brash and bluster and she felt his anguish as his faith slowly failed him.

They had much in common. They both disliked bullies, indifference, clutter, and mess. She, like him, was usually on deployment in distant lands, mostly in impoverished countries where her skills are most desperately needed. She, like him, hated people who hurt other people, anywhere. They both hoped for a better world, for an end to suffering, and they both worked diligently to achieve it. Both had an inherent love of humanity, a sense of calling, and a disciplined approach to professional duty.

LeMonte had been her big brother and her unfailing backstop. She loved him in a non-sexual way. He had watched her evolve from a confident and self-contained young woman into a love-stricken matron, an outcome he had carefully nurtured over recent years. Parnell had come into her life quite by happenstance but her present entanglement was no accident. The aging prelate had been a skillful match-maker and the fruits of his wiles were beginning to emerge. He saw that it was good.

Le Monte's efforts were rewarded when he quietly married Jackson Parnell and Elsie Chambers in a small private ceremony at a little chapel on the banks of the Central Fork of the Clearwater River in the fall of 2036.

Chambers hated violence. It was Parnell's attraction to nonviolence that had attracted her to him, despite his obvious personal strength and his profession. But she sensed that he also had a sound grip on reality and could see he accepted the notion that sometimes you have no choice but to fight, that sometimes it is necessary to achieve the greater good.

She sensed that was how his mind was working now, and desperately hoped he was wrong. She had to get back to Canada and try and keep the hotheads under control so would not be around to support him with the upcoming APA council meeting. But for now, all she wanted was to catch Parnell's attention. She wanted at least some private time with her husband before she departed in the morning.

Rouleau was oblivious to her needs.

But the wily old cleric was a little more astute. He yawned, stretched, gulped down his remaining scotch, and said: "Well, big day tomorrow. I'm off to bed."

"Yes, me too," said Chambers, and slid her unfinished drink into the center of the table in easy reach of the big French Canadian.

Council of War

Parnell sat silently, keenly observing their body language as he waited for the council to scan his latest draft strategy document. The document outlined how Parnell and the other leaders of the American Patriotic Association sought to force the illegal Frazer dictatorship in Washington to the negotiating table and to the ballot box.

The balding headmaster from the Wyoming Education Association sitting two seats to the right of Gillian McCloud was a little more composed than his more agitated colleague but he also showed significant levels of concern as he scanned the text. He was sure the 6,800 teachers he represented would be similarly worried. Halfway through the second page he paused, cleared his throat and inquired of Parnell:

"You're not seriously considering doing any of this … are you?"

"I'm not suggesting that we do any of it at this point," said Parnell. "I'm just laying out the range of options we could employ if we consider any of them appropriate."

"I can answer that in just three words," said the fuming McCloud as she flicked to the fourth page of the document.

"None of it …" she said then added hastily: "None of what's listed under 'Military Wing' anyway. Have you forgotten that this is a peace movement?"

Several of the rest of the group spread around the donut-shaped conference table nodded in sympathy with this last statement.

"No, I haven't forgotten," said Parnell, "and, as I said, I'm not suggesting we do any of it. All I'm doing is laying out for you the range of options available to any organization that is trying to effect regime change in a body politic."

"Then why are you even presenting this paper?" demanded McCloud. "This stuff that you've got listed under 'Military Wing' is nothing less than terrorism. So is much of what you got listed under 'Political Wing' in terms of the definitions laid down in the Patriot Act. Not only is it highly dangerous to be even reading a document like this, it's also totally contrary to everything that we profess to believe in."

"Look," said Parnell, "I'm supposed to be on this council because of my military expertise and that's what I'm presenting to you, a range of options including military ones."

"We didn't ask for military options!" fumed the redhead. "We asked for a political strategy. We want to know how to get the regime to change its political position. We're not interested in finding out how to start a war."

"What do you think military options are?" asked Parnell patiently. "If you think military operations are only about how to fight wars then you really don't understand what military operations are all about. Military operations are all about getting your opponent to change his or her policies, to get them to change their mind, especially when they've given you the clearest indications that they have no intention of doing so."

"Well if it takes going around blowing up innocent people to get governments to change their policies then I want no part of it," retorted the redhead. "And I doubt that anyone else here does either!" She glanced around the room in search of support. And got it.

"Blowing up people is the last thing I would recommend," said Parnell. "And believe me I've seen enough real combat in my lifetime to know that option is a really bad idea given the objectives of this group and of the greater movement generally. You may not believe it, but the last thing that experienced military people want is to fight wars. It's usually people who know nothing about warfare that advocate fighting wars."

"Then why are you presenting it as an option?" inquired the headmaster.

"Because it's part of the range of options, but I would like to stress that, in my opinion, actual military operations involving real live shooting at other human beings are the last thing on my list of priorities."

"Good," said the redhead. "Why didn't you say that at the outset? We could have torn off the front couple of pages of your paper and thrown it in the trashcan before we even started."

"Well, not quite," responded Parnell. "You still need to give some thought to them."

"Why, if you said that we weren't going to even consider them?" inquired a grey-haired matron from the far end of the table.

"Because others will consider them," said Parnell. "You are all aware as much as I am that the APA is a very broad-ranging movement. Most of the members, active participants as well as more passive supporters and sympathizers, feel the way that most of us here do. They want to achieve the change by peaceful, non-violent, legal means. But we're facing a regime that has no conception of the rule of law and they have demonstrated time and time again that they're prepared to engage in the most brutal of activities to maintain their rule. It is going to take an enormous amount of courage, patience, and dedication to achieve our goals by peaceful means alone. I don't doubt that those assembled around this table have what it takes to see that kind of a strategy through to its fruition but we would be extremely naive if we were to assume that everyone in this movement has that degree of courage, patience or resolve. Many will give up along the way. Others will despair at the peaceful approach and opt for more aggressive tactics, especially some of the younger ones. We need to have some control over those who take that path even if we don't take that path ourselves. Otherwise, we will lose control of this rebellion and the radicals will take over."

"So you're saying we should resort to terrorism before someone else does?" demanded the redhead.

"No!" said Parnell. "I'm suggesting we consider the full range of options available to us. Let's consider those options that we can live with and are likely to be successful in achieving our goals. Then let's consider how we are going to handle those more radical types who are not content to keep things non-violent and legal and decide how we're going to manage those groups. If we simply bury our heads in the sand and say that we'll have nothing to do with them then we'll have no influence over their activities and we'll get tarred with the same brush as them by the regime and the media."

"Well, I want no part of it." The redhead again.

"Me neither," chimed the headmaster.

"Nor me …" came from a few other participants. But not all. A few delegates remained silent.

The leader of the Eastern Longshoreman's union, in particular, looked thoughtful. His members were descended from the militant workers who had fought for workers' rights in the early twentieth century and they cherished that heritage of courageous resistance to overbearing authority.

Rouleau said nothing.

Neither did Chivers.

And neither did Antonio Alveraz, the president of the Southern Californian Workers Union. They, and a couple of others, just stared intently at the paper before them and said nothing.

Parnell had quietly noted who they were.

It was not that Parnell had lied about his reasons for including the military options in his paper, nor that he was not sincere about recommending a resort to violent methods as being his last resort. As much as he hated to think about it, he was sure that some kind of 'kinetic' activity would eventually be required. His main objective was to keep this to a minimum, particularly the number of human fatalities.

As the APA council meeting moved into its second hour, the neatly-dressed middle-aged matron at the end of the table asked openly: "How feasible is a nation-wide general strike?" She was obviously well into the list of Political Wing options although she'd been amongst those who had joined on the "nor me" chorus earlier in the meeting.

"Industrial action doesn't work too well these days," said Alex Gerenco, mentally massaging the lump he still carried on his head from a police baton. "Last time we tried it a lot of heads got broken. The goons were vicious right across the country. A lot of people are unhappy but they're not that keen to relive the experience."

"Difficult," added the headmaster. "Most of the union leadership – those who haven't been completely bought and paid for by the regime that is – is still in re-education. Union membership is now down to eight percent of the formal workforce and, of course, illegals and contingents dare not formally join any organization for fear of attracting attention to themselves. A low-key civil disobedience campaign is more likely to be successful than any overt, formal strike. Unions just aren't a part of American life anymore."

"I wouldn't say that," said a smartly dressed Canadian woman whom Chambers had asked to deputize for her. "Teachers and hospital service workers are still pretty strong and also pretty militant."

"They're mostly the eight percent," said the headmaster. "Even the teamsters have been bought off to a large extent. In any case, Frazer is not averse to bringing in the military, private contractors, and even foreign workers if he thinks that any vital government services are going to be disrupted. No, civil disobedience is definitely the way to go but I think it will need to be a lot more subtle than a formal general strike."

"What about military and police personnel … particularly the more junior ranks? There are an awful lot of unhappy service people out there and most veterans I know think they've really been stiffed by Frazer and his gang."

"That's veterans and other ranks," chimed in Parnell. "Most of the officer corps and most of the senior NCOs are still pretty solid when it comes to the policies of the current Government. Frazer makes sure the backbone of his key professional forces is well supplied and given pretty much everything they want."

The council members paused to ponder his last remark. But to their surprise, Parnell then contradicted his last statement.

"Although," he mused, "I will say that I've been surprised at how many of my old comrades, both senior serving officers, and retired officers, have made subtle suggestions from time to time that they don't think that Frazer is deploying the military or the police the way they were brought up to believe a defense force or a police force should be deployed. I think there could be a significant minority of that group who thinks the regime is more interested in protecting the privileges of the regime and its cronies than actually serving the national security and internal order of the nation as a whole."

"I like the idea of a consumer boycott," interjected a twenty-something young woman whose infant was quietly sleeping in a carrycot near the wall behind her. "But what can you boycott that's produced by the Federal Government?"

"Tax assessments," shot back McCloud.

"Classes," added a young man who'd previously introduced himself as the president of the student union at the Santa Cruz campus of the University of California.

"I think a consumer boycott would be more successful if it was targeted against commercial organizations that are known to support the regime, particularly those companies that have substantial divisions that supply consumer goods and military supplies. They'll scream like hell to Frazer if their bottom lines start to suffer."

The discussion continued for another two and a quarter hours in more or less the same free-flowing exchange of ideas with nothing specific being proposed or decided. Clearly, there was a lot to think about and most at the meeting had given considerable thought to what type of tactics the movement should use. There was a general consensus that nothing tried to date had been particularly influential in putting the country back on the path to democracy, and most attendees felt something a little more robust than peace marches, and writing to your congressmen was going to be required. It was also felt that the key issues had been fairly well aired in the underground press, if not in the mainstream media, and most felt the general public was well acquainted with the corruption and malfeasance of the Frazer regime.

Few around the table had approached the issue of strategy to the extent and intensity Parnell was now asking them to do. And Parnell had emphasized several times it was they who had to recommend and adopt the grand strategy the movement as a whole would adopt. Most seemed to accept that as their role and were prepared to commit the time and resources to do that.

The general feeling though, so vigorously espoused by the dynamic and diminutive redhead at the outset of the meeting, was that only the 'Political Wing' options were up for consideration. There was no support, subtle or otherwise, expressed by those assembled for the 'Military Wing' options.

But Parnell suspected the rejection was not as absolute as the formal exchange might have suggested. Not all had vigorously joined in the "nor me" vote. He left the meeting with the quiet expectation that one or two, maybe more, of those attending might subtly broach the subject with him in a much less public forum. He was also far from convinced that military action was the right path forward. He was aware that controversy over pure nonviolence versus mixed tactics was huge in social movements seeking radical change. Some activists said a 'diversity of tactics' was the best approach and allowed for a common front among people with different values and ideologies. A mix of nonviolence and violence is perfectly natural they would argue and that this is what happens in any case in most revolutionary movements. On the other hand, some people, such as the American theorist Gene Sharp, who Gary

Knight seemed to revere, said that diversity of tactics in this sense is a terrible idea because you 'pollute' your nonviolent actions with even one violent action. Even with that one incident, it could ruin your cohesion. It could result in an acrimonious split in your movement.

Both arguments made sense to Parnell. Much debate and discussion on tactics, including the nonviolence versus violence issue, would be required before a final policy decision could be taken on his draft strategy. Parnell was torn by the dilemma more than most of his fellow councilors due to his personal experience of the horrors of war and the divisiveness of civil war in particular.

The main problem, though, was that not all APA members were as patient as Jackson Parnell.

First Strike

Andre Martin, second in command of the Deep Forest Division of the Western Canadian Command (also known as *Can-West*) turned his head to the left and spoke into the radio handset pinned to his left lapel. "*Contingent Three* ready," he said.

"Stand-by," replied Barbara McDowell, division commander and the leader of *Contingent One* of the strike force.

"*Contingent Two* ready," squawked Allan Denton's voice through McDowell's radio speaker.

"Stand-by," ordered McDowell again.

McDowell glanced at her watch: "05.59.15" it read. She paused and waited a further 45 seconds then shouted to the driver of the lead vehicle: "Right, let's go!" He swung back up into his cab, started the motor, dropped the clutch and the *Stryker* lurched forward.

The Deep Forest Division struck the Eielson Air Force Base just outside Fairbanks, Alaska at dawn on the 9th of September 2037. Its main target was the squadron of F-22 fighters of the 354th Fighter Wing and the two squadrons of Unmanned Aerial Vehicles (UAVs) stationed there. Prime amongst these latter targets were the twelve MQ-7b *Terminator* Extended Range Multi-Purpose (ERMP) drones because these posed the greatest threat to mobile rebel soldiers and their thin-skinned vehicles. Also of high priority were the tanker aircraft of the 168th Air Refueling Group and their fuel storage facilities which would make a spectacular sight in their demise if they could be struck effectively. However, it did not matter what targets *Can-West* hit. As long as the force could penetrate the base and inflict significant damage the strike would be successful from a political point of view. Or so McDowell,

Martin, and Denton believed.

Parnell would have counseled against the strike had he known of it. Chambers would have also. She sensed something was brewing and had cautioned against any military strike but her three Deep Forest Divisional field commanders had thought otherwise and acted anyway.

Foot traffic was practically impossible in the Alaskan terrain except for close-quarter fighting in heavily wooded or mountainous terrain and that did not describe most bases of the United States military complexes. Most were located in wide, open plains to provide safer flight paths for military aircraft. From a tactical point of view, assault operations had to be conducted from mobile platforms. Defense was a different matter. The rugged terrain favored the rebels, which was why most of the Deep Forest bases were located in heavily wooded or mountainous locations.

Mobile approach proved a problem, however. Sensors were deployed miles out from the base perimeter so an accumulated body of vehicles moving in the early hours of the morning was bound to raise suspicion within the base. Therefore, the initial approach to the rally point for each vehicle was staggered intermittently throughout the night and final convergence only achieved in the last few minutes before their strike.

Another key dilemma was timing. Darkest night would have aided surprise and cover but would have made target identification more difficult. In any case, night vision equipment was standard issue for sentries so attacking under the cover of darkness was largely negated, for them anyway. It would have also required the rebels to acquire night vision equipment. On the upside, base personnel not on duty would not have been so equipped, initially anyway. So, night cover would have inhibited base response times.

Further, the unusual nature of many of the strike team vehicles was bound to raise questions if seen in daylight so their approach had to be concealed as much as possible from the general populous as well as base personnel.

The strike team leaders pondered these dilemmas and opted for an approach just before first light and attack as dawn broke. But all these factors increased the risk and would have been further reasons why Parnell would have advised against the strike had he been aware of it.

But the rebels got lucky that morning. They descended on the base undetected from three different directions. Each contingent comprised four vehicles. The first contingent, McDowell's, came at the base directly down the main road from Fairbanks. It was led by an aging M1126 *Stryker* Infantry Carrier Vehicle (ICV) the insurgents had liberated from a somewhat slothful and totally surprised squad of Oregon National Guardsmen on deployment to Alaska and in unfamiliar territory. Behind it came McDowell and three other fighters in an equally aging Ford *Trans-Territory* followed by a Mitsubishi one-ton light truck. The latter had two fighters manning 50 caliber heavy machine guns standing on the rear tray, swiveling their weapons about on home-made mounts welded to the corners of the rails and arching across the front of the tray immediately to the rear of the cab. Bringing up the rear was a Chinese *Snow Minx* ten-seater *people mover* with its three passengers brandishing their automatic weapons out of its rear windows while the fourth drove the vehicle. *Contingent One*'s main target was the rows of aircraft lined up along the main runway to the base.

The second contingent, Denton's, came in from the east out of the darkness of the mountain's shadow in the distance. It comprised four standard half-cab four-wheel-drive vehicles, two American, one European, and one Indian in origin, all rather aging and each with a flat rear cargo tray. Each of their four-person crews comprised a driver and three crew members, one with an automatic weapon, two with a three-inch mortar and ten mortar shells. This group had advanced quietly to within three miles of the base's eastern perimeter fence, arriving just before dawn. It was scheduled to commence its run to position just outside the eastern service gate immediately on hearing firing from the lead force on the main road.

From there the mortars would target the fuel storage tanks several hundred yards to the east of the main runway while the drivers and *shotgun* passengers would provide covering fire if required until the full thirty-round mortar salvo had been fired.

The third group, led by Martin, came in from the south. It was led by a small lightly armored two-ton truck that had been stripped down and rebuilt with one-sixteenth inch plate steel across its passenger cab, engine compartment, and sides of its rear tray. Mounted in a swiveling makeshift turret on the passenger's side of the cab were two thirty-caliber machine guns in tandem. A make-shift periscope hung down in front of the driver replacing the windscreen's forward view. The steel plates on each side of the rear cargo tray contained three firing slits, two fore and aft comprising six inch by four inch holes, the third being a vertical plate twelve inches by six inches, hinged to drop-down so the Rocket Propelled Grenade (RPG) carriers could fire their weapons.

Behind the lead armored car came the bulk of the infantry force carried by two standard commercial trucks, a Ford five-ton low-sided truck with ten insurgents, four with semi-automatic weapons and hand grenades and six with RPGs, and a Volvo six-by-six heavy truck with fourteen fighters, four with semi-automatic weapons, four with RPGs and four with side arms but carrying plastic explosives. The final two rear passengers of this vehicle manned a single machine gun, each mounted on the corner rail of the truck tray.

The fourth vehicle in the group was a Ford F750 tow truck with an extendable main derrick – more usually seen on mobile cranes – and configured to fold to an extendable bridge that could span obstacles, ditches, bollards and other impediments to vehicular traffic.

The aging *Stryker* ICV of *Contingent One* slowed to a modest twenty miles per hour as it negotiated the fifty-yard S-curved section of the entrance drive leading to the guardhouse at the main entrance to the Eielson Air Force Base. Then, as it cleared the last of the curved sections of roadway, its driver gunned the engine. The vehicle leaped forward towards the gap in the concrete crash barrier behind which stood a solitary security guard.

The startled air-force sentry instinctively jumped back but kept his wits sufficiently to yell a warning to his colleague still inside the guard post: "Code Red! Code Red! Terrorist attack! Terrorist attack!"

As the ICV crashed through the thin metal drop-down road barrier near the guardhouse door its more robust cable companion was already rising from its subterranean bed six yards further down the road.

The speeding lead vehicle was now committed to its designated task. It crashed through the heavy-duty vehicle barrier that stretched across the roadway to the rear of the guardhouse. The barrier was designed to stop a vehicle of 15 tons traveling at 50 miles an hour, its designers not anticipating it would need to stop a 16.5-ton armored military vehicle, particularly one fitted with an ingenious vertical V-shaped scythe that had been hastily welded to the leading edge of its bow. This home-made attachment was designed to slice through the flexible impact-absorbing cable that had risen to impede its progress. The two made contact, the unstoppable force meeting the immovable blockade. The latter blinked first as it was intended to do, then its multi-strained tentacles snapped with a resounding twang. The force sent its severed strands flying outward as their elasticity dragged their stretched lengths back into stable form. Many of the strands slapped hard into the concrete crash barrier either side of the gap through which the ICV had raced. But one strain took a different trajectory and sliced through the chest of the now recovering air force corporal, almost cutting him in half.

"We're through," yelled McDowell. "Keep going, Driver."

Behind the speeding armored juggernaut, the remaining three vehicles of *Contingent One* sped unimpeded, their passengers poised, weapons ready to repel any defenders who might challenge their progress. But no challenge came. Of the only two defenders who had witnessed their rude and abrupt entry to the base, one was two masses of blood, the other was heaving violently at the sight of his stricken comrade, unable to raise the alarm or fire the semi-automatic weapon that now lay across the same crooked arm that nursed his convulsing stomach.

The small fleet sped on toward its allotted target, the main north-south runway of the airbase. A full thirty seconds passed before McDowell, traveling in the following *Trans-Territory*, realized the lack of shooting had failed to sound the signal for her eastern and southern comrades to commence their runs.

"Open fire," she bellowed as she raised her machine pistol. She aimed at a row of drums neatly stacked alongside a large hanger some fifty yards to the left and fired a long and sustained burst. Her companions in the rear of her vehicle and in the following *Mitsubishi* and *Snow Minx* did likewise. A few seconds later the turret of the leading armored *8x8* swiveled to the left and its chain gun began to rake the passing building with a long and sustained staccato of 50-caliber shells.

Contingent One reached the main runway within two minutes of crashing through the arrestor barrier at the main gate. The ICV now headed straight for the first row of aircraft lined up along the eastern edge of the runway. Without reducing speed, it raced down the full row of twelve F-22 aircraft smashing the tails off each as it hit them. Meanwhile, the *Trans-Territory* and the Mitsubishi raced along the outer side of the twelve aircraft on the western side of the runway pausing long enough for their occupants to fire four RPGs into the engine intakes of the first four aircraft before leapfrogging on to the next four then the next four. From there the lead vehicles sped on to join the *Snow Minx* which had driven straight to a second aircraft parking area further south along the main runway. It proceeded to fire an RPG into the avionics pods of the first three *Terminator* drones before similarly leapfrogging onto the next three in the squadron.

"Phase two!" yelled McDowell.

The three vehicles then proceeded to a second group of UAVs. This one contained three long-range RQ-4b *Global Hawk II* patrol drones, five MQ-9 *Reaper* ground attack drones, and an RQ-3c *Dark Star III* high altitude surveillance drone. They each fired an RPG into these remaining aircraft. Meanwhile, the ICV raced to the main UAV service hanger and raked the whole building and its contents of smaller observation and surveillance drones with 50-caliber cannon fire.

The three conventional vehicles drove back to the take-up station alongside the ICV, signaling that the mission was now complete.

"Right," yelled McDowell, "job done! Retreat!"

The whole contingent then wheeled north and sped out of the main gate, turned off onto the highway, and headed away from the base. At North Pole, they turned right and sped off into the mountains to the east. They had been inside the base for just 17 minutes. In that time, they had completely wrecked sixteen F-22s, severely damaged eight more, destroyed nine *Terminators*, two *Global Hawks*, two *Reapers*, one *Dark Star*, seventeen smaller assorted drones, and seriously damaged most of the rest of the aircraft on the base.

Meanwhile, *Contingent Two* had moved to within fifty yards of the eastern perimeter entrance to the base. There three of its flat-bed trucks turned one hundred and eighty degrees to the east so that the three-inch mortars mounted on the rear of the trucks faced the fuel storages tanks eight hundred yards to their west. Denton mounted the hood of the middle vehicle and surveyed the target area.

"Commence firing!" he yelled.

Each mortar squad fired its ten mortar rounds in quick succession at the giant tanks in the distance. Seven tanks received direct hits and immediately exploded, sending up spectacular balls of flame. Denton surveyed the fiery scene through his binoculars. "Cease firing!" he yelled needlessly. "Withdraw."

The entire contingent then sped off to the east, returning from whence they came. The only resistance they encountered was from the two air-force sentries at the entrance gate who opened fire on them with their semi-automatic weapons. The two machine gunners on the lead truck which still faced the gate had returned fire, killing one outright and grievously wounding the other. The mission of *Contingent Two* was over in just twelve minutes. In that time, they had made the whole fuel storage precinct of the base a firestorm.

Contingent Three commenced its run the moment it heard firing from the north. Within five minutes it had reached the southern perimeter of the base. The three lead vehicles then paused while the Ford F750 raced straight past them. It executed a one 180° turn before halting in front of the lead two-ton truck carrying Martin. Martin jumped from the cab, ran to the Ford driver's door and yelled: "Okay, back 'er up."

The driver complied, reversing the two-ton truck up to within one and a half yards of the row of five-foot-high, one yard spaced, concrete bollards that were laid around the entire perimeter of the Eielson Air Force Base, ten yards from the perimeter fence.

"Halt," yelled Martin. "Set 'er up."

The three-man crew deftly deployed the whole weird contraption, each having practiced this drill a dozen times in the previous two weeks. The mobile girder bridge unfolded. One rear span, sitting snugly behind the inner one for easy transportation, swung out and was lowered by its cranes, winches, pivots, hawsers and girders. It formed a low arch spanning ten yards long, six feet high. When fully deployed it could carry a ten-ton truck. The specific traffic it was designed to carry on this particular Sunday morning was the three vehicles of the southern strike force that had preceded it to the rally point, plus the tow truck itself.

Martin checked the deployment. "Right," he yelled. "Back 'er up."

The tow truck quickly reversed up and over the bridge picking up speed on the downward span. With the vehicle still in reverse, the driver gunned the motor and sent the vehicle crashing backward through the chain-lock perimeter fence. The rest of the vehicles in the southern contingent then crossed the bridge and drove through the hole in the fence then on into the base to execute their mission, with Martin now back in the lead vehicle directing the attack.

Contingent Three's initial targets were the aircraft lining the base's southern runway. Immediately they were taken out, the southern force raced to the heart of the southern workshop area. Here it disbursed on foot for fifteen minutes, wreaking as much havoc as possible with grenades and pre-primed explosives with timers set for ten-minute. Martin waited with his command vehicle watching the raid, checking his watch periodically. At exactly fifteen minutes from his initial crossing of the bridge, he started beeping the vehicle's horn, short three-second bursts every thirty seconds. The raiding party returned to their vehicles within two and a half minutes ready for their Phase Two.

"Mount up!" yelled Martin. "Let's go. Phase Two."

Contingent Three proceeded south to the base runway that hosted the aircraft of the 168th Air Refueling Group. There sat a line of three aging KC135Y *Stratotanker* aerial-refueling aircraft and three more modern KC 45c *Thirst Quencher* tankers. The whole strike group paused only long enough to fire two RPGs into each aircraft before heading off toward the main base workshop while the armored truck headed for the base control tower.

At the northern workshops, the invaders dismounted and disbursed throughout the complex planting plastic explosive charges on anything that looked expensive and arming the detonators timed to explode in eight minutes.

Meanwhile, the armored truck arrived at the control tower where three of its passengers dismounted and headed for the main stairway. But that is as far as they got.

By this time the Base Duty Officer and the two Air Traffic Controllers, aware of what was happening, had unlocked the tower armory and distributed automatic weapons among themselves. The two lead insurgents as they mounted the final section of the stairwell ran headlong into a hail of fire from the tower's occupants. The third, realizing this part of their mission had failed, turned and fled to the armored car. The driver gunned the motor and sped away to the rally point at the southern end of the runway.

The remainder of *Contingent Three* completed its mission and returned to its vehicles as planned. By now a chorus of sirens howling the alert had woken practically everyone in a five miles radius of the base. Vehicles and running figures emerged from all directions. All three strike vehicles of the southern contingent, now accompanied by all but two of its members, wheeled out of the workshop precinct and roared south towards the rally point.

They never reached it. Blocking their path at the shattered section of the perimeter fence was an armored sentry drone, its twin machine guns firing directly at the approaching convoy. Off to the left, about one hundred and fifty yards, a second similar remote-controlled vehicle sped along the outside perimeter service road towards the now unattended mobile bridge span. Three hundred yards to the right of the obstructing drone an ageing *Bradley* Infantry Fighting Vehicle was speeding along the same track towards the same entry point.

Martin assessed the situation quickly and accurately as his group sped towards their exit point. Their escape route was blocked.

He barked a quick order to his driver and the armored vehicle made a long arching curve; headed back the way it had come; headed north again towards the main gate. His followers took his lead and followed.

But too late. The entrance from which the first contingent had entered and escaped was now blocked. Another *Bradley* IFV and a *Stryker* ICV both had their turrets pointed directly at Martin's makeshift contemporary. This time Martin did not have time to bark an order. A shoulder-launched anti-tank rocket slammed into his vehicle – he and his compatriot died instantly.

The three remaining vehicles in *Contingent Three* screeched to a halt. Everything suddenly went silent. Except for the wailing sirens from all sides of the beleaguered group.

"Give it up," a loudspeaker barked from somewhere beyond the main gate guardhouse. "You've got nowhere to go. Give it up or I'll order my soldiers to fire on you."

Silence prevailed for a further ten seconds or so. Then a sub-machine gun rocketed up into the air above the Volvo; clattered to the ground with a muted metallic bounce. Within seconds, a rain of similar hardware followed suit. Then a single pair of hands appeared above the cab of the Volvo followed by an apprehensive call:

"Don't shoot. We surrender."

As an ashen face rose slowly between the two rising hands a deafening roar of exploding munitions erupted from the workshops a mile or so to the south. A pall of black smoke rose from the site to join the many plumes spiraling to the heavens to the south, while their grander cousin billowed like a volcano to the east.

"Mission successful but casualties high," texted Western Command Headquarters to a now furious Parnell thousands of miles to the south. *High indeed!* Of the sixty-two insurgents that had embarked on the raid on the Eielson Air Force Base that crisp Alaskan morning four were dead and twenty-six were prisoners of the United States Air Force. Their adversaries had suffered two dead and one badly wounded.

In consolation, the Military Wing of the American Patriotic Association could boast a spectacular strike costing the Frazer government over ten billion dollars in lost military assets. But Parnell knew even a casualty-free result would have been a political disaster. Now all he could manage was damage control. Now Frazer and his gang could, and legitimately so, label the whole APA a terrorist organization.

The folks in Fairbanks knew about it, of course, so rumors of a terrorist attack circulated throughout the state and into the wider North American and world communities via the underground press. But all the American and Canadian general population heard officially from their respective governments or mainstream media – heavily censored as usual – was that a terrorist plot had been foiled; four terrorists had died in the attack; twenty-six had been captured and two brave American airmen had lost their lives in the service of their country. Each of the latter was awarded the Silver Star posthumously.

Frazer, though, heard the full details and so did Fifth and the rest of his Global Security Commission. It unnerved them; shook them to the core. This was a military strike; carried out on American soil, executed by Canadians but, if the captured insurgents were to be believed, this new rebel army was commanded by a former American army officer.

They were not aware, of course, or, if they were, chose to ignore it, that Parnell had not authorized this raid. This was exactly the hot-headed reactionary initiatives he had warned about when the bulk of the APA council decided not to consider his Military Wing options. But they were thinking about them now. And they were horrified and fearful of what retribution might follow from Frazer's ruthless regime.

An APA Manifesto

Modest attempts by some American activists to win international support for the APA had proven largely ineffective but their disappointment was subdued due to their having more pressing domestic concerns to deal with. Their efforts, however, had not gone entirely unnoticed particularly by a former Prime Minister of Australia, Talbot Macintyre, whose interest had been piqued by Parnell's old friend Andy Wilks. The former politician could not proclaim his feelings publicly but he could privately, particularly within his own home. There his real passion was noted approvingly by a quick-witted, energetic, and purposeful young student of journalism, Julia Macintyre. Ms. Macintyre took up the call with gusto laying the foundations for a manifesto for the APA that neither Parnell, LeMonte, Chambers, Rouleau nor any of the APA leaders across North America had yet had time to create.

The young Macintyre's call was primarily to her own people, but it was penned in such a way as to stimulate the development of a global movement Parnell and his APA patriots would find increasingly valuable in their own indigenous struggle. Macintyre's initial draft was titled *American Patriotic Association Sympathizers – A Manifesto.*

It read:

> *"I propose that we found, here in Australia, a movement known as "American Patriotic Association Sympathizers" (APAS for short) or something similarly named. The purpose of this movement would be to show support for and give encouragement to, those Americans who are now congregating all over the United States of*

America to press for, advocate, and inspire a return to grassroots democracy in that country.

I propose that state branches of the APAS be established in each Australian state and territory and that each branch, or chapter, campaign actively to raise funds, publicize goals and encourage support amongst the Australian population for these American patriots.

I further propose that we approach our Canadian, British, New Zealand, Irish, and other cultures of the English-speaking world, to found similar organizations within their respective polities with similar aims and activities to our movement. I can see no reason why such activity and support organizations should not be encouraged and founded in every country of the world that cherishes freedom, democracy, the rule of law, and human rights. It would be particularly appropriate in those countries whose forebearers have provided the bulk of emigrants to North America over the past four or more centuries and from whose seed the same cultural and traditional values were born, aspired to, transported to the New World, and were further enhanced by their North Americans descendants.

But, of course, America is not only peopled from immigrants from Europe. Immigrants to that new society came from all over the world, particularly from Africa and Asia, where the values embodied and articulated in the European Enlightenment did not manifest themselves quite so clearly. The journeys of some of those immigrants have not been quite as pleasant and benign as those of their European counterparts. But all these peoples that now form that polyglot society which, together with indigenous peoples of that hemisphere, now collectively calls itself 'American'.

What Americans like to think of as American values are derived, in essence, from the values of the many, many peoples who have crossed the seas and trudged the land to locate in what is now called the United States of America. Those immigrants took their hopes and dreams with them and in that vast expanse between the Pacific and Atlantic oceans they melded those values into a unique blend of philosophical thought that their descendants think of as 'American Values'. That mingling was achieved, mostly by peaceful discourse and compromise, but not always, and sometimes not gently either. Even though American history is punctuated with a few bursts of great violence – the Revolutionary War, the Civil War, the Indian Wars, the Civil Rights Movement, and numerous other minor wars and conflicts within the American body politic – there has been a steady advancement in what we now globally think of as 'Human Values', particularly since that daring and profound declaration of the late eighteenth century that begins with the words: "We the people hold these truths to be self-evident … that all men are created equal".

What the American Patriotic Association in the United States is trying to do today is to win back for the common people of that land the embodiment that was proclaimed in law and born in trial, espoused so eloquently by one of America's most famous sons: "Government of the people, for the people, by the people".

I'm not sure when that principle left the American Republic; if indeed it was ever fully realized at all. Even as the phrase: "all men are created equal" was first uttered, it was never intended to extend to women, slaves, or indigenous Americans. It was not even meant to include all 'white men' given that most of the first thirteen states of the new republic had restrictions on the right to vote based on property ownership.

But it was, nevertheless, a momentous step for the whole human race in its quest for social justice for all peoples, as momentous as Magna Charta, the document that enshrined into English law the principle that the sovereign was not above the law but subject to it like all other people in the kingdom. And the struggle that ensued immediately following the Declaration of Independence was as momentous as the struggle in England over a century before in which a king lost his head and the principle was established in that realm that the people's will, as espoused by their elected representatives, should prevail over that of the head of state. The American proclamation inspired the French Revolution which introduced to that land the concepts of citizenship, nationhood, and "liberty, equality and fraternity".

America has come a long way since 1776 and much of its progress towards the ideals espoused at the founding its republic has been approached encouragingly. That republic was never perfect but America has, probably more than any other great power in the history of the world, made more progress to creating an egalitarian commonwealth for all of its citizens than almost any other nation. It would be a great blow to all people who value freedom, democracy, human rights, and the rule of law if she regressed now.

And that's what seems to threaten at this precarious time in its history. Whether by malicious design, benign neglect, or an increasing sense of helplessness on the part of many, the republic appears to be drifting steadily and inexorably away from being a democratic republic towards becoming a plutocratic emporium. Wealth is being concentrated increasingly into the hands of fewer and fewer members of the elite and the nation has taken on an increasingly militaristic tone in its domestic as well as its international affairs.

The war drums have not stopped beating for most of the last century. Indeed, they seem to be getting louder, and not just in the embroiled trouble spots of Iraq, Afghanistan, Yemen, Iran, Taiwan, and Canada. The unchecked growth in American military technology, domination of space, automation of firepower, and extension of global reach, marches ever onward; it seems the American militarists have no limit to their ambition.

Why should Australians, Canadians, Britons, Germans, and all the other aspirants of "life, liberty, and the pursuit of happiness" care what happens to the American republic? Because, whether we like it or not, the United States of America is the pre-eminent nation in the world today. It certainly is the leader of the Western world, even if some Europeans are reluctant to acknowledge that fact, and it is doubtful that any other aspirant to that role can, or will, rise to replace it within the next several decades. Even in the re-emerging civilizations of China and India, there is not, in their historic traditions, anything that resembles a liberal democracy of the type that we in the West have come to regard as being the most advanced form of social development yet devised from the point of view of the common man or woman, traditionally that section of society that forms the bulk of all earlier civilizations, the peasantry.

Imperfect though she is, the United States of America is still the best hope we have for leadership to a benign civilization for ordinary people. If America goes down the road of fascism, militarism, and imperialism, then it is the citizens of our own countries who will also become the subject peoples of the American elite, aided and abetted by *a handful of Quislings within our own regional elites.*

So, if our American friends are now motivated to rise up as they have in the past, in the Populous Movement of the late nineteenth century, the IWW movement (the "Wobblies") of the early twentieth and the Civil Rights and Feminist movements of the late mid-century, then it is in our best interests to see them succeed.

No-one in the American Patriotic Association is advocating armed insurrection or violent rebellion in the United States; they have made that mistake in the recent past and seen its grievous and unproductive consequences. Nor is this paper advocating violence, such strategies are not only morally wrong but also counter-productive. Furthermore, they are unnecessary. Non-violent protest and advocacy have proved to be successful strategies for achieving social and economic change in countries as diverse as India, the Philippines, Eastern Europe, North Africa, and many other places in the world over the past century. They can be so again.

The current United States Government may not be an inherently malicious or malevolent entity. It may just be a lapsed devotee, an errant practitioner, a neglectful overseer, but not irredeemably bad or deliberately willful. Active, lawful, and relentless protest and advocacy by a determined, dedicated, and patriotic people can remedy its shortcomings. Those who form the body politic of the American Patriotic Association certainly think so.

It is important for our American compatriots to know they are not alone in their struggle. And they need to know that they do not struggle for themselves alone. They struggle for us all, all of us who value what they value, values that many, many peoples around the world share with them in common. And when they march, they need to

The Australian people responded enthusiastically and within three months of Julia Macintyre's draft appearing in the national electronic newspaper *The Australian On-Line* there were forty-seven chapters of the APAS established across the country.

In Canada, Rouleau seized on the Australian draft and simply transposed the words "Canada" and "Australia" in the text and posted the draft on the *Free Canada* website. A vigorous online debate ensued and a final draft penned by a linguistics professor from McGill University was voted by the on-line forum as the final version of the Canadian APAS manifesto. It did not differ markedly from the Australian version. More importantly, chapter establishment of the APAS was even more vigorous in Canada than in Australia with no less than ninety-three chapters being established across the country by year's end.

In Britain, the process was a little slower, with British enthusiasts preferring to incorporate more of their own cultural heritage into their text. Quotes from Shakespeare and Churchill figured prominently. Chapter establishment was also vigorous although not as prolific as that in the former dominions in North America and the antipodes.

The French took to the French Canadian version of the Canadian text with enthusiasm also. Many saw the spirit of Lafayette in the draft and were keen to reaffirm the principles of their own republic's birth and revive their ancestors' support for the American rebellion.

And so it went globally. The German's seized on the English text but modified it by replacing the English heroes with German ones. The Poles did likewise. The Japanese crafted a distinctive version that incorporated their Emperor and cast him as the benign protector of modern Japanese democratic aspirations. A Spanish version, developed initially in Nicaragua, was rapidly adopted with minor local modifications throughout Central and South America.

Within twelve months of Macintyre posting her initial draft of the Australian manifesto, there were more chapters of the APAS around the world than there were chapters of the APA within the United States of America.

New American Patriots

Francoise Toulemont and Jalan Nanakinilli glanced at each other and then back into the glowing red face of Jackson Parnell as the three of them huddled around the roaring log fire in the common room of the Berkley campus of the University of California. Parnell had just outlined his idea for a daring non-kinetic strike against the Frazer Government's key revenue source, the Inland Revenue Service.

"Well we can't actually do that," said Toulemont.

"Why not?" asked Parnell.

"Because they're using quantum cryptography," said Nanakinilli.

"I thought you both knew all about that stuff," said Parnell.

"We do," asserted Toulemont, "or at least we like to think we have as good an understanding of Quantum Mechanics as anyone does."

"And we know enough about quantum cryptography to know that you can't break their code," Nanakinilli chimed in. "No-one can," he added quickly to establish that their ignorance was not something to be ashamed of.

Francoise Toulemont had become fascinated with the call of academia at an early age. She loved the smell of the old university buildings of the Sorbonne, their quintessentially French architecture, the feel of its deeply textured books, and the ambiance of French culture that they all exuded. Her choice of physics allowed her to pursue its enchantment through to doctoral level. The success of her thesis on quantum cryptography led to her being headhunted by the University of California, Los Angeles where she had met Dr. Jalan Nanakinilli.

In contrast to her gentile upbringing, Nanakinilli had been the product of the Indian slums, and also of an emerging and increasingly confident nation that had always cherished education, particularly after it had achieved its independence from the British. Nanakinilli's talent was obvious even in his primary school years. By the time he had finished high-school a place was waiting for him at the prestigious Bangalore University. There he studied Information Technology and Quantum Computing. It was his Ph.D. in the latter that won him a post-doctoral fellowship at UCLA.

In his graduate years, a blissful summer romance, which went nowhere serious, lured him to Perth in Australia where he was invited to attend the Christmas function of the local branch of the Australian Institute of International Affairs. At that meeting, he had met an enigmatic Australian with white hair and white beard. The old man had wandered over to him and simply started chatting. During the conversation, the old man mentioned that he'd just written a bullet point summary of an investigation he'd made into the events of 11th September, 2001 in New York City and Washington DC. Nanakinilli had heard of 9/11, of course, but hadn't given much thought to it. He wasn't that interested in politics. But the old man had made the astounding comment that he thought the Americans had orchestrated it. Nanakinilli had been the soul of politeness and allowed the old man to ramble on.

"What do you mean: they had a hand in it?" Nanakinilli had asked.

"I mean 9/11 was an inside job," said the old man.

Nanakinilli's eyebrows had raised, something the old man undoubtedly expected as he'd immediately launched into a ten-minute dialogue of the evidence, concluding with: "The evidence is irrefutable."

To extract himself from the conversation Nanakinilli had given the aging skeptic his e-mail address, the old man offering to send him his paper summarizing his evidence. It arrived a few days later. Nanakinilli scanned it, thought it was an interesting viewpoint then promptly forgot about it. He gave it no more thought until, while on an extended weekend seminar on the UC campus, he was invited to an evening lecture by the Northern California 9/11 Truth Alliance in Santa Cruz. The keynote speaker was an aging American architect, Richard Gage, the same architect the old man had referred to in his paper [*See Appendix 2 for a copy of this paper*].

Nanakinilli started to wonder about some of the strange goings-on he'd witnessed at UCLA since his arrival there a year earlier. These events were explained a few years later by Parnell when he had come seeking clarification of Toulemont's initial 9/11 revelations in the light of Parnell's advice from his Australian friend Andy Wilks. Now Nanakinilli's 'old man' story had corroborated Toulemont's and Wilks' sources and had led to Parnell's latest conversation with the two physicists and his plans for a non-kinetic strike against the Frazer Regime.

Parnell had diverted his return trip from his APA board meeting via Los Angeles where Gillian McCloud had arranged for him to meet the two celebrity scientists.

"You're saying they have an unbreakable code?" queried Parnell. "I didn't think any code was unbreakable. It is, after all, a product of human creation, so I would have thought that, with enough effort and enough resources applied to the problem, it should be able to be broken."

"That's just the point," said Toulemont. "It's not a human creation. It's a natural phenomenon."

"A natural code?" Parnell frowned as his suspicion rose

"Well, not exactly a natural code," Nanakinilli corrected. "It's more like they have harnessed a natural phenomenon to create a message medium that cannot be intercepted without destroying it."

Parnell's frown deepened. "You've lost me," he said.

Dr Francoise Toulemont assumed the condescending air of a university lecturer delivering a lecture in Quantum Mechanics to a lay audience. She'd made these presentations countless times since she and Nanakinilli had been nominated for the Nobel Prize in Physics for their ground-breaking work on Quantum Entanglement and its Macro-world Implications. They now had near rock-star status in the world of American science. Invitations to explain their discoveries had come from all over the country, particularly from the military and from Capitol Hill.

Job offers had come fast and alluringly, particularly from the military which was keen to see these two intellectual wizards and their knowledge did not fall into the wrong hands, or under the wrong kind of influence. Private industry was equally siren-like with its lucrative offers of salaries, perks, research resources, and idyllic locations.

But to no avail. Toulemont and Nanakinilli were true scientists. Their devotion was to science not to mammon or power.

That's when their real difficulties began. And at first, they hadn't realized what was happening. They suffered unexplained delays in the renewal of their research grants. Then they were refused release from mundane teaching duties which would allow them to attend important conferences – they thought this was all just part of the system of declining academic standard and intellectual decay. Then came the excessively pedantic scrutiny of their research papers and endless rejections by reviewers and editors. But after three long years of these ever-increasing obstacles, the message was crystal clear: "Play ball our way or forget about any further advancement in your careers, both in North America and in Western Europe".

India had been welcoming. So too had China. Toulemont had expected her native France would be also. She was stunned when the French academy rebuffed her inquiries on her prospects of returning to France to continue her work.

That had finally brought them to Parnell. There were more than a few disgruntled academics in the American Academy. Most American scientists yearned for a return to the old days when knowledge was not sought for the power of the state or the profits of the private sector. Many academics were members of the American Patriotic Association, and the great majority of those academics who were not, were sympathizers of the movement. Toulemont and Nanakinilli were among this group.

"Every code needs a key so it can be decoded," explained Toulemont. "Without it, the more sophisticated codes are almost impossible to break and even those which can be broken are usually decoded long after the information contained in their messages is useful."

"I am familiar with cipher activities," interjected Parnell. He did not want to be taken back to military kindergarten at this point in his career.

"Yes, of course," said Nanakinilli. He nodded a little disapprovingly at Toulemont not to be too patronizing.

"Well, the challenge in cryptography, as you know," Toulemont continued, more respectfully, "is to convey the key from the encoder to the decoder without it falling into unauthorized hands. The most secure way of doing that is by personal courier. But personal couriers are slow, expensive, and vulnerable. And, if you're not very careful, their messages can be intercepted and read, without the courier even being aware of it. Key delivery can be sped up, and be made much cheaper by electronic delivery, but that makes them even more vulnerable to interception. And they can be read without the decoder ever being aware the message was intercepted. That's the biggest challenge in cryptography."

"Security of codebooks and keys has always been a high priority in the military and civilian affairs," agreed Parnell, impatience growing at the banality of the explanation.

"Precisely," said Nanakinilli. "Quantum cryptography offers the opportunity to encode a message so the receiver will know instantly if the message has been observed before it reaches the decoder."

"How?"

"Because the encoding of the key is done at quantum level where normal laws of nature don't apply – it's a whole different world to the macro-world. In the quantum world, the very activity of observing something actually changes it".

"What? You can change something just by looking at it?" queried Parnell.

"Exactly," chimed in Toulemont. "In the quantum world things are so small that bouncing something off of them, like light, or an electron, or some other elementary particle, actually changes its position or trajectory so that, by the time you observe the light particle, or whatever you're bouncing off that tiny particle, it's no longer where it was when you first observed it. As a result, you don't really know where it is or what direction it's traveling in."

"Well, how does that help in coding messages?" said Parnell.

"In quantum cryptography, the message is sent using single elementary particles, or photons – elementary packets of light that have a particular spin on them – spin up, spin down, spin left, spin right, et cetera. If they are observed, either by another photon of light, or another elementary particle, the spin on the message particle is reversed. Then the receiver reports back to the sender what the spin of the message particles received was and the sender confirms which, if any, are different from what was sent.

'If any are different, then both the sender and the receiver know that the message has been intercepted. It's actually a bit more complicated than that, and, of course, this is all done at a micro-micro-level with special equipment, but that's the essence of it."

"Can't the interceptor change the message back to what it originally was before they observed it?" asked Parnell.

"Non," said Toulemont. "That's the beauty of quantum cryptography. It's foolproof. There is no way known to do that. As Jalan said, the quantum world is a very weird and special place. It runs according to its own rules, not the normal rules of physics that apply in the everyday world we live in."

"So you can see, there is no way we can intercept the Treasury Department's messages by tapping into their communications networks, or hacking into their computer networks, especially if the information is encrypted using quantum technology." Nanakinilli shrugged. That was the way it was.

Parnell's shoulders slumped. He abruptly broke off the conversation.

"I have to water the horse," he said and rose and headed for the men's room. As he stood at the urinal, he pondered his dilemma. He had dearly wanted an intervention that would break into the regime's main source of funding, something that would severely disrupt the dictatorship's economic base without any Americans, civil or military, being physically hurt. Something that would deal a devastating blow to the regime while providing a great financial boost to many struggling American families.

He had not worked out exactly what to do, the financial wiz-kids would do that, but his thinking went along the lines of giving every American family a year's average family income as a tax refund. Dumping that amount of money into the public's hands at once would deal a huge fiscal blow to the elite. It would cause panic in the government. While it would probably be quickly reversed, given that most of the money would be going to the poor, the destitute and the needy, a fair amount of it would immediately flow out into the food, clothing and general retail outlets long before it could be stopped. And it would be next to impossible to recall much of it. Those who spent even some of the money simply wouldn't be able to pay it back and even this draconian government could not bankrupt tens of millions of people.

"So there's no way we can penetrate the Treasury Department's computer systems then?" Parnell said as he rejoined the group.

"I didn't say that," said Toulemont. "All human systems have weaknesses. Just because technology has effectively made one part of the system tamper-proof doesn't mean the whole system is tamper-proof." She smiled mischievously. "There are probably a dozen different ways we could penetrate the system."

"Ahh, the code cannot be broken, but we can get around the code?" Parnell clarified, his eyebrows lifting. Toulemont's statement rekindled his hope that the two young geniuses might be able to aid the cause after all. He leaned forward and engaged the pair with growing interest.

"Yes," said Toulemont.

"Certainly," chimed in Nanakinilli.

A broad grin spread across all three faces.

Two hours later each lifted their head, straightened their bent torsos, and stretched their tired arms. This now looked promising.

Imperial Expansion

Fifth's business interests had taken a severe hit during the 2008 Financial Crisis, particularly its banking interests. The Darcy family bank, the largest in the United States, had not been quite as greedy as some of its other industry contemporaries – not significantly so – but enough to avoid the type of catastrophe that befell some of the smaller institutions. One filed for bankruptcy immediately, two others were taken over by larger rivals at fire-sale prices. Fifth's position as de facto head of the industry had something to do with that but also the collective power of the major industry players, many of which were members of the Global Security Commission, virtually ensured its survival.

The United States Government came to the rescue with political donations to both major parties, and to members of both houses of congress. This ensured the appropriate levels of concern and sympathy for an industry proclaimed "too big [to be allowed] to fail", by injecting, ultimately, trillions of taxpayers' dollars. An appropriate level of 'tapering' of public support was introduced after a respectable period – of course, if one considers ten years of continued support to be 'reasonable' – but by that time the bulk of the collective losses of the industry had been 'socialized'. It was then deemed by most respectable economic and political commentators time to 'normalize' things, to return to traditional market-based, for-profit, private enterprise, capitalism. And, of course, before the myriad of small bank depositors, pension fund investors, insurance policyholders, and fixed income earners had stumbled onto the essential understanding that the purchasing power of their life savings had been seriously eroded by the 'rescue mission'. It had been 'taxation without representation' on a scale that would have made an eighteenth-century English tyrant blush with embarrassment, a currency debasement that would have made an ancient monarch proud.

The scam had not been confined to the United States either. The Japanese and British Governments saw the wisdom of the policy and followed suit early on. Other European governments were a little slower but as the fifth and sixth years of the practice of money printing – well, no one actually printed much money anymore, it was all money supplied out of thin air through the wizardry of fractional bank systems – the European Central Bank emulated its American counterpart and also came on board. As for the Chinese Government, they'd been with the Americans all along, much to the chagrin of the latter.

The Americans had hoped to redress their ballooning foreign exchange deficit by paying their creditors back with dollars of diminished value, but their inscrutable oriental debtors were having none of it. They fixed the exchange rate for their indigenous currency, the Rimini, to the US dollar and insisted on being paid back the same purchasing power they had loaned to their errant and gluttonous debtors. The American Government screamed 'currency manipulation', of course, but those who understood international finance knew it was the Americans who were manipulating their currency and that the Chinese were just protecting their interests to avoid being robbed blind.

Fifth and his council understood all of this, mainly because they had orchestrated it. They sat back somewhat bemused at the public discourse on the issue. Indeed, most financial professionals understood it. But they said nothing because it suited their purposes. The gullible public was who did not understand, especially those whose savings were being whittled away month by month. All they knew was their meager fixed and investment incomes did not keep pace with the rising cost of living. They grew poorer day by day but didn't know why. And they didn't know 'who', although vilifying 'greedy bankers', or 'banksters', as the money manipulators were now called, became a national, and international, pastime.

There had been public protests, particularly when the International Monetary Fund, the bankers' global enforcement instrument, dictated stringent 'austerity' measures on desperate national governments. They, in turn, were forced to reduce pensions, welfare support, and wages to public employees to comply with those loan conditions. But the average citizen, in almost every country, did not understand who was pulling the strings, or how. Most had never heard of the GSC. Most had never heard of Fifth or anyone within his inner circle. And that's the way Fifth liked it.

The COVID 19 pandemic of 2020 was an even greater bonanza for the Darcy family due mainly to its earlier retreat from hospitality industries and avoidance of transport industry investments and its heavy investment in the health care and pharmaceutical industries. Fifth, along with other leading entrepreneurs of the day had seen it coming and had positioned themselves advantageously beforehand. Some European GSC members had not been so farsighted and suffered serious losses due to their tardiness.

"Cyprus was fine," said Gerhardt after 2008. "So was Greece. Nobody really noticed and those that did didn't care," he added. "We were lucky with Spain because everybody attributed that fiasco to the Catalonia independence ruckus. And if Italy goes then no one will be surprised there either, and for the same reasons. But Britain, France, and Germany will be a different story. If they go then people will really start getting curious about what is happening."

"Germany is rock solid," said Fifth. "There's no problem there. Britain and France?" Fifth held his right hand up and waggled it a few times. "Would they really be missed? All the weight has moved eastward so they would not be any great loss these days," he said.

The Dutch prince was not so blasé after 2020.

"We've still got a lot of money tied up in Britain and France, especially our European members," protested Gerhardt. He meant: that's where the bulk of *my* family's wealth is still deployed.

"Hmm," mused Fifth with an air of nonchalance – he really didn't care too much about that particular Ancient Regime. Darcy money had already been redeployed elsewhere. But he would display an appropriate air of concern at the upcoming GSC board meeting just to placate the European councilors. They still seemed to think they were important. In any case, he had regularly warned Gerhardt of the inherent instability of the British and French economies so if the slow-moving prince had left himself exposed then that was hardly Fifth's fault.

The thin edge of the 'taper' that finally started to penetrate the tracks of the gravy train towards the end of the second decade of the twenty-first century spelled the beginning of the end of this particular phase of super-profit reaping, although banking still remained a lucrative business to be in. Banking was only one of many businesses in the Darcy business empire but it was Fifth's favorite haunt. Banking could be done anywhere; geography was largely irrelevant when it came to instant funds. And the Covid19 stimulus by various governments around the world reiterated the trillions dollar boondoggle to the banking industry once more in 2020.

As the third decade dawned, the Darcy family's alternative energy business took over as the great bonanza. The Darcy wealth base continued to grow exponentially. By this time 'shale gas' and 'tight oil' had supplanted traditional oil sources as the second major leg of the family's energy portfolio. This was facilitated by the wondrous technology of 'hydraulic fracturing, 'fracking'. The key twentieth-century traditional sources of the fossil fuel resources that had poured into a North American energy network dominated by the oil majors, of whom the Darcy-controlled group had been the largest and most influential. It was now largely dominated by more source-proximate predators, mostly of Chinese, Indian, and

East Asian domicile, particularly in the Persian Gulf and Central Asian regions. Fifth's control of these was now somewhat diminished.

In Europe, alternative energy sources were increasingly prominent, especially wind, solar and nuclear, although Russian-sourced fossil fuels still played an important role, albeit through the mist of the hot and cold running political relations with that former, steadily declining, great power. The European members of the GSC, particularly those controlling the traditional oil giants from that continent, were still influential in energy distribution, mainly because energy products were more constrained in that theater, and hence more crucial to local political economies. Energy efficiency had become the prevailing paradigm in that geopolitical space so technologies relating to that prevailed and the Europeans were still the masters of that game. Gerhardt may have been a little slow but Krupp, Phillips, and the other leading European industrial dynasties had not. They were doing very nicely in that closely controlled market.

But even the newly evolved hydrocarbon technologies and sources provided a short reprieve; the writing was clearly on the wall for fossil fuels. In North America 'fracking sites' had long exceeded 100,000 in number and were a ubiquitous sight across most states and provinces. It was becoming increasingly clear that the yield per site was not going to meet initial exuberant expectations. In the early bonanzas, two-thirds of fracking gas had come from just three major plays: Barnet in Texas; Haynesville in Eastern Texas and Western Louisiana; and the Marcellus play of Pennsylvania and West Virginia. Darcy interests dominated in all three. But production had peaked in both Barnet and Haynesville by the end of the second decade and, by its end, all three were clearly in terminal decline despite the prolific growth in the number of operating wells at each location. They were replaced by other lesser plays but by then it was readily apparent that shale gas and oil was not the long-term answer to America's energy dilemma. It was a reprieve at best.

In Canada, the Alberta Tar Sands continued to produce world-beating volumes of bitumen-based products but at fearful environmental costs, a fact not lost on Fifth but of no great concern to him. The local backlash, in particular from the indigenous First Nations communities whose traditional homelands were being decimated, became increasingly more strident and numerous. Resistance from non-indigenous Canadians, who cherished the wild beauty of the Canadian countryside, was intensifying. Indeed, much of Chamber's activist cohorts were filled with angry environmentalists who despaired at the avarice of the southern-based energy conglomerates, among which Darcy interests dominated.

Fifth was not perturbed. Business was business. He knew, as did his GSC comrades, that this particular opportunity would not last forever. If resource depletion did not bring it to an end then something else would, something like political agitation from disgruntled locals. Better to make hay while the sun shone. Cloudy skies in North America would, no doubt, give rise to clearer skies elsewhere. Or at least they always had, and he had no reason to believe there had been any significant change to that particular law of nature. There were still good profits to be made in the meantime.

The third major leg of the Darcy Empire, arms production, had also suffered a significant decline in profitability by the end of the second decade. The heady days of 2003 to 2008 were a thing of the past. Western publics had begun to signal their resistance to unbridled defense-spending by their respective governments. European governments had responded almost immediately to the 2008 financial crisis putting a severe check upon their discretionary spending policies overall. Defense spending was one of the first to suffer their austerity measures. It was so again in the 2020s.

In the United States, the initial ax fell on welfare spending. This saw drastic cuts as the tail end of the second decade unfolded and the third emerged. The bluff of the external threat maintained defense cut immunity for well into the third decade through the promotion of regional wars, terrorist atrocities, school shootings, and assorted bogeyman scares ranging from religious zealots in the Middle East, to crazed megalomaniacs in Africa, fascist nationalists in Eastern Europe, to political scare campaigns at home. Threats, it was asserted by all manner of establishment mouth-pieces, were everywhere and military spending was the only antidote that could reliably keep the citizenry safe – that, and increased surveillance of every move anyone might care to make. A "we've gotta get them 'fore they gets us" mentality held sway for almost twenty years from the initial 'great crime' of 9/11 but supplemented spasmodically by lesser stimulatory episodes. By 2020 it was civil disorder that was the great bugaboo, particularly race relations spurred on by police brutality and ever widening income disparities. The GSC's media juggernaut worked overtime and effectively kept public fear at fever pitch.

But even that did not last. Gradually cynicism crept into every Western society. The general populous increasingly began to realize that, despite its huge investment in 'national security', it didn't feel any safer. Indeed, it felt considerably less so. So most began to feel that increased defense spending was not the answer and even the contemporary level of military spending could probably be redirected to better effect elsewhere.

"No matter," reasoned Fifth. "All good things come to an end. It was time to move on to something new."

Like what? he thought.

'Well', he answered his own question, 'Aged Care looks promising – nothing like a health scare to open a wallet.'

'In fact,' he reasoned, 'you don't even need a scare to open a wallet. All you need is the passing of time. There's only one alternative to getting old and no one is keen to resort to that. People will pay almost anything for a few more years of life.'

So the Darcy family diversified into Aged Care and Health Care. And a new gravy train left the station bound for Tomorrow Land.

COVID 19 gave that strategy a significant boost, not unexpectedly from Fifth's point of view, but fortuitous for Darcy family interests nevertheless.

Though even this was not the greatest business opportunity to become available to the Darcy family and the other great houses whose patriarchs filled the membership of the GSC. No, that came from another phenomenon which they, and their ilk, were largely responsible: anthropomorphic climate change.

By 2025, after the pandemic disruption of five years earlier, world trends had largely settled back into their long-term trajectories. There had been a boost to pandemic preparations world-wide immediately thereafter but they tended to wane as memory of the disruption faded and new more current concerns surfaced in people's collective milieus, particularly the political restrictions in many countries and the increasing effects of climate change. Carbon dioxide levels in the atmosphere above the Mauna Loa Observatory in Hawaii exceeded four hundred parts per million. Disastrous forest fires, annual river flooding, storm surges, rampant tropical disease outbreaks, and numerous other climate-change-induced disruptions were mounting. All the ecological disaster chickens were coming home to roost and Fifth and his cohorts were ready for them, thanks to the commercial genius of its urbane patriarch, John Davyd Darcy the Fifth.

The Darcy family had exited the insurance business in the early years of the second decade of the twenty-first century. Fifth could see it would not be a particularly profitable business from there on in. Instead, the Darcy family invested in a broad swathe of industries offering global warming remediation technologies. Fifth bought heavily into construction companies offering levy bank and flood control services, into pharmaceutical companies with leading-edge technologies combatting tropical diseases and the surprisingly frequently novel pandemic scares which now seemed to be a permanent feature of the global health environment, and into energy efficiency research. And he established a broad property portfolio of land in Canada and Alaska with its promising potential for future agricultural production. He established the world's biggest portfolio of sea farming ventures, hatcheries, deep-sea fish farms, aquaculture processing facilities, and land and sea transport fleets to service them and distribute their output. His energy industry portfolio now included seven of the world's largest solar energy farms, and he had already negotiated access to promising areas of the Australian outback for a giant solar energy power station that could generate electricity and channel it via submarine power cables to the Indonesian archipelago and the Malay Peninsula and further on into Asia. He and a small handful of GSC compatriots cornered the market for lithium, a key ingredient to renewable batteries, those outside the control of the Chinese and Russian captive markets. His companies were on the cutting edge of large-scale electrical storage technology, so the generation of electricity from solar sources via electrical storage systems could be preserved for use during non-daylight hours.

Although Fifth and his compatriots had had a significant hand in creating the problems now facing the world, he was, they were, also determined to be a significant player in finding a solution to global warming, or at least the remediation of its worst effects, provided it was profitable to do so, of course.

In truth, though, Fifth's first love had always been Banking. Here he had cut his teeth as a budding business graduate. It was the business he understood best. Money, trade, exchange, stores of value … these had always been at the center of civilizations from the dawn of time and Fifth was convinced they always would be. To be the conduit through which the world's exchange of values was processed was an interminable source of wealth, the opportunity to skim a few percentage points of value off the top of every transaction ever made, through some means or another, for every party to every transaction on Planet Earth, that was the source of eternal wealth, and Fifth was a master of that game. No amount of technological change threatened the basic character of this system even if the medium of exchange varied, be it coin, notes, paper, precious stones or metals, electronic impulses, or technology. The basic idea of measuring and transferring value from one soul to another would always exist. Financial intermediaries, and their services, no matter what they were called, would always be in demand.

Fifth's great uncle, a former president of the Darcy banking empire, had explained it to him during a heart to heart conversation just after Fifth's ninth birthday: "The key to profitability in any business," he said, "lies in the ability, not only perceive an opportunity but to control who can and cannot take advantage of that opportunity. Of all the principles of business that ensure profitability, monopoly, or as close to it as you can practically get, is the most important. The greater the demand and the narrower the supply the higher will be the price, irrespective of the costs involved."

"The other key principle that ensures profitability," he continued, "is timing, when to get in and when to get out. If revenues do not exceed costs, or they don't appear if they will be, then get out. If it looks like revenues will exceed costs, and in good enough margin to make the opportunity better than any other available opportunity, then it is time to get in."

Fifth had listened intently that day and he never forgot those pearls of wisdom from the great old master who'd done so much to enhance the Darcy family fortune. So, in the contemporary environment, he reasoned, it was time to get out of fossil fuels, and military hardware, and it was time to get into alternative energy and into new technologically advanced intensive food producing ventures especially now that many of the traditional food-producing methodologies were failing. But banking? Always stay in banking.

Fifth called the meeting to order and asked:

"The Chinese have dumped another trillion dollars of US securities onto global bond markets," he said in earnest. "What do you suggest we do about it?"

He glanced around the room at the assembled council. Blank faces stared back.

"Well?" he challenged.

Then they all spoke at once.

Cracking the Bank

As Parnell well knew, cryptography had come a long way since the start of the twenty-first century. Actually, it had come a long way throughout the previous century with techniques like letter substitution being a thing of the distant past even as that earlier century had started. But the breaking of the Japanese cypher prior to the Second World War by American codebreakers and the equally impressive breaking of the German Enigma codes by their British counterparts during that same conflict had demonstrated that having unbreakable codes, or as close to that ideal as humans could get, were going to be indispensable to military operations from then onwards. Added to this, the emergence of the telecommunications revolution in the later twentieth century with most financial and commercial activity taking place over broadcast media meant that simply avoiding snooping interlopers from listening in was a luxury that was no longer possible. From that point on, anyone sending a message they wanted to keep private had to work on the assumption that someone would be listening in no matter what surreptitious encoding device was used.

Parnell had certainly worked on that assumption most of the time.

But as the twenty-first century dawned two new and exciting technologies had greatly enhanced the already impressive achievements that the invention of the silicon chip, the ever miniaturizing circuitry, and enhanced computing capacity spawned in the previous decades. Those two new realms were Chaos Theory and Quantum Mechanics. Parnell knew very little about these except their names.

Quantum Mechanics had been around since the beginning of

the twentieth century, although few people, even leading physicists, really understood it. As for Chaos Theory, since its emergence in the second half of the 1900s, most people simply assumed that it meant what its name implied, that what was being described was randomness, unpredictability, chaos, something that could not be used to any great effect because of its sheer unpredictability. But, by the time Toulemont and Nanakinilli were introduced to these theories, scientists were starting to realize that both provided new insights into the real universe that human beings had never really thought about before.

Theoretically, both Chaos Theory and Quantum Mechanics were incompatible because they were based on different mathematics. If cryptographers could combine the two incompatible phenomena, they would have a system that was both unpredictable and detectable if intercepted, a truly secure messaging system. That's what Toulemont and Nanakinilli had achieved and that's what brought Parnell to them for this meeting. They had spent most of their Ph.D. theses researching how to combine these two theoretically incompatible natural systems. It had taken them the best part of five years but by 2027 they had succeeded. Their research was ground-breaking and the publication of their findings rocketed them to near stardom in the scientific community. By 2030 most of the global financial and business communities had also discovered them and their amazing discoveries. Within a few short years, the whole civilized world was using their algorithms. So was the United States government.

Parnell had realized after the debacle at the Eielson Air Force Base that his revolutionary strategy was going to have to be much more subtle than merely mounting military operations in the traditional 'kinetic' fashion. The northern operation had been a disaster on several levels. Firstly, a significant portion of the attacking force had been captured and their subsequent interrogations had led to further losses through follow up counter-insurgency operations by Frazer's forces.

Secondly, the operation had resulted in the deaths of two United States soldiers. This distressed Parnell – he was, after all, a former United States soldier. More importantly from a strategic point of view, the death of these two soldiers had provided a tremendous propaganda victory for the Frazer regime. It allowed the regime to portray the APA movement as a terrorist group when it was imperative to Parnell's strategy that it be seen by the American public, and indeed the whole world, as a heroic liberation movement. To be successful, the APA needed the support of the American public. He could not afford for it to be seen as the enemy of the people.

That's what turned Parnell towards cyber warfare. In cyberspace, he could be just as disruptive to the Frazer regime's capacity to govern America as he could be by mounting physical attacks. Moreover, provided he did not damage or disrupt vital safety features of computer-controlled infrastructure, he could deliver devastating blows to the regime without physically hurting anyone. Properly targeted, he could also avoid inflicting disruptive financial and economic harm on the civilian population whilst simultaneously wreaking havoc upon the structures of government and its support agencies. He could even thwart the regime's efforts to exploit the civil population by frustrating its predatory tax collections and economic plundering schemes. He could even deliver real benefits to the civil population by plundering the regime's financial and economic resource, by redistributing them from the powerful to the weak, from the rich to the poor, from the haves to the have-not. He could become a modern-day Robin Hood. And that would pay enormous dividends to the APA both politically and logistically.

But he needed the expertise of Toulemont and Nanakinilli to do so. It was they who had the skills to break into the secure systems their technology had spawned. He explained his plan to the two scientists. They both looked a little skeptical. Then Toulemont spoke:

"One hundred thousand dollars to over two hundred million taxpayers?" queried Toulemont.

"Yes," said Parnell. "That's the general idea."

"But that's twenty trillion dollars," said Nanakinilli. "That's nearly fifty percent of the whole Gross Domestic Product of the country. It's more than the whole Federal budget in one go."

"That's right," said Parnell. "It would be hugely disruptive to the Federal Government. And it wouldn't hurt anyone. In fact, it would do a lot of people a very big favor, to all those poor people who are really struggling daily to make ends meet, they would have money in their bank accounts, many for the first time in their lives. They could actually spend it on things they genuinely need."

"But the government will know instantly what's happened," said Toulemont. "They'll immediately nullify the payments."

"True," said Parnell, "which is why we will accompany the payments with a wide-ranging social media campaign just to let the people know the money is there in their bank accounts and encourage them to go out and spend it. As you say, the government will try to stop any withdrawals but they won't get it all back. An awful lot of people are going to go out and spend that money just as soon as they realize it's there to be spent. And as for those who are in debt, this money will either pay off those debts or substantially reduce them. Do you really think the people who are owed that money are just going to give it back once they've got their hands on it? I don't think so. The banks and the other greedy institutions are going to hang on to it. It will take the government years to go through all the legal proceedings to get the money back. No. I think that in the long run, the government is just going to have to suck it up and wear the loss. And it will put a huge hole in their budget".

"But won't they just print more money?" queried Nanakinilli. "I mean, that's what they do, don't they? They've been doing it for decades with their so-called 'Quantitative Easing' policies. They just print more money, or, more accurately, they just pass a few more accounting entries and create more money out of thin air. It will be wildly inflationary, won't it?"

"Yes," said Parnell. "And you're right. That's what they've been doing for decades. That's why the people don't have any money. What money they did have is now almost worthless because all the QE policies have debased the currency so much that a thousand dollars won't buy much anymore. That's why the middle class is now rubbing shoulders with the underclass. That's why it's only the very rich, the people who run the show, Frazer' cronies, have got all the money."

Toulemont and Nanakinilli both still looked perplexed. Economics was not their forte. Economics was not Parnell's forte either so he was relying on the quick course in Finance 101 that he had been given by his APA financial whiz-kids to enlighten them.

"Look," he said. "Who do you think benefits most from inflation? Who benefits most from the debasement of the value of the dollar?"

The two scientists looked back at him blankly.

"It's the people who owe money," explained Parnell trying hard not to sound patronizing. "If you borrow money that has a certain value and the real value of that debt goes down then you actually have to pay back less value than you borrowed in the first place. So, the lender suffers a real loss and the borrower gets the corresponding benefit. Leading business entrepreneurs do it all the time. They borrow lots of money, wait for inflation to jack up the value of the real assets that they buy with that money, then they sell the assets at the higher inflated prices and pay back the money they owe at its now debased value. Governments do it too. They have been doing it for centuries. They borrow money in the form of long-term bonds. They create inflation. Then they pay back the money decades later in the same nominal sums, now worth much less in real purchasing power than they originally borrowed. Even though they pay interest on the borrowed money, they take back a slice of that interest in taxes, and they pay the principal back in debased dollars. It depends on the rate of inflation, of course, but if they get enough inflation into the system, they can get to borrow your money for nothing. They can even come out in front if the inflation rate is high enough."

The two scientists look back at Parnell with mild understanding.

"But … I don't see how that helps with this plan," said Toulemont.

"Well," said Parnell, "the flip side to the inflation effect on borrowing applies to lending. The people who lend money are really the ones who suffer most from inflation. They have a stock of wealth in the form of their bank accounts, bonds and other financial investments. They lend money at a certain value but, if inflation is high, they get paid back in reduced value, in debased dollars. That's why all of those people who saved diligently for their retirement are now broke. They still have the same amount of dollars in their investment portfolios but those dollars are now not enough to buy the necessities of life. The cost of everything has gone up too much."

"So how does it help the people to debase the currency further?" asked Nanakinilli.

"Because, as I said before, the middle class has largely now been wiped out. The only people who have any money nowadays are the super-rich. Everyone else is broke or deeply in debt. If we reward the debtors and punish the creditors, who are all now mostly all the super-rich anyway, we relieve the burden on the poor people and we hammer the super-rich. And the super-rich are the people who are standing behind the Frazer regime. Frazer is really just a stooge for them."

Suddenly a huge grin appeared on Toulemont's face. Nanakinilli had got the message too. His grin was a little more reserved but was definitely there.

"So you want us to hack into the Treasury's computers and give every taxpayer in America a one hundred thousand dollar tax refund?" queried Nanakinilli.

"Yes."

"And this will deal a mighty blow to Frazer and his gang and also to the super-rich that back him?" asked Nanakinilli again.

Parnell nodded.

"And this will help the poor people?" queried Toulemont.

Parnell nodded again

"Love it," said Toulemont.

"Love it too," reiterated Nanakinilli.

Parnell had just recruited his new expert cyber warriors.

Parlay

"It looks like a trap to me," said Father LeMonte.

"Could well be," responded Parnell.

"And you're still going to go for it?"

"I don't see that we've got much choice. The whole point of our campaign has been to force them to the conference table. Now it looks like that's precisely what they're asking us to do, to negotiate. How can we turn it down when that's what we've been trying to get them to do from the start?"

"I thought the main objective was to get them out."

"Yes, but in a legal and traditional way, by forcing them to hold proper elections," replied Parnell.

"They're not likely to do that," retorted LeMonte. "They know they would never be re-elected after what they've put the country through. They got away with it when they orchestrated Frazer's election but then look what he was up against, Chadwick, another one of their stooges. Even they can't seriously think they can get away with that again."

"They might if they thought they could rig things sufficiently in their favor to engineer their own re-election."

"But we wouldn't let them do that. Any elections would be closely scrutinized by us and we would insist that it be overseen by international monitors next time. How could they rig that and get away with it?"

"They might not care," said Parnell. "Or they might think they could be clever enough to make it look genuine even though it was rigged. I don't think that they're short of confidence in their own cleverness nor are they short on bravado. They just might think they could get away with it, especially if we give them the impression that there is a good chance they could."

"I don't know," said LeMonte. "It all looks very risky to me. We would be totally exposed to their scrutiny not to mention being almost completely under their physical control. This could be the mother of all double-crosses."

"I know," said Parnell, "but, if we pass on this invitation, we're effectively saying that we don't want to negotiate."

"I don't. I just want them out, and out for good. They're evil, Jackson, pure evil. We have to be rid of them. I don't believe we can trust a single word they say. And I certainly don't feel comforted by their assurances of safe conduct."

"I know," said Parnell for the third time, wondering how many times he had to acknowledge that he appreciated the risks.

The discussion went on for a further three hours with every conceivable outcome, contingency and possibility being explored. In the end, Parnell's reasoning prevailed.

"I know Frazer and his gang will probably do everything in their power to stall, cheat, lie, fudge, delay, and whatever else they can do to delay surrendering power back to the people," said Parnell, "but they're hurting. Both their legitimacy and their strength are waning the longer this campaign drags on."

"They know we're winning," broke in LeMonte. "They need an 'out' so they can salvage at least some of their ill-gotten gains … and to avoid future prosecution," he added as an afterthought.

Parnell wrapped up the conversation: "It may not be justice but it just might bring peace and an end all this suffering."

The final APA delegation to meet with the Frazer regime comprised Parnell, LeMonte, Chambers, and Rouleau. Parnell had asked Gary Knight to lead the group but he'd declined, explaining that publicly he could not be seen to be associated with the Military Wing of the APA; it would jeopardize the APA claim of being a non-violent organization. *Politicians*, mused Parnell. *Or is Knight just being more prudent than I am?*

The Frazer delegation comprised Frazer himself as president of the American republic, General Hedley Darcy as Commanding Officer of North American Military Command, Fifth officially in his capacity of President of the Council on Foreign Relations, and Sixth as the American Secretary of State. There was no official Canadian delegate, subtly confirming that country's status as a puppet state. But they were all thinly-veiled pretexts.

All present were acutely aware that Sixth and Hedley Darcy were there as their father's lieutenants, and Frazer was there as Fifth's lapdog. Few had any real illusions as to who was who at the gathering save, perhaps, for Chambers who had hitherto been regarded by Frazer's security people merely as Parnell's girlfriend.

The venue for the meeting was, somewhat to the rebel team's surprise, the boardroom of the New York Yacht Club headquarters on 44th Street, in the heart of New York City. It was not surprising it was in New York given the city's status as the financial capital of North America and the seat of power of Fifth's global financial empire. Parnell had expected a more intimidating venue, a military base, or political institution perhaps. But Fifth was much more subtle than that. His choice was deliberate. His message was more one of 'you're dealing with the elite of the world here not merely its hired henchmen' than any attempt to make his interlocutors feel as ease.

So, this is the Global Emperor, thought Parnell glancing at Fifth.

Parnell sat in the central position at the rebel delegation's side of the table, indicating his seniority in the group.

Rouleau sat on Parnell's left suggesting his rank as senior military commander of the rebel forces. The French Canadian made no particular effort in respect to his dress but his appearance was imposing nevertheless. A big man and very fit, his manly frame filled out his attire impressively. His fiery red hair added to his fearsome countenance, as did his full untrimmed beard. He still wore hiking boots and combat fatigue trousers, and a checked lumberjack's waist-length jacket completed his woodman's look. His piercing green eyes amplified his intimidating gaze. He looked every inch a rebel leader.

LeMonte sat on Parnell's right and Chambers on the far left. She was dressed in a smart but unremarkable skirt and matching jacket.

On the government side, President Frazer, dressed in a business suit of the highest quality, sat directly across the table from Parnell, apparently as leader of the government delegation. General Hedley Darcy, fully uniformed with four polished stars on each shoulder and a chest brimming with medals – most of which Parnell immediately recognized were mostly honorary – took the seat to Frazer's left, sitting directly opposite Rouleau. The two military commanders now directly confronted each another.

Fifth sat on the far left, directly opposite LeMonte, suggesting that he was the most junior of the Government delegation. He wanted to eyeball LeMonte as closely as possible. He suspected there was much more to the lapsed prelate than was readily apparent and Fifth did much of his evaluation of people from personal scrutiny. LeMonte had resisted his urge to wear his priestly attire. It might have added to his image as a man of peace and a champion of justice but in the end, he had concluded that such attire would have been hypocritical in the present situation.

Sixth, also dressed in an impeccable business suit, took up the remaining position on the far right, opposite Chambers.

To Parnell's surprise, General Darcy opened the conversation: "Well? What do you want?" he blurted out.

Fifth, dressed in relaxed attire featuring an open-necked sport shirt and a pair of casual slacks momentarily flinched at the crudity of the outburst, but did not interject. His benign poker-face returned almost immediately.

Parnell, dressed also for comfort and convenience in a simple lounge suit, was a little taken aback as well but his composure also rapidly returned. "Well," he began cautiously, "if you recall, it was you who invited us to this meeting. As such, I would have thought you should begin with presenting your proposals."

He turned his gaze directly on Frazer as the supposed leader of the government delegation, effectively dismissing the brash young general in subtle but firm tones. "Do you wish to begin the conversation, Mr. President?" he inquired politely.

Frazer shot a glance in Fifth's direction, to be met with the very slightest of affirmative nods. The aging and devoted lieutenant took the cue from his master and commenced:

"Our disagreements have progressed at ever-increasing tempo over several years now," began the president carefully, "but in all that time you have never really outlined exactly what your grievances are. It would seem to be a useful place to start if you were to do so." He paused, his eyebrow rising as he looked directly at Parnell.

Parnell knew the puzzlement was phony: Frazer knew exactly what the demands of the rebels were, but, in a spirit of cooperation, went along with the charade.

"Our prime requirement," he said calmly, "is that your Government submits itself to the popular judgment of the people and hold democratic elections as required by the law of this land. They are now four years overdue so they need to take place immediately."

"We all want a return to normal," responded Frazer adopting a condescending classical politician's put-down tone matched with a fake genial face, "but we are currently in a state of emergency. Significant violence has been perpetrated against the people of the United States and your organization has largely been the instigator of it. The Government's prime requirement is that you cease all terrorist activity."

The discussion ensued in this diplomatic vein for a further twenty minutes mostly with Parnell and Frazer exchanging accusations and claims more suited to a propaganda campaign than serious negotiation.

"Civilian casualties are not receiving adequate medical care,"

Chambers interrupted at one point.

"It's your rebels that are responsible for those casualties," countered Hedley Darcy.

LeMonte and Sixth each made a couple of interjections on minor points of 'clarification' neither of which was accepted by the other side. Hedley Darcy's contributions were more substantial but mostly accusing. Their blunt aggressiveness was successfully parried by Parnell. On two occasions Rouleau responded with vigor and firmness equal to that of the accuser. Throughout Fifth remained silent. Finally, he spoke.

"This is going nowhere," he said, looking at Frazer. "I think it's time to get a little more formal with our inquiries." His non-threatening expression held the slightest touch of menace but his prearranged prompt was clearly understood by all his lieutenants at the table.

"Yes, sir," responded Frazer. "Guards!"

It happened so quickly the rebel team was completely taken off guard. Parnell had anticipated, exactly as LeMonte had pointed out, that the whole meeting could have been a trap. He'd tried to mitigate the risk by having the New York Yacht Club buildings closely watched in the week before the appointed time. He even had sympathetic supporters inside the building but nothing untoward had been reported. The venue had looked unthreatening and provided ample access and escape routes should they need them. But that was also one of its weaknesses. Any venue in the heart of a large city would have favored the establishment side with its access to streetscape surveillance, unrestricted subway access, unchallenged control of traffic flows and street and building access. In any case, with the President of the United States of America in attendance, security was extreme as a matter of routine.

The half dozen heavily armed, black-clad figures that emerged from the adjoining anterooms could have come from any one of a dozen different security agencies. Rouleau instinctively jumped to his feet, his chair flying back and clattering on the floor. Parnell also rose quickly, but in a more controlled manner. He adopted a Karate-type stance as his unarmed combat training had instinctively primed him to do but moving forward to protect Chambers as he did so. LeMonte was also quick to his feet and, for a supposed man of peace, quickly adopted a defensive position.

Rouleau moved forward to confront the intruders.

Parnell quickly appraised the situation.

"Piers … Piers!" he snapped again. "Stand down! You'll only get yourself killed."

Rouleau paused, realizing to resist was futile. He stopped, lowered his fists, and glared at the now smirking General. "Salaud," he hissed in his strong French-Canadian accent.

In the spring of 2040, in the regime's twelve-year reign, 'formal' interrogation within North American security institutions had moved well beyond the controlled and closely supervised interview techniques of the century's early decades. They now used the 'gloves off' approach. American and Canadian interrogators had learned well from their Middle Eastern allies. Disappearances were by now quite common so there were few holds barred once suspects had entered the confines of the 'national security' realm.

The security forces, prison guards, and members of the prison management practiced torture, humiliation, profanity, deprivation, blackmail, ethnic and sectarian and political discrimination, and the raping of both men and women without exception. Privations extended well beyond denial of family visits, phone calls, any kind of contact with the outside world or with other prisoners. Health care, sanitary needs, legal rights, legal representation, sunlight, soap, clean clothes, detergents, and disinfectants were all deprived. Redress of grievances was non-existent. Control was absolute. Rights were none. Appeals non-existent. Hope totally absent.

This was the realm that Parnell, LeMonte, Rouleau, and Chambers now entered as 'formal inquiries' began of each of them.

Fifth, of course, did not indulge in any of the sordid practices designed to extract information about the rebel cause and its capabilities. Nor did Frazer. As President of the American Republic, the latter's authorization was required but merely as a formality. His disposition was more nuanced though. As a professional military man, with a West Point pedigree, honor had always ranked high on his self-image. But he had been in the services long enough, and at a rank high enough to know that all military operations had their darker side.

Sixth's responsibility was Foreign Affairs so, since two foreign nationals were involved, it fell within his portfolio of responsibility but since the policy of their home country was in lockstep with American policy on 'terrorism', no complaint was likely to be forthcoming. He therefore effectively washed his hands of the whole distasteful affair.

As a result, prime responsibility for extracting the necessary intelligence from the captives fell to General Hedley Darcy. And Hedley Darcy was a different kettle of fish to his urbane father and cautious brother. To his brother's surprise, and the indifference of his father, a sadistic streak emerged from the young general. A frequent visitor to the detention centers where suspects were interrogated, he was an active participant in some of those interrogations, especially when pack rape was on the agenda. He did this for enjoyment and to demonstrate to his subordinates that 'anything goes' – although, of course, his sexual participation excluded male prisoners. That would have been 'unmanly'.

"Where is your headquarters?" asked General Hedley in a calm, almost soothing tone.

"I can't tell you that," said Parnell.

"Why not?" asked Darcy. "You know you're going to tell me in the end. Why not tell me now and save yourself and your comrades any further discomfort?"

"I don't think you'll get much out of them," said Parnell, grimacing as the ropes securing his hands and feet started to bite into his flesh. "And you'll get nothing out of me …"

"Really?" said Hedley. "We'll see. More water?" he asked as if offering refreshments.

The towel went back over Parnell's face and another bucket of water gushed from the upturned receptacle. Parnell spluttered and gasped as the torrent surged through the thin toweling, down his throat, into his gullet then down his bronchial tubes into his lungs. He thrashed on the tabletop trying to avoid the flow but the restraints held firm so all he could do was try and hold his breath. It didn't work. The centuries' old technique perfected by the Chinese had long ago been mastered by American interrogators. He swallowed as best he could; coughed to expel as much of the liquid from his lungs as he could but not all exited. This was the seventh time today and he could feel himself slowly drowning.

Hedley waited patiently for Parnell to cease coughing. "Where is your headquarters?" he asked again softly, almost motherly.

Various techniques were applied to the prisoners over those next tormenting weeks. Some were mere irritants, some just stressful. Some lingered for hours while others were short, violent, and agonizing. Disorientation was constant. Timing was irregular. Sleep was sporadic, unpredictable, frequently interrupted, and sometimes denied for days on end.

In the end, all four prisoners divulged 'useful intelligence', or so Hedley Darcy described it. Few people could have withstood such an onslaught, but precisely how 'useful' the information gained was open to question. Each victim tried to relieve their suffering by offering up something that might momentarily alleviate their immediate plight. Each readily confessed to absurd allegations they knew were not true, their confessions also easing their immediate torment. In practical terms, even the most experienced interrogators could never be sure whether their victims were telling the truth or whether they were just being told what they wanted to hear. Only rigorous cross-checking of claims, admissions, and facts with those of other victims, or with previous sessions, could give them any confidence as to whether 'useful intelligence' had actually been gained.

So, the unrelenting process proceeded. All the while each of the rebel leaders was kept in isolation. From time to time each could hear the distant screams of another victim although whether real or staged, or whether a compatriot or stranger, they couldn't be certain. Their lack of information about their compatriots was probably the most excruciating of all their trials, particularly Parnell's concern for Elsie's wellbeing. He agonized over her fate. He had no reason to believe that she would be treated any more gently than he was being treated. Should he offer some useful information to his captors in exchange for their guarantees that she would not be further harmed? played heavy on his mind.

Then he thought: *No! This gang has already proved that it cannot be trusted.* In any case, how could Elsie forgive him if he betrayed all that she stood for? All he could do was hope that this vicious crowd had some semblance of decency. *Some hope*, he thought. But what else could he do?

Their prison was the penthouse of a twenty-four storied office block in Newport, approximately two miles from the New York Yacht Club's Harbor Court facility in Rhode Island. Fifth wanted his four prisoners kept close so he could drop in on them from time to time if he felt the need, which he rarely did. It suited Sixth and Hedley Darcy for the same reason. It suited Frazer. In Rhode Island they were out of sight and out of mind, well away from Washington, so he need not trouble himself with their 'processing'.

The more physical aspects of the interrogation were conducted in the basement of the building specially modified for its purpose. Access from the penthouse to the basement was via a dedicated service lift. The lower venue was used for the more 'personalized' activities — the 'party' type activities were carried out on other residential floors, depending on their nature and how much noise they were likely to generate and how many people were likely to be involved. It also contributed to the general anxiety and disorientation of the prisoners as they could never be sure whether an upcoming session was likely to be excruciatingly painful or deeply humiliating. And they could never be sure whether the sound of the lift would bring sustenance or torment.

Troops from the Washington Army National Guard, 'acting on information received', raided a fish hatchery complex on the northern banks of the Colombia River believing they had located the APA's military headquarters — this from the 'intelligence' extracted from the hapless four. All it revealed was a bewildered pensioner caretaker who the raiders soon realized could not be any sort of revolutionary. Royal Canadian Mounted Police were similarly embarrassed when they, 'acting on information from a credible source', raided a property ten miles northwest of Grand Mere in Quebec. They found the property entirely deserted, apparently for years. Beyond those 'credible leads', Hedley Darcy's interrogations yielded little other than four exhausted, traumatized and suffering human beings.

Cover

The APA's guerrilla war had unnerved many members of the GSC but Fifth was quite unperturbed by it. He had always believed the capture of the rebel leadership would take the wind out of the movement's sails and that is what he had advocated as GSC policy. Other key GSC luminaries had been more circumspect. They'd felt that, given the broad nature of the rebel movement, with its multiple and widely disbursed factions, the elimination of any particular junction of them would cause a reconfiguration into a new combination which would simply pick up where the previous structure left off.

Since Fifth always liked to give the impression of being a consensus leader – he, therefore, indulged the philosophical debate within the core council membership, but he had not risen to prominence with this group, or any other for that matter, by being indecisive. So, while the council as a whole dithered, Fifth did not. He moved forward with the strategy he thought best and, in the process, subtly bypassed the armchair strategists. While he knew he could count on the loyal and obedient Frazer to do as told, he also needed a couple of other loyal lieutenants to rely on.

He had them in his two sons. While they had not always been 'good' boys, they had grown up under sufficient oversight by their father to appreciate he was an exceptional man; that he had always ensured their rewards and punishments were sufficiently generous and restrained respectively for them to truly believe that they were better off going along with the old man rather than challenging him.

Sixth, now in his late thirties, was nearing that pinnacle of personal achievements most men of modest talent and reasonable opportunity might be expected to attain if properly guided by wise mentors. He had never shown great talent in any particular field of activity but had been modestly competent at most things he tried. He'd not been a great sportsman, charming companion, hilarious wit, or intellectual genius, but most people who knew him liked him. Most had come to accept and rely on his word if he had given it and had not been disappointed. He had a relaxed demeanor and a lack of belligerence. What he did lack was Fifth's killer instinct, however subtle and refined that might have been. It was therefore doubtful that he would have progressed much further than the middle-ranking achievements of upper-class society had his father's wealth and influence not been there to elevate him higher. Fifth had found a useful role for him in the family's banking businesses and it was up through this avenue his career had been shaped.

Hedley, on the other hand, was entirely different. Brash, aggressive, ambitious and intellectually rather stupid, what he lacked in brainpower he more than made up for with vigor. Fifth had found for him a very useful role in his sprawling empire, the non-business end, essentially as an attack dog. He had crafted his development to enhance those natural talents. After college, he was accepted, with Fifth's puppet-mastery smoothing his path, into West Point Military Academy from which he subsequently graduated in the lower third of its year's output. He then commenced a career as a military officer with the rank of second lieutenant. Of course, he didn't stay at that rank for very long, not with Fifth's connections. By his thirtieth birthday, Hedley had an eagle perched on each shoulder and a service record much of which was unavailable to most inquirers due to the clandestine nature of his many missions. It was a career that suited both his temperament and natural talents, given that brutality and ruthlessness were key ingredients for success in many of the roles he played. Much of his work was outside of North America, in the Middle East, where his instructors and collaborators were equally endowed and his education was deep, thorough, and very practical. Now he was busy diligently applying those talents.

"Do you have to be so brutal?" Sixth had asked after one of his rare visits to the Newport prison.

"You can't make an omelet without breaking a few eggs," Hedley had replied.

"Eggs are one thing," responded Sixth, "we're talking about people here."

"They're not *people!* They're rebels. Don't you realize, John, these people are trying to tear down everything that our family built up? They're wreckers. That's all they know how to do. They have to be smashed! End of story!"

Others were involved in the development and implementation of GSC policy. To be sure, that was Fifth's greatest talent: to make people believe they were being consulted and their ideas included, even when they were not. For a man of Fifth's capabilities that was not usually difficult given the egos of many of the upper-class prima donnas with whom he plotted – not to mention their general timidity born of a lifetime of pampered existence and a sense of entitlement devolved from generations of privilege that preceded their birth. Prince Gerhardt and King George, of course, were royalty. Their sense of superiority had always been clear to them even if they consciously chose to ignore the great imperial regimes of their ancestors had long been surpassed by more vigorous clans. Van Kleist, on the other hand, was descended from only minor European nobility, and had always been taught to defer to his betters even though his achievements were more a product of his hard work and studious upbringing than those he'd been taught to defer to.

The rest of the GSC council was not generally part of the inner coterie Fifth consorted with as he orchestrated the agenda and policy development of the council. This inner circle comprised almost exclusively of Fifth, Sixth, Hedley, Gerhardt, and van Kleist, ably supported by Henri and Biggy. The balance of the various sub-committees comprised lesser councilors or GSC members according to the contacts and skills required for each unique project.

"Oh, I think this one is yours, Gerhardt," Fifth would announce, "and I think George and Hardigan would be good resources to deploy on this one also."

It was usually Fifth who recommended the composition of each sub-committee, at the international level at least. For regional and national councils, the local president would usually retain that prerogative, unless, of course, Fifth had a special interest in that particular project. The North American rump of the GSC council there were modestly talented individuals who could be called upon to contribute from time to time, people more of Sixth's equal rather than of the raw entrepreneurial talent that had built their family dynasties. But the third and fourth generations of these elite were less inquisitive and more cautious. Similarly, much of the European general GSC membership, and a goodly portion of its lower governing structures, was also populated by what the more disrespectful and crudely outspoken of the English tabloid press called 'upper class twits', those with any money left, that is. So the bulk of the GSC membership merely went along with whatever the council decided, and that suited Fifth just fine.

Escape

The flexibility of the interrogation routine Hedley Darcy had set up for processing its APA guests turned out to be its greatest weakness. On the fourth morning of the seventh week of their captivity, the monotonous routine was shattered by a series of explosions. The blasts splintered wall-length tinted windows of the 'residential' wing of the Newport prison and created openings for nine black-clad ninjas sporting balaclavas and automatic weapons. In Parnell's 'cell' the intruders nearly landed directly on top of him. As he blinked and stirred, the nearest of them looked intently at him.

"General Parnell?" the intruder inquired.

"What?"

"Brigadier General Jackson Parnell, former Commanding Officer of the 1st Brigade of 1st Cavalry Division?" The voice again demanded.

"Formerly, yes," said Parnell.

The black-clad figure dragged the balaclava from his head.

"Major Andrew Macintyre, sir," he said, "Australian Army Special Air Service Regiment. My father sent me. We have to get out of here now. We have a chopper on the roof. Ms Chambers and Mr Rouleau should be on their way there as we speak."

"Your father ... Australian ... what's going on?" Parnell blinked with bewilderment.

"Talbot Macintyre, sir. Former Prime Minister of Australia. I believe you know him. He sent me to get you out. We have to go now, sir."

"Tal?"

"There's no time now, sir, we have to go. They'll be on us any minute. Ms Chambers and Mr Rouleau are already moving. Please come quickly, sir."

"Wait," said Parnell. "There's a fourth member of our group, Father LeMonte. He must be here somewhere. We have to get him out too."

"I'm sorry, sir," said Macintyre hesitantly. "You obviously haven't been told. Our intelligence reported that Father LeMonte died under interrogation three weeks ago. I'll ask my men to do a quick sweep of the floor before we leave just in case we're wrong but I won't have time now to do more than that. We have to go now, sir."

Parnell sat somewhat disorientated but not for long. Macintyre and his colleague grabbed him by his elbows and lifted him to his feet. Then briskly they dragged him from the room and up the stairs to the roof terrace and the waiting helicopter. Parnell did not resist. He was too stunned to do so.

When they reached the chopper, his dazed state was abruptly shattered by the sight of his two long-suffering compatriots Rouleau and Chambers. He slid in alongside Elsie in the rear seat of the aging Blackhawk and wrapped his arms around her. His initial horror at her desiccated visage slowly turned to an inner rage. *They will pay for this!* he vowed inwardly, and that transition rejuvenated his flagging strength into a determined resolve.

Fifth was also bewildered by the audacity of the rescue. His visit to the now deserted penthouse suite an hour later was brief. It did not take him long to take in what had occurred and quietly rebuked himself for allowing his second son the latitude he had on this project and for not taking greater care to ensure the adequacy of the security arrangements. But beyond those pangs of regret the daring rescue had taken the entire GSC inner council by surprise. They had no idea the APA and its ragtag network of disparate groups was capable of such a sophisticated military operation. Its coordination and efficiency were uncanny. It looked too professional to be the work of untrained, inexperienced rebels.

Frazer thought so too.

"If it was professional," queried Fifth, "then who?"

"It's the sort of thing I would expect our top special ops teams to pull off," said Frazer, and his Chairman of the Joint Chiefs agreed with him. Unless it was some rogue element within the American Armed Forces, it must have been someone of comparable competence and there were not many of those.

"It could have been the Canadians," ventured Sixth. "Two of the prisoners are Canadian."

"No. I can't believe that." His younger brother shook his head emphatically. "The Canadians are rock solid with us, or at least their military is. Damn it, John, you're talking about people under my command."

"Yes, I agree," said Fifth. "I don't see the hand of our northern neighbors in this."

"Well," suggested Sixth, "The Brits could do it. So could the French ... a lot of the French are sympathetic to the French Canadians and their inclinations. The Germans could do it too. So could the Russians. And the Chinese."

"In fact," concluded Fifth, waggling his head, "it could have been any one of a dozen or more different groups." Then he turned to Hedley:

"Find out!" he commanded. Then he turned and strode to the private lift that would take him directly to his waiting limousine.

Had General Hedley Darcy and his team of interrogators been a little less crude and a little more nuanced they might have been able to accommodate Fifth's command. While they had gleaned the 'western mountains' part of the APA headquarters location correctly, and the 'river bank' part, they had assumed the mountain range was the Cascades and the river was the Colombia. They were wrong. So the APA headquarters location was still unknown to the

GSC and so was Parnell's winter retreat on the other side of the Lolo Pass. It was that refuge Parnell retreated to with his newly liberated wife and French-Canadian comrade to recuperate from their ordeal.

Now safe, Parnell leaned back and scanned the latest outline of his grand plan for the overthrow of the Frazer regime. His draft document had grown considerably in the months since he'd settled into his Clearwater Mountain retreat. The fleshed-out draft now was entitled *An Overview of a National Resistance Movement*. [*See Appendix 1 for the content of this document*].

The APA Supreme Council had reviewed his initial draft, given him a vague indication as to what types of activities they were prepared to authorize and those they would definitely reject but no clear directive, yet. He was still sure the majority of the council would reject most, if not all, of the activities he had listed under 'Military Wing Activities'. Nevertheless, he was also quite sure that ultimately the APA would have to pursue some of them because the Frazer regime had demonstrated quite clearly that it had no intention of compromising with the APA or any similar organizations – so he sensed the bulk of the non-violent and strictly legal activities the APA 'peaceniks' would favor simply would not be effective in removing the Frazer Regime.

And given his, Elsie's and Rouleau's treatment at the hand of the Frazer Regime he was in no mood to compromise. His grief at the loss of his closest friend weighed on him even more than he realized and he was outraged at the rape of his wife even though Chambers had said little about her ordeal since their rescue.

"The gloves are coming off," he mused out loud as he scanned the document for the umpteenth time. "All options are on the table.".

Now, he thought, *let's see if the APA Supreme Council is willing to do what it takes to win this war or whether they're all just a bunch of armchair heroes.*

Global Alliance

The intervention of Talbot Macintyre through the deployment of his son, the daring Australian Army Special Forces major who affected Parnell's and his compatriots' rescue, opened a new chapter of the resistance. It extended its reach and influence beyond the North American continent and began the construction of a global alliance of resistance movements. Initially, they were confined to the English-speaking countries – England, Australia, and New Zealand – along with the initiators of the movement, United States and Canada. But their activities soon drew interest and support from other dissidents further afield. It was not a surprising development. After all, the Global Security Commission, chief antagonist to the American Patriotic Association, was also an organization of international composition. It was therefore likely only to be a matter of time before the blowback from its greed should emerge worldwide.

Macintyre Senior's initiative had, of course, been largely personal. He'd been retired from any political role for over a decade so his former role as the Australian Prime Minister did not feature in his involvement. Indeed, the Australian Government, allied closely as it still was to the United States government via its now almost century-old ANZUS alliance, would have been, and indeed now was, outraged at his actions. It effectively meant that an Australian citizen was now an active supporter of what was regarded throughout the concord of Western governments as a terrorist organization. That his eldest son, Andrew, was a serving military officer in his country's national defense force was largely coincidental but was also now a severe embarrassment to the Australian Government. Macintyre Senior had turned to his son

Andrew mainly because he was one of the few people he knew and trusted who had the necessary skills to do the job.

From Andrew's perspective, his involvement caused a dramatic dilemma: loyalty to government or loyalty to family? In the end, he'd favored family, mainly because of his enduring love and respect for his father but also because of his moral principles, most of which he'd learned from his parents. Like many people amongst America's wide network of friends and allies around the globe, he was unhappy with the concentration of wealth into the hands of an ever-shrinking class of the super-elite, the current nature of global commerce, and the increasingly violent domination by military forces driven largely by the American elite in close collaboration with the super-elites of foreign allies.

Canadian dissidents, of course, had been with the APA from the start. They were co-founders of the movement, mainly because their lands and resources were most prominently in the path of American exploitation. While Canadian corporations were amongst the exploiters, it was American companies that dominated Canadian commerce.

The British experience was somewhat different. Although American-based companies were well ensconced with the British economy and had been so since the end of the Second World War, the bulk of British corporate dominance was indigenous. Scotland and Northern Ireland had, by now, largely become separated from England politically. Wales was hedging along similar lines but economically was still largely tied to the united system – although they still smarted after severing ties with the European Union after Britain exited the EU. Scottish and Irish lords still populated the ranks of the British aristocracy which, in turn, still dominated the British super-rich class. But the most significant facet of the British elite was its close alliance and collaboration with its North American counterpart. It was the junior partner, to be sure, but a firm and obedient compatriot no less. With King George and Lord Hardigan as key members of the GSC, it was likely to stay that way.

Further afield in the Commonwealth realms, Australia and New Zealand were different again but also similar. Both were more linked into the Asian economies in terms of their export markets, but on the supply side their key producers, particularly in their resource industries, and their non-bank finance, insurance, and manufacturing sectors, they were closely allied to the British and American cousins since their major corporate owners were part of the GSC network of interests. Agriculture remained largely in local hands, and to an increasing extent Asian, but by now agriculture was a relatively minor sector of Australian economy. Indeed, the only significant sectors of the Australian and New Zealand economies that were predominantly locally owned and controlled were the small service sectors, the rural sector in New Zealand, and the public sectors of both which all tended to be the less economically lucrative. Even the military in both countries was largely a foreign legion under direct American control.

In the non-English-speaking countries of Western civilization the social structure mirrored that of the British system with the old aristocrat families still dominating economic and political life with their respective royal families, those that had them, being key participants in the GSC network although, again, as junior partners to the North American clique. That Prince Gerhardt and van Kleist were members of Fifth's executive committee attested to the closeness of their relationship.

Similarly, Japan and South Korea were still dominated by ancient aristocratic interests.

And in the Middle East, those countries that had not yet thrown off the yoke of Western domination were policed by monarchies propped up by Western, particularly American, military might.

Indeed, for the global economy and political system as a whole, practically the only regions that were not under GSC or affiliated dominance were mainland East Asia, South Asia, South East Asia, and South America. Most of Africa was by now under North American, and to a lesser extent, re-emergent European, colonial domination with the Islamic north being the only real resister in what were still highly contested spaces.

So, although Macintyre's initiative brought Australasia into the orbit of the North American resistance, a move that did not bring much in terms of geopolitical weight, the potential for resistance from other GSC dominated regions was highly potential. Resentments simmered in the European and Middle Eastern monarchies, in Africa where the dominance of the white men was again becoming habitually brutal and its predecessor victims vividly remembered, as were the colonial experiences of the Philippines, Indochina and South America.

This unrest was not unnoticed by the great rivals of the West – China, India, and Russia in particular – all of who subtly encouraged and supported the growing unrest. To them, the Macintyre raid was a wakeup call, and whilst Fifth and Frazer would have liked its daring to remain secret, it was not long before the whole world was enlightened to it. It was a fuse that had now been lit and its trail was many-destined.

That fuse had long been simmering in the Islamic world, not only via the Iranian Revolution but also with the rebellion of the Palestinians against the bar to their return to their former lands from which they had fled when the State of Israel had been proclaimed in 1948. The Jewish State had been at perpetual war ever since, both with its neighbors and with the Arab peoples within its original, and now significantly extended, borders. This tussle had become a long-running sore that periodically invited the upsurge of hostilities by both the direct participants and by their extended networks of supporters and sympathizers worldwide.

A brief respite promised in the early years of the twenty-first century, known colloquially as the 'Arab Spring', proved ephemeral and most of the sparks of promise had soon dimmed and a return to authoritarianism quickly followed. Nowhere was this more pronounced than in the largest Arab country, Egypt. But even in that ancient society, the reinvigorated tyranny did not endure for more than a few decades. The aspirants of change came back with a vengeance led by no less than Parnell's old nemesis-turned-friend Mohammed Ishmael, the quiet-spoken archaeological scholar-turned-rebel, spurred on by the brutal treatment of his wife and daughter by the Egyptian security forces.

By the early thirties the Egyptian rebels, led by Ishmael, had overthrown their indigenous despots and installed a popular democratic government leading a moderate Islamic State. Ishmael was not a supporter of the North American rebellion in any material sense, but he was aware of his old friend's leading role in it and was quietly relieved when he heard of Parnell's miraculous escape from his brutal captors. And he made his delight known to his North American emulators through quiet back channels, along with a subtle hint that he could be called upon for support if needed.

Other subtle offers of support were also forthcoming. Parnell had made many friends and acquaintances throughout his long military career and, although at the time many of those he met were adversaries, his inherent decency and humanity, even in the performance of his duty, the objects of which were often less than noble, he had won respect and appreciation from those with whom he had dealings. Two of particular note were his old adversary Demetri Medlevkov in the Russian lands and Li Chi Tung in the China space.

Parnell had first met the Russian in Xinjiang. There Parnell had demonstrated an almost tender concern for the beleaguered Uyghur peoples whom the Russian government of the day had been subtly supporting with Medlevkov as its point man.

Parnell had met Li on the western shores of Taiwan in 2026, where Parnell had negotiated the surrender of Li's beleaguered Chinese invasion force that Taiwanese, American and allied forces had pinned down on the beaches. A more brutal adversary could have ruthlessly crushed the abandoned Chinese soldiers but Parnell had negotiated their surrender with Li and had honored all of the terms of that surrender with humane treatment of Li's hapless Chinese vanguard.

Both Medlevkov and Li had long since fallen out with their previous masters and were, each in their way, seeking to effect changes in their respective homelands. Within their own cultures, economies, and political systems they were in rebellion. Although their struggle was not related in any direct way with those of the North American rebels, they both knew and understood the nature of their struggle and sympathized with it. They both, again each in their subtle way, reached out to Parnell to indicate their support and to offer what help they may be able to render.

It was not much, though, in any concrete way. All resistance movements were under pressure from the overwhelming power of their respective governments; each needed help from a substantial source beyond their domestic borders. Each had precious little surplus of anything to share with others. If anything, the North Americans were in a better state of supply than either the Russians or the Chinese. They at least had a well-armed indigenous population even if their arms were mostly of light caliber. The Asians were not unarmed but much of their weaponry was obsolete and ammunition for it was scarce. All three potential allies needed heavy weapons, particularly anti-aircraft and anti-armor missiles.

None of the governments of the other great powers – the European Union, Russia, China or India, nor any of the medium-ranking powers like Brazil, Turkey, Indonesia, Japan, Britain and the like – was particularly interested in providing material support to the resistance movements of North America or the Asian mainland, although many of them secretly enjoyed the discomfort that the rebels brought to their respective rivals. But none wanted a confrontation with those powerful rivals either. So their official response to the rebellions was mild disinterest and their unofficial one of mild amusement. In each of their respective realms, the rebels were largely on their own and any support from their contemporaries in other realms was largely encouragement and sympathy but little else.

Macintyre's initiative was not an indication of support from his native second-ranking middle power, Australia, despite his still considerable local standing as an elder statesman.

But they met anyway; Parnell, Chambers, Rouleau, Macintyre Senior, Macintyre Junior and a handful of lieutenants from the African-American and Mexican American communities that formed part of the Southern and South Western Commands of the APA, and a delegate from each of Medlevkov's Russian and Li's Chinese embryonic rebel armies, and Ishmael's Egyptian inner circle, albeit in an unofficial capacity.

"Tal, what can I say? Thank you," said Parnell, not knowing how to make the sincerity of his appreciation more clear than mere words could express.

"No worries, mate," responded Macintyre.

"How did you know where I was?" asked Parnell.

"Bob Inglis gave me a call. Then I called Andy Wilks who confirmed you were missing. Then Julia started tracking down your movements and that's when we found out where you were being held. I asked Andrew if rescue was possible. He said 'yes'. Then he took it from there. It's him you really should be thanking, Jackson. He's really gone out on a limb for you. I doubt he can go back home now, not before this is all over."

"Right," said Parnell. "But thanks anyway." He would get back to Macintyre Junior later.

Mutual embarrassment curtailed further comment and each looked quickly away to their other newly arrived guests.

"Commodore Hua, we've not yet had the pleasure," said Parnell, extending his hand to the Chinese delegate. "How fares General Li? I haven't seen him since, God; don't tell me, it must be over fifteen years."

"General Li is fine, sir," said the Chinese sailor. "He sends his highest regards."

"Please convey mine in return," said Parnell. "Have you met

Mister Macintyre, from Australia?"

"Your name is well known in China, Mr. Macintyre. I'm honored to meet you," said the Commodore graciously. The two shook hands.

Parnell turned to the other stranger. "Major Komorov?" he enquired, hand outstretched in greeting.

"Da," replied the Russian. "Marshall Medlevkov sends his respects," he added in heavily accented English.

"And I understand you have not yet met Mr. Macintyre either," Parnell said motioning to the Australian. Komorov turned to Macintyre and the two shook hands. "Your fame has spread to Russia also," he assured Macintyre.

"Shall we go in?" Parnell inquired, gesturing to the wooden steps of the cabin. "The others are already here," he added.

The group proceeded inside. There Parnell quickly introduced Chambers, Rouleau, the Mexican American delegate Rodrigez, the African American delegate Cousy, and the Egyptian delegate and Ishmael's right-hand-man, Anhuri Awi Djadao, who declined to shake hands but merely placed his hand on his heart and bowed slightly.

Their cabin was on a cold secluded island in the Aleutian group far from prying eyes. And there they explored what might be possible in terms of mutual support. For their part, the North Americans could offer more modern arms in small quantities and the Russians could offer small quantities of man-portable anti-aircraft and anti-armor weapons they'd been able to buy from veteran jihadists who had pilfered them from the flood of stocks that had poured into the Middle East during the more frantic years of the Arab uprisings. The Chinese rebels had some access to this vast store, also via sympathetic central Asian dissidents, most of who were Muslim and were in close contact with their Middle Eastern devotees. The two Australians, with no movement at all beyond themselves and their initial raiding team, had less to offer, other than the not-insignificant example of their daring rescue. So the flow of materiel supply was meager. It demonstrated goodwill and sympathy more than anything else.

The encounter was valuable nevertheless. The exchange of military doctrine and practical experience was more useful than the small flow of materiel. All represented movements had stories to tell, accounts of what had worked and what had not, and that was very valuable. The Eielson Air Force Base raid was an APA example of what not to do. They all had stories like that. The main outcome of the meeting was the exchange of liaison officers, observers to accompany each other's fighters in their respective battles, to learn new tactics, gain new insights and to spring more surprises on their adversaries. It was not much, but it was a start.

Squeeze

The morning sun had just peeped over the horizon of the Labrador Sea as Rouleau ducked below the crest of the small mound between him and the pipeline. Once there, he twisted the handle of the detonator generator. Instantly, a loud but muffled bang came from the direction of the iron snake.

He peeped back over the peak of the rise. The charges had done their work. A dozen or so long sections of the pipeline had disappeared and oily black goo spurted profusely from each end of the severed conduit. That was enough. It would not take long before the refinery operators 850 miles to the southwest would notice the rate of flow into their receiving tank slow to a trickle then stop. Within minutes they would be on the air to the pumping stations at the well-head storage tanks at Davis Inlet, telling the operators there to turn off the giant taps that controlled the flow. Within minutes they would also be on the telephone to the Energy Secretary in Washington telling him they had been forced to shut down oil supplies to the Eastern seaboard due to an as-yet-unknown breach of their main energy channel. And it would not be long after that that an emergency meeting of the GSC would be called.

Frazer had warned the council of such a possibility. Indeed, it did not take a great deal of imagination for anyone, even the most dull-witted of the GSC's more supercilious 'upper-class twits' of the global elite, to realize just how vulnerable the United States of America was to a disruption of its most valuable source. By this time most of the shale oil and coal seam gas resources on the North American continent were approaching depletion, leaving only the more distant sources available in any significant quantities. The

Canadian tar sands of Alberta were still in production although much of the surrounding countryside was devastated as a result. Further afield in the West, a few new oil and gas fields had been found and tapped in the Canadian and Alaskan Arctic but they too now relied on long and vulnerable overland pipelines. They had not yet been attacked, although that possibility was now highly likely.

To the East, the Western Greenland offshore fields had been the main source of hydro-carbon supply to the Eastern industrial and population centers. Their disruption would have serious economic and political effects. The suppression of peoples was almost a norm in human history, but stability usually required maintaining the standard of living the masses were accustomed to, however miserable that might be. Any sudden disruption to that living standard usually resulted in a violent response. Fifth and the more enlightened members of the GSC grand council were well aware of that.

There was an alternative source, of course. Even further east, the East Greenland offshore fields were still operational. They were still reasonably safe from sabotage by the APA rebels because the APA had next-to-nothing in the way of maritime assets. And the US Navy still ruled the waves, in the Western Hemisphere at least. But those fields were in Danish territorial waters and some degree of diplomatic decorum was needed to access them. Not that tiny Demark posed any sort of threat to American maritime dominance, but Demark was part of the European Union so leaning on the tiny West European country would have broader implications: the other great European powers, particularly the Germans who had been cozying up more and more to the Russians of late ... well, it was complicated.

Therefore, the severing of the West Greenland flow was serious, and Fifth and his GSC grand council knew it. So did Parnell and his APA Revolutionary Command Council, which is why they chose it as the next phase of their strategy to oust the Frazer dictatorship. And 'Yes', they had thought of the Western supply channels. Unbeknown to Fifth, not that he did not expect something like it, at this particular time, Chambers and her Western Canadian Command was already positioned to strike along that route.

"It's pretty serious," said Frazer. "They have essentially found our Achilles heel. They know how dependent we are on oil imports, especially from Canada and Greenland. They also know the state of our fracking wells and that they're well past their peak. They kept us going for a couple of decades after the cheap oil ran out but we always knew it was a temporary fix. They also know the nuclear waste issue has not been solved. We should have moved to solar and poured more money into geo-battery storage. So, they know we're still highly dependent on fossil-fuel energy. They know that our grip on the Middle East is all but broken. These people are very well informed, sir."

"There's a good reason for that," retorted Fifth. "We don't have a monopoly on solar technology. We do on fossil technology. What do you think we should have done? Walked away from our most lucrative businesses?"

"No, sir," replied Frazer, sensing the irritation in his master's voice. "But perhaps we should have hedged our bets a little more."

"Well, bellyaching over what we should have done is not going to solve our problem now, is it?" Fifth's irritation surfaced. "Can't we buy them off?" he suggested.

"Not likely, sir," said Frazer, somewhat defiantly. "Not after our last attempt."

"What the devil are you trying to say?" demanded Fifth. "Are you saying I stuffed up last time?"

Frazer squirmed. He had never doubted Fifth's resolve in getting what he wanted but he'd always noted Fifth's composure in even the most challenging situations. He was not used to overt aggression from Fifth, even if he had always expected that beneath Fifth's charm and politeness lay a ruthlessness he had no desire to receive. That ruthless side was now peeping out from behind his master's façade.

"No, sir. It was a judgment call on your part which I did not wholly disagree with. I would have said so if I had considered your choice of strategy to be ill-advised." Frazer trod carefully now. "All I'm saying is that I think that particular approach is likely to be unsuccessful in the future. We need a different approach now."

"Like what?"

"I'm not sure, sir," confessed Frazer. He quickly changed the subject. "There is also another dimension to our current situation, sir. In addition to being remarkably well informed about our current situation, they also appear to be remarkably well informed about the more sensitive aspects of the council's historical development. For instance, they know about the Kennedy assassinations and about the council's involvement in the 9/11 initiative. We didn't get a lot out of them about their current organizational structure or the disposition and composition of their forces but they were quite frank about what they knew of the council's history and the basis of its power."

"That's right, sir," Hedley chimed in, avoiding the more familiar term of 'Dad' when in Frazer's company. "Most of the ravings of the rebels we interrogated went over the heads of their interrogators, but on those occasions I sat in on they were quite forthcoming about what they knew of our previous operations. Naturally, I downplayed them to keep our people in the dark but they were pretty spot on with what they believed had happened over the years."

"All the more reason to crush them now," asserted Fifth. "We just can't afford for them to succeed, not at any level."

"That may be easier said than done," responded Frazer. "We've been trying to do that for almost a decade but they just keep getting stronger."

"Damn it, Frazer!" blurted Fifth. "You're supposed to be in command of the most powerful military machine that has ever existed in the history of the world. Are you seriously telling me you can't squash a few cockroaches hiding in the Canadian wilderness?"

"It's a very big wildness, sir," reminded Frazer. "And it's not just a few rebels in Canada. They've got an entire network of sub-units right across North America and we think they are now getting foreign support."

"Foreign support?" queried Fifth. "Who from?"

"Well, sir, our intelligence thinks the leader of the mission that rescued the rebels was led by an Australian."

"An Australian?" blurted Fifth. "What the hell are the Aussies doing sticking their noses into American affairs?"

"We don't know, sir," said Frazer. "The Australians deny any knowledge of it. They say it's not any of their people."

"So why do our people think they're lying?" queried Fifth.

"We don't think they are," said Frazer, "but the CIA has picked up a connection with a former Prime Minister of theirs who has a son who is an officer in their Special Forces. He would definitely have the skills for a rescue operation like the one that was carried out. The CIA thinks that it may have been a private initiative, by the ex-Prime Minister."

"I see."

"There's more," continued Frazer. "It seems that a meeting took place a few weeks ago in the Aleutians between this ex-Prime Minister and the rebels …" He paused to let the information sink in, then continued, "… and some rebels from the Central Asian groups that are currently challenging the Chinese government …" He paused again, then added, "… with some rebels from the Russian resistance movement. It looks like the rebels are starting to build a world-wide resistance network."

"That won't help them much!" retorted Fifth. "The US Navy still controls the seas. Neither the Russians, the Chinese, nor anyone else for that matter, is prepared to venture too far out into the oceans even if they do dominate their immediate coastal waters. Colombia still rules the waves! Anyway, foreign insurgents shouldn't be much of a threat to you here on the North American continent."

"That's true," agreed Frazer. "But it does complicate the situation even further."

Given the sensitivity in dealing with the Europeans over the Danish energy concessions, further complications were the last thing Fifth needed. He said nothing, just grunted.

Frazer knew Fifth well enough to know that grunt was not a good sign. Fifth usually disarmed his disputants with reasoned argument and he usually won. If he agreed with the superiority of their argument he usually conceded although that didn't happen often. But if Fifth did not prevail, and he did not concede, that meant he had not agreed and Fifth did not tolerate dissent either. Though nothing further was said on the issue, Frazer was now a worried man.

Chambers and her Western Canada command struck the Keystone XL pipeline a week later. It had initially been planned that she would coordinate her attack to coincide with that of Rouleau in the east, but particularly diligent activity by the Alberta Mounties had forced her armorers to go to ground for a while. The delivery of the charges for the strike had therefore been delayed. This turned out to be fortuitous for the rebel cause. Frazer had largely been able to deflect the adverse publicity of the eastern strike by insinuating it was primarily the work of Quebec separatists. Therefore it was a 'foreign' matter as far as the American Government was concerned. He had 'leaned' on his Canadian counterpart, Andre Anglaises, the Canadian Prime Minister, who had responded indignantly at the virtual impossibility of securing the entire length of the Greenland Connection pipeline one hundred percent of the time. And he had publicly brushed off the American leader by insisting the attack was a purely internal Canadian matter.

Chambers strike merely reiterated and emphasized the embarrassment to both Governments. It did, indeed, effectively demonstrate the inability of Canada's small internal security forces to cope with armed dissent of such wide-ranging reach. This forced Frazer into a more drastic response. The strike was still inside Canadian territorial jurisdiction but impacted vital American interests.

Frazer could not publicly ignore the weakness. He ordered the 317th and 174th Infantry Divisions to cross the border and take up defensive positions along the length of the Keystone pipe north of the border, the full length of Alberta to its wellhead in the north of the province. This inflamed Canadian public opinion even though Anglaises had gone on Canadian television and announced he had requested American support in the light of the upsurge in 'terrorist activity' his country was now facing. Canadians had long resented the dominance of their southern neighbor but the actual presence of armed American troops on their soil was a stunning insult to their national pride. Protests broke out from Vancouver to Halifax, from Whitehorse to London. For Fifth and the GSC, it was a severe embarrassment and an insolent provocation from a somewhat previously docile population.

But Fifth's worries did not end at either the Pacific or Atlantic coastlines. Within days of the Alberta strike, Lithuanian rebels lowered two ancient World War II depth charges onto the seabed either side of the Baltic South gas pipeline just west of Memel. Their coordinated detonation severed the line with a five-yard gap that sent gas profusely bubbling to the surface and brought an immediate pressure drop in the line as far away as Danzig. Frantic calls to the main pumping station at Klaipeda resulted in its immediate shutdown. The German government immediately initiated gas restrictions for domestic use for the 10 pm to 6 am time slot except for emergencies. It put industry onto an immediate six-hour working day and limited gas usage during those times to seventy percent capacity.

Two days later Uyghur separatists blew up a fifteen-yard section of the Kabul-Urumqi section of the Gwadar-Beijing oil pipeline, the main oil supply route from the Middle East to the People's

Republic of China. Again, the breach brought the entire flow to an immediate halt.

Neither of the two North American strikes nor the Western European or the Central Asian ones, was fatal or even seriously disruptive to the respective economies upon which they impacted. All were repaired within weeks. But not without some disruptions; some Government embarrassment, and, more importantly, considerable disquiet from inconvenienced populations. Their psychological impacts were significant. Firstly, it demonstrated that the authorities within their respective jurisdictions were not in firm control of their respective territories. And secondly, the strikes demonstrated that a global dissident movement was now in action and its coordination was quite professional.

Precision Strike

Parnell had not really believed Toulemont when she'd first suggested the US Government's official narrative on the so-called terrorist attack on New York City and Washington DC in 2001 was rather questionable. He'd been aware of some controversy in the ensuing years but had understood that centered on the apparent failure of the security services to see the attack coming. In any case, to him, and to most other Americans of his and younger generations, the whole issue was largely just a quirky quandary of history, much as the Kennedy assassination had been half a century earlier. He, like most, had more pressing contemporary problems to be concerned with. It was only his admiration and respect for the young French physicist that gave him any reason to consider the matter at all.

But consider it he had – in just the way Toulemont had suggested he do – by a little casual reading of the various hypotheses that addressed the event. Some people called them 'conspiracy theories' but Toulemont had preferred the term 'hypotheses. She said none of them would have met the standards of the scientific definition of a 'theory'. But she had also pointed out the official narrative on the event was likewise merely a 'conspiracy theory' since the hard factual and scientific evidence that supported it was scant and unconvincing. The only sound authority supporting it was the 'official' version of the event as told by the American Government, so it relied almost exclusively on the credibility of that source.

In earlier times that last-mentioned authority would have been all Parnell, or for that matter, any other patriotic American, would have needed for him to accept the account without question.

Toulemont, on the other hand, was French and not bound by such an imperative. She was also a scientist. She required some form of credible, impartial, and unbiased evidence before she accepted almost any point of any issue. That was one of the things Parnell admired about her. If Toulemont said the evidence supporting the official 'theory' was 'scant' and 'unconvincing' then Parnell felt he should at least respect Toulemont's skepticism.

So he had done some casual reading on the matter, not furiously, nor obsessively, nor even in any sort of dedicated or diligent manner, initially anyway, more in a casual, read-it-in-your-spare-time way as one read's a novel while travelling on a train or while waiting for a doctor's appointment. But read he had. And the more he'd read the more he'd begun to see the point Toulemont had been making. The 'official' story appeared to rely mostly on the belief that the American Government would not lie.

Parnell knew from his military career that the American Government was just as capable as any other in carrying out dastardly deeds and dirty tricks — 'fun and games' as they were known within the security services — now and in the past. Few Americans had any doubts that the Chinese, the Russians, the Iranians, the Germans, particularly during the Nazi era, the Japanese during their militaristic phase, even the British, had carried out what was known in military circles as 'false flag' operations, but most Americans did not believe or did not care to consider that the American Government might also do such things. Parnell knew otherwise.

He knew that before Pearl Harbor, the FDR administration had been trying to goad the Japanese into making a first strike against the United States to give the US an excuse to get into the Second World War. Former President Hoover had reported as much in his long belatedly published memoirs. Parnell doubted that the Roosevelt Administration had been aware that Hawaii was the target; a more rational strategic analysis would have suggested the blow would fall in the Philippines. So FDR's indignant claim that the 'day that will live in infamy' was a sneak attack was not entirely so – the target may have been but the event was not. It was, in fact, a pre-ordained, pre-planned, and keenly awaited response to American diplomatic pressure.

Parnell was also aware of other well-proven examples of American 'skullduggery'. Like the Gulf of Tonkin incidents: the second of which did not actually happen but was presented to the US Congress as a statement of fact to secure congressional approval for an escalation of the Vietnam War. Clandestine operations like 'Operation Gladio' in Italy in the mid-twentieth century and the 'Operation Northwoods' proposal to the then President Kennedy to attack American ships, planes, and personnel with American military assets to be able to blame it on a neighboring dictator were also well known and understood within the inner circles Parnell had moved in during his long military career. These and other, less than honorable orders, he had seen or even received during that time. They very much supported a contrary view to the one that said: 'an American Government would not do such a thing'.

Parnell had not confined his research to that one source Toulemont had brought to his attention. He'd asked others about the issue. He'd found engineers and architects who very much doubted the explanation by the National Institute of Standards and Technology as to why the Twin Towers of the World Trade Center had fallen, or its account of why World Trade Center building number seven had collapsed that day. He'd found lawyers' accounts of the flimsiness of legal evidence available to support the official narrative. This included the inadmissibility of evidence that had been extracted by interrogators by methods described by lawyers world-wide as constituting torture, or which were inadmissible as expert testimony because they failed the Daubert Test, the Federal Court's standard for admissibility of that type of evidence. He'd found physicist reports proclaiming that some of the official explanations defied the Laws of Physics and chemists' reports that described the finding of traces of chemicals used only in sophisticated explosives in dust samples collected shortly after the fall of the New York buildings. He'd read over 150 eye witness accounts of explosions being heard before and during the collapse of the buildings. And he also came across the Professor Leroy Halsey simulation which proved conclusively that Word Trade Center building number seven could not have collapsed solely due to office fires as the National Institute of Standards and Technology had said that it did.

As time unfolded in the ensuing years Parnell had come to three main conclusions about the 9/11 event. They were:

1. The official United States Government's account of what happened that day could not possibly be true,

2. The 'Controlled Demolition' hypothesis was a more plausible explanation as to why the three New York buildings had collapsed on that day than the official "Progressive Column Failure" hypothesis, and

3. The most definitive thing that could be said about the 9/11 event was that it remained an unsolved mass murder.

To this particular issue, however, he could now add a further glaring and impressionable insight. His treatment at the hands of the current American Government at its Rhode Island 'retreat' had convinced him, if he had had any doubts previously, that *his* government was indeed capable of anything. He had experienced it first-hand, so had LeMonte to his sad demise, so had his wife – although she'd not spoken in any detail about what she had gone through and Parnell had not pressed her on the matter – and so had Rouleau who was also not forthcoming with any details, but his rage was clearly apparent in the set of his jaw and the fire in his eyes. None of them now had any illusions of what they were up against and this surviving rebel clique was determined the Frazer regime and its elite backers had to go, by whatever means necessary.

The public reaction to the ordeal of the former captives was less intense though. APA supporters were outraged and plastered their revulsion in graphic detail across all the media at their disposal. In the international sphere, the Russian, Chinese, Iranian, and like-minded American critics also trumpeted the news, while the Europeans dismissed the issue with the same diplomatic 'tut-tut' they had criticized the Guantanamo prison camp procedures. But the wider general American public simply preferred not to know. The 'patriots' were sure it was just foreign propaganda but to the skeptics – and there was a growing army of those – particularly those who had experienced police brutality first-hand and those whose extended families had been 'guests' at 'immigration detention facilities', it all sounded rather familiar. But what could one do about it?

Parnell knew what to do about it. It took him a few weeks to finally tie Rouleau down to an agreed meeting time and place. The big French Canadian was constantly on the move these days, both for personal security reasons and to provide some degree of coordination between his disparate forces on both Eastern and Western Canada. But he finally managed to agree on a meet in Trois Rivieres in Rouleau's native Quebec.

The meeting was brisk and business-like. Little was said by either man about their ordeal at the hands of Hedley Darcy and his goons. There was no need. Both men quietly fumed inside but both knew that overt anger at this point would serve no useful purpose, so they simply pushed it to the back of their minds and focused on the task at hand. Over the space of three-quarters of an hour Parnell quietly, deliberately, explained about the need for an alternative strategy to the irregular warfare approach Rouleau had been pursuing for several years now.

Rouleau did not argue the need for a revised approach.

"Oui," he said at measured intervals throughout Parnell's situation analysis. When Parnell finally drew breath and looked intently into the lumberjack's eyes, the latter simply said "J'accepte", then quickly added: "I agree. I've been thinking along the same lines too."

"And?" Parnell prompted. In response to Parnell's encouragement, Rouleau outlined the essence of his targeted assassination strategy. Five minutes later, he paused to appraise Parnell's response. Parnell was a little taken aback at the extent of Rouleau's detail; the big man had obviously given a lot of thought to this strategy.

"Isn't that a little ambitious?" inquired Parnell. "Two hundred high profile targets, that's a big ask." Parnell had planned a few Special Operations during his military career and this particular plan sounded decidedly bold.

"I don't think so," said Rouleau. "We're planning to achieve this penetration over five years. And we expect to start off quite modestly, only about ten or twelve hits in the first year. It will take six months to set up the first hit and then we'll be lucky to get in another two or three in the following three months. The next half dozen or so will take another three months. And it will take another twelve months before we're up to our normal quota of about a dozen hits every three months. After that we will probably experience some attrition, probably about twenty percent casualties a year thereafter, so I doubt that we'll achieve more than fifty hits a year even after we're up to full strength and operating at peak level. If Frazer's gang is not amenable to discussions after two hundred successful strikes then they probably will never be and we'll have to raise the strategy from one of decimation to one of total annihilation."

"I still think you're being optimistic," said Parnell. "Remember, the American Government hung on in Vietnam for seven years after it became obvious they could not win after the Tet Offensive in '68. And also remember that Afghanistan dragged on for over twenty years even though they said they'd be out by the end of 2014. These guys don't like to admit when they're beat. Look how long it took them to get out of the Horn of Africa and the Congo. They were there for nearly twenty years."

"Oui, but they were sideshows in distant places, being run

largely in covert operations. Most Americans didn't even know they were going on, especially the African campaigns. In any case, they were plays in which poor dumb kids from the ghettos and the dependencies were being killed. Here we're talking about hitting the elite personally, not just their cannon fodder. I think they'll move a lot quicker when they realize that it's their own miserable hides that are on the firing line."

"What makes you think they won't just go to ground and leave all of the fighting to their lackeys? There's no shortage of ambitious young punks who would love to get a bit of brass on their shoulder and a bit of color on their chests for ducking the odd bullet or two. It's amazing just how brutal you can get people to be if you pick them up out of the gutter and give them a bit of power. Especially if most of the actual danger is being faced by even poorer dumb shmucks who've got even less than the local college heroes directing them," said Parnell.

"We don't plan to engage the college kids and their poor peasant cannon fodder," said Rouleau. "They're not the target. We'll be going directly after the Patricians, the aristocrats. Not their wives, not their kids, not their servants, not their lackeys and certainly not the foot soldiers of their armies and police forces. That's why we only need two hundred hits. We're not looking for casualties in the tens of thousands."

"Maybe not," Parnell countered, "but their armies and police forces will be coming after you. You'll be trying to avoid making contact with them, of course, but there'll be times when you won't be able to just slip away after a strike. There'll even be times when they actually anticipate your strike and they'll be lying in wait for you. Then you'll have to engage them."

"Oui, but I think it will take them a couple of years to get their counter-strike mechanisms into place, not just the protective forces but also the intelligence gathering and counter-intelligence assets. And we'll be constantly changing our doctrine and modes of operation so they will have to be constantly adapting also. I think we can keep them off balance for at least three to five years. As I said, if they're not ready to start negotiating by that time then they probably never will be."

"They're not going to just give up running the world, you know, just because they lose a couple of their buddies. Remember what we're dealing with here. We're talking about people who are mostly psychopaths. They don't feel anything about the suffering of others, not even their own kind. All they think about is their own miserable skins," said Parnell.

"That's exactly the point," responded Rouleau, nodding. "It's not just their buddies who will be in the firing line. It will be every one of them, personally. It's because they only care about themselves they will want to negotiate, especially once we have demonstrated we can get to anyone anywhere, even them. They'll negotiate because they'll come to realize that, sooner or later, they will be the next corpse on the slab if they don't."

Parnell was not entirely convinced the strategy could work. But he could see Rouleau's point: the Patricians didn't care about anyone else and that's why indiscriminate terrorism simply wouldn't work against them. Targeting them personally was the ultimate price — if they could not hide effectively and defeat the rebels that very personal threat was their own survival.

Parnell also knew that specific targeting was immensely difficult to achieve. How many assassination attempts were made on Adolf Hitler, forty-five or something like that? What about 'decapitation strikes' against Saddam Hussein? How many of those had there been? This type of operation required up-to-date intelligence and precision strike skills of the highest order. Simply putting together enough teams to carry out the multiple missions would be a challenge. And Rouleau was right about the attrition rate. It would be significant, probably higher than twenty percent in Parnell's estimate, more like thirty or even higher. In his experience, both American and Canadian Special Forces were already pretty good at counter-insurgency and counter-terrorism. Losses could go even as high as fifty percent in the third year and that would really put the strategy under strain.

He glanced down at Rouleau's handwritten concept paper again.

"Twenty teams of five people per team, one hundred operatives in all; replacements at twenty per year from year three onwards; precision strike of the designated target only; a five-year campaign resulting in two hundred hits in all. That's it?" he asked.

"Oui," said Rouleau. "Twenty teams each comprising: a striker, an observer, a logistics specialist, a researcher and a scrounger/financier. Six months to train and deploy the first team and another three months to train and deploy two more. Then three months to train and deploy six or seven more. A further ten teams up and running by the end of the following year. Then an ongoing training and deployment program of at least four or more additional teams thereafter to replace the casualties and retirements."

"Well," said Parnell, "I've always believed in the adage that it always costs twice as much and takes four times as long as whatever your best estimate is at the start of any operation so, if I was you, I would treble every one of your estimates then sit back and see how feasible you think this strategy is at that level. If you think it's still possible then I'll support you in council when you present it. I'll even present it for you if you like. But I think that when you really get into the detailed planning for this you'll find that it's going to be a lot harder than you think. Your strikers, for example, aren't just going to be sharpshooters with sniper rifles. With some of your targets, you are not going to get anywhere near them to get a clear rifle shot. You're going to have to have a whole bag of tricks to hit them, kinetic and otherwise. Your strike teams are going to have to be multi-tasked. Where are you going to find people like that? And as for the security aspects of this operation, it gives me a headache just considering it. The Special Forces and Intelligence community is pretty close-knit, you know, even worldwide. It's not going to be long before word of this gets out once you start trying to recruit people of this caliber."

"I never said it was going to be easy." Rouleau smiled.

"No, you didn't," said Parnell. "I'll give you that at least. It's certainly not going to be easy.

"There's one more thing," he added. "I assume that the hit list will be highly targeted. You're not just planning to draw it randomly from the Forbes list of billionaires, are you?"

"Non," said Rouleau. "It will be highly targeted. There will have to be a judicial process first."

"And who is going to do that?"

"Judges. We do have some of those, don't we?"

"Judges usually believe in the Rule of Law," said Parnell. "Killing people is not usually considered legal in polite society."

"Well there will have to be some sort of tribunal to try them first, I suppose," said Rouleau. "I don't know much about that sort of thing."

Parnell decided to leave it at that for the moment. He had many more reservations about Rouleau's plan but he had to agree that in terms of achieving the maximum political and military impact, while at the same time minimizing the number of casualties, both civilian and military, it had considerable merit. He had hoped, as had most of the APA supreme council, that this movement would be able to achieve its objectives through non-violent means. But the Frazer regime, and GSC generally, had clearly demonstrated that non-violent protest was not going to move them. Indeed, their brutality had only increased despite the obvious levels of restraint being displayed by the vast majority of the movement's activists. Calling in the SWAT team was becoming the standard response by police forces across the country to any armed standoff and once deployed, those teams usually drew blood in resolving the confrontation. And 'enhanced interrogation techniques' were also standard practices around the country.

As for those in the APA movement who believed that military force was the only way to achieve the movement's objectives, their efforts had generally only succeeded in playing into the hands of the GSC's propaganda machine, allowing it to portray the whole movement as being extremist, so Parnell and the APA supreme council did their best to keep those hotheads in tow. At least Rouleau's strategy would result in relatively few low-level regime personnel – foot soldiers, servants, clerks, and so on, ordinary people just trying to make a living – from being hurt. This way, only the seasoned policymakers, and the ultimate beneficiaries of all this tyranny would be physically hurt.

Parnell ended their meeting with a brief instruction: "Give me a suggested target list for your first year of planned operations," he said. "The council will want some faces attached to this proposal so they can make a gut feeling judgment about whether it has merit or not."

"You mean they will make a gut feeling judgment about whether these people deserve to die," said Rouleau bluntly.

"Yes," said Parnell. "Quite."

Two weeks later a courier from Rouleau delivered a list of fifty names together with a typewritten summary of his assassination strategy. Parnell had not studied the target list in great detail but a glance down it suggested the names on it were indeed the leading luminaries within the American patrician class. Many of the names comprised household names of the leading families that had descended from the robber baron days of the nineteenth and twentieth centuries, as well as some of the more recent Nuevo Riche dynasties. There were also some of the more prominent empire builders who had come up through the ranks of their respective public sector, military or academic empires who had ruthlessly clawed their way to the top, decimating compatriots and civilians alike in their rise.

This was the first time Parnell has seen such a list in such personalized detail. Many members of the APA talked about the 'American Elite', the shadow government, the 'Deep State' and similar socio-political entities, but always in generalized biographic terms, not specifically as identified individuals. The consensus was that this class of people, the 'Superclass', the one percent of the one percent of the one percent of American society, comprised about two thousand individuals and Rouleau's strategy proposed to decimate this specific class … literally, in the true sense of the word – to kill one in ten – ten percent of them. With this display of resolve, Rouleau believed the remaining ninety percent would clearly see their very existence being threatened if they did not reform.

Parnell could see the logic of the big French Canadian's reasoning. Two hundred victims; that did not seem too high a price to pay to see freedom and democracy returned to his beloved homeland. His parental upbringing would have once dismissed such considerations without hesitation, but since his Rhode Island experience, Parnell was a changed man. The rape of his wife and the murder of his friend outraged him. Now he firmly believed that evil had to be fought with the same level of evil. His inner self struggled through sleepless nights and his waking moments were filled with doubts. Could he be partially ruthless? Could he be selective in his wrath? How would he know when to stop? Who would hold him in check once he crossed the line into barbarism?

Plutocrat

Fifth's move to replace Frazer came in two stages. Stage One was to install Hedley Darcy as Vice-President of the American republic. Stage Two was his elevation to the presidency itself. The latter was not a foregone move but contingent upon Frazer bowing to the will of his mentor and master. It was not so much that Fifth was a fair man who liked to give the impression he was giving an errant servant time to reform. It was more that, even in the case of his own immediate family, he still liked to hold all of his minions expectant and obedient, even those who had not done anything, yet, to incur his displeasure. So he knew that dangling the presidential prize before both Sixth and Hedley, without indicating who would ultimately get the prize, would keep both of them loyal and obedient while at the same time threatening Frazer by their very proximity to his throne.

All three responded exactly as Fifth expected, but ultimately Frazer failed to measure up to the task that Fifth had assigned him. He was too honorable, too decent a man. Despite his long military career, which had sometimes involved obeying orders he found distasteful but which he had felt duty-bound to carry out to the best of his ability, Frazer still, in his self-image, carried the romantic refrain of 'honor, duty, country' that had been drummed into him in his formative years at 'The Point'. Even with his well-practiced, iron self-discipline, he could not enthusiastically carry out orders he found repugnant, and that ultimately impacted on his effectiveness. His subordinates sensed when his heart was not in his policy directives, and they held back in sympathy. It was a small flaw in his otherwise well-disciplined character but not one Fifth could tolerate from his most senior lieutenant, even if that subordinate carried the rank of Commander-in-Chief.

Sixth did not measure up either. He was useful, competent, and effective in his role as Secretary of State but Fifth knew his eldest son well and knew he did not have that streak of ruthlessness needed to crush the rebellion. Better to keep him where he was. But also better to give the impression that he was still a contender if only to keep Fifth's second son, Hedley, in a state of apprehension – if not yet anointed, he would be doubly diligent to ensure he would ultimately be his father's choice.

Stage One was not difficult to achieve. Frazer had chosen, at Fifth's suggestion of course, a southerner, Alexander Carter, a distant third cousin of a former president, as his Vice President to give the impression that the South was included in the power elite in Washington. But the man was a dandy and a fool and was given no real power or role in the affairs of the empire. He merely kept the seat warm and attended to the more urbane and irksome political tasks Frazer could not be bothered with. In that respect, he was fairly typical of such incumbents when the key officeholder was a true loyal subject of the power elite, as Frazer was. When the latter was not, of course, when it was the figurehead that was the clown, as was also often the case, then his immediate subordinate had to be that loyal subject. And in Fifth's latest assessment, Frazer's quaint honorability had now reclassified him into the 'clown' class. So he had to go if he could not be brought to his senses. First though, Fifth wanted to see if he could rise to the occasion. It would be so much more convenient if he could, so, for now, it was the subordinate 'clown' that had to go.

Carter had few virtues and many vices, stupidity probably being his worst – in Fifth's eyes at least. Among others were a talent for getting involved in endless sex scandals, with both males and females, often very young ones, which had to be constantly hushed up and injured parties paid off. A prime example was his dalliance with an eighteen-year-old Hollywood starlet which then turned to a ménage à trois with her brother – the gutter press had a field day with that one.

"Get rid of them both," bawled an enraged Frazer, conscious of the rebuke he was sure would come from Fifth when he found out about it, which he surely would.

Then there were Carter's often unimaginative and indiscrete business dealings especially involving shareholdings and option entitlements in publicly listed companies and publicly prominent land transactions. A more talented person would have made sure these types of rewards would remain undisclosed and unpublished but Carter seemed to have a devil-may-care attitude to their notoriety and extracting him and rescuing the Government from scandal was an annoying distraction for both Frazer and Fifth.

"Our family has always had a flair for business," Carter had boasted to an inquiring television reporter, quite oblivious that what he had done was illegal. It took considerable arm twisting and favors redemptions by Frazer to get him out of that one without a criminal indictment.

By the time Fifth heard of this little scam he'd had enough of this bumbling idiot. "Get rid of him," he ordered Frazer who had promptly complied. It had not been difficult to set up a clandestine kickback that somehow became leaked to an eager young journalist. This time, Carter, at least, had the sense not to contest the allegations, especially after Frazer had told him: "You're on your own with this one," and he'd had the 'decency' to resign the Vice-Presidency 'for the good of the country'.

With the Vice Presidency now vacant the next in line for executive leadership, in strictly legal terms, was the Speaker of the House but since the house had not met in over six years the prospect of that lineage being followed was questionable. As to who beyond that was next in line was also uncertain. Some legal scholars suggested it was Secretary of State. Some said it was the Secretary of Defense. To Fifth, the issue was academic. He had no intention of allowing Congress to reconvene, and with a son in each of the two key cabinet posts he had both bases covered anyway. He promptly chose his second son for the Vice-Presidential role, due mainly the Hedley's inherent ruthlessness but also to Sixth's obvious mediocrity. And, with a Darcy now yapping at his heels, it was readily apparent to Frazer that he was clearly on notice to 'measure up' or 'move on to a different role'. He had reason to be worried.

Tommy Frazer's final demise came with almost a whimper. He stood down with all the aplomb and dignity of former dismissed military chiefs, Douglas MacArthur and David Petraeus in their time, and of former presidents, Lyndon Johnson and Richard Nixon, in theirs. All it took was for Fifth to suggest to Frazer that it was time to activate the secret citadels they had both agreed would be needed by the fleeing aristocracy when their hold on power was no longer viable. Frazer had long advocated such a move but Fifth had resisted as long as he dared. Now even he could see the end was a distinct possibility. His cool charm and flattering demeanor contributed to Frazer's easy acquiescence but, in truth, it was Frazer's intimate knowledge of the underlying ruthlessness of the Global Emperor that convinced him he should do as he was bid or he simply would not survive. So he lamely announced to an incredulous public that for the good of the nation, 'to calm its troubled soul', as his speechwriters spun the narrative, that he should step down.

And with that, he was gone, to the public anyway. Oh, there was a job for him to do, of course. He was the new ambassador-at-large to the new president, his former enthusiastic and much junior vice president, Hedley Darcy.

The elevation of Fifth's second son to the presidency was a natural promotion for a vice president but a disappointment for his first son, Sixth. Fifth soothed the loser's ego with a diplomatic explanation:

"I need a man of your calm demeanor in the foreign affairs portfolio. Hedley is too aggressive for that role. He'd have us at war with half the world if I put him there. Besides, I need the

Commander-in-Chief to kick some heads here in North America and for all of your talents, John, 'head-kicker' you are not. Hedley is." And that was the end of the matter.

Ambassador Frazer was tasked with numerous delicate foreign policy initiatives most of which, strangely enough, seemed to focus on the Pacific, particularly in Guam, American Samoa, and in the South Island of New Zealand. These were the preferred retreats of the GSC executive when the time came, which Fifth now realized could be closer than most of them realized. The first choice of most of the European executives was Switzerland but the English aristocrats preferred the antipodean location. Frazer's first choice was Guam where he could surround himself with former military comrades. Fifth's personal choice was American Samoa.

Frazer's redirected focus was timely for another reason. It coincided with a resumption of the APA's 'kinetic' campaign.

When Rouleau launched his assault on the Western American energy and food networks in the spring of 2037, in a third attempt to force the GSC capitulation, it fared better than the two previous attempts – with oil and gas flows to both the Eastern and Western seaboards of the North American continent being severely disrupted. It brought them both to a halt in a matter of weeks. Queues lengthened at gas stations almost overnight and air travel soon followed as east, south, and Caribbean coast refineries felt the impact of dried up supply pipelines. Supplies from the Danish East Greenland fields kept military and Government users in feedstock but little else moved, and a rampant and very lucrative black market soon developed to service those with the money and the connections to tap the diminished sources. Public anger mounted but with little respite. Americans and Canadians alike were not surprised. They had come to expect little in the way of sympathy from the Frazer regime and they were rapidly learning not to expect much improvement from their new president. Both countries rapidly drifted into chaos.

Fifth immediately ordered his newly appointed vassal to crush the dissident movement once and for all. President Darcy proceeded with relish after a half-hearted attempt at reassurance to an increasingly belligerent population that the rebels would soon be trounced, and a thinly veiled threat that anyone who felt inclined to join them or professed any sympathy with them, would be severely dealt with as a terrorist. Dawn raids became the norm across the entire continent and football stadia filled to World Series capacity as anxious relatives flocked to seek news and reassurance of the safety and health of their relatives who now huddled in pathetic groups in fields where once sporting heroes gathered.

Two weeks after the crackdown began journalist networks estimated that one hundred and forty-seven thousand hapless citizens had been seized. Little was left unmarked in the long lists of suspected dissidents that Frazer and his security brigades had compiled over the preceding years. Almost every member of the APA Supreme Council knew someone who was now a guest of the Darcy government. Among them was the fiery California redhead, Gillian McCloud, who had enlivened APA council meetings so vigorously in the past and who now shrieked defiance at her bemused captors.

Rouleau and his widespread army, however, were little affected by the brutal response to their death-like grip on the lifeblood of the continent. His forces were well provisioned and well supplied over wilderness trails that his forces alone dominated. The Government controlled the towns and cities but its forces were under siege and, although the army trucks rolled well enough, the civilian transports did not. It was the general population that went short. Looting began in earnest by the second week as hungry households sought meager sustenance, and those with dwindling stockpiles turned their homes into fortresses. Many a long, ensconced firearm was retrieved, cleaned, loaded and placed at the ready.

Hedley Darcy cared little for the besieged masses. His fury drew on indignation known only to those whose sense of superiority and entitlement is born from a lifetime of privilege and plenty. He was outraged that common woodsmen, farmers, tradesmen, and servants should dare to challenge his authority. He had a mandate from his master to crush these minions, and crush them he intended to do. He was oblivious to the fact that his brutality and repression yielded a bitter harvest, a widespread resentment amongst the civilian population both in the United States and in Canada. It grew especially amongst those with friends and relatives who were now his guests in a thousand jails across the continent.

Rouleau was not oblivious to the public mood, of course. He knew it worked in his favor. The more brutal the Darcy regime became, the easier his recruiting became. He always had to be careful. Thanks largely to Hedley Darcy, there was no shortage of willing supporters.

And Parnell was not oblivious to the favorable trend of public sympathy either. But his seasoned practicality had a humane tinge to it that the powerful French-Canadian lumberjack lacked. Although he could see, and largely agreed with Rouleau's assessment that inciting brutality upon the civilian population by the incumbent regime would only serve to strengthen the cause, Parnell nevertheless could not forget that his primary goals, indeed his sacred oath, was to protect and defend the people who were now suffering mightily under this repressive onslaught.

As the weeks turned into months with no resolution in sight Parnell realized the time was right for a different strategy to be implemented, a strategy involving fewer casualties, less kinetics, and decidedly fewer people. The targets needed to be narrowed from the board front to the precise, from the little people to the big fish, from the suffering masses to the elite itself. In short, it needed the strategy precisely akin to that which Rouleau had proposed to him at Trois Rivieres several months earlier.

With Parnell's support now secured, Rouleau outlined his targeted assassination strategy to the APA's Supreme Council. The effect was electric and, to many on the council, the target list bewildering.

"Who are all these people?" inquired Toulemont. "I've never heard of most of them."

"Most of them are part of the one percent of the one percent of the one percent, the malignant part," chimed in Parnell.

"You've got the names of some of the wealthiest families in America on this list," said a Southern Command delegate, Angela Orman.

"Who did you think the 'one percent cubed' was?" responded Parnell. "By definition, if you rank the population by personal wealth then the top one in a million is going to be the richest people in the country."

"So we're going to kill people because they're rich?" inquired Chambers.

"No," said Parnell incredulously, "we're going to kill the people who are killing our people. Some of them are rich. Many are not, they're just bad. It's not usually the rich that do the killing. They leave that to others. But most of the people on this list are those who are authorizing who is to be killed by the regime and who is not."

"I thought Darcy did that," said Chambers.

"He does," said Parnell, "But he takes his orders from these people. Most of these people are members of the Global Security Commission in one capacity or another. Darcy's father leads that group so he is the real power behind the throne."

"Who's this guy … Solamonson?" asked Rouleau surprised at the inclusion of a further candidate to his initial list.

"He owns half of lower Manhattan," said Parnell.

"So we're going to kill a man because he owns real estate?" Chambers was clearly having trouble understanding why the movement was drawing up a list of people to be assassinated. She was generally averse to violence in any form and was struggling to understand why the man she loved so much was now recommending they engage in the most extreme form of violence you could perpetrate on another human being. She wanted at least to understand his reasoning and to know the criteria upon which these particular people had been singled out for such extreme treatment.

"No," said Parnell. "He's a member of the council of the GSC. His family has a long history of involvement in state crimes against the people. His parents on his mother's side were involved in 9/11 and the family business has long been involved in financial fraud including having a big fat finger in the Global Financial Crisis of 2008."

"So we're going to kill him for what his family has done in the past?" Chambers pursued her line of misunderstanding.

"No," said Parnell patiently. "Let's just say he's been carrying on the family tradition. We have solid evidence that he was involved in the Chicago Massacre and also the Atlanta Strike. As I said, he's an influential member the GSC's American Security Committee and he's as guilty as sin when it comes to violent crimes against the people."

"Never heard of him," said Rouleau again.

"You probably haven't heard of a lot of people on this list," said Parnell. "Anonymity is a cornerstone of the elite lifestyle. Many of them try very hard to stay inconspicuous. You won't find too many of these people appearing on the Forbes Rich List. They spread their wealth around. They own the controlling interest in many of the leading corporations of the world but their holdings are held in private companies and trusts and their investments channeled through private equity, bond and real estate vehicles, often through offshore tax havens and the like specifically so there is no direct money trail to them. But the dividends go through to them via these vehicles and much of their wealth accumulates and compounds through various foundations and charitable organizations which purport to be non-profit benevolent bodies but whose activities promote the interests of their elite controllers."

"So how do you know these are the people who are behind the

corporations plundering the planet?" asked Chambers.

"We've done a lot of research and intelligence gathering over the past few decades on this issue," said Parnell. "Our academic colleagues, in particular, have been delving into specific identities for decades although they usually only talk in generalities in their published works. We've also got quite a few inside sources as well."

"Inside where?" queried Richard Orman, Gillian McCloud's replacement and cousin to his Southern Command namesake.

"The Government," said Parnell. "We've actually got almost as much access to commercially classified material as Darcy does. Most of the people who work for the bureaucracy are not rich, and many of them are just as disgusted by the activities of the Darcy regime as we are. We actually discourage public whistleblowing, it only turns the whistleblowers into targets of the regime, but we have a fairly extensive network of contacts who can quietly let people who are unhappy about what their bosses are doing know that there is an avenue where they can get information about fraud and illegality out to people who will actually do something about it. They know they can't go to the authorities because the authorities are as corrupt as hell anyway but there are a growing number of people in fairly sensitive positions who are aware that we exist and that we're prepared to act."

"How long have you been at this?" asked Chambers, scowling. She thought she knew this man intimately. It was not just his strength of character that she'd come to admire, nor even his gentleness in their most intimate moments. It was his inherent goodness as a human being that captured her love, his enduring proclivity to minimize harm and to promote good, even for the most miserable and dastardly of creatures, even when his calling demanded that he resort to the use of the full arsenal of his impressive military capabilities. Even then he was careful, measured, compassionate, and sparing. And above all, she had come to admire his honesty. Had she been wrong to be so trusting?

"Almost a decade, Honey," said Parnell. "I'm sorry to

disappoint you but anyone marrying a military person needs to understand that there are some aspects of their work that cannot be shared, even with your closest confidants." His lips thinned as he looked at her, and he shook his head. "I thought you understood that. Everything is on a need to know basis and up until now none of you have needed to know. But you do now. As the head of the Military Wing of this movement, I need your approval before my team action any of it. To date, all we have done is gather information. We have an extensive dossier on every one of the people on this list. That's why I know so much about Solamonson."

"Well, I'm sorry, Jackson," said Chambers, "but I'm not prepared to sanction the killing of anyone until I'm quite sure they are guilty of some heinous crime and that they continue to pose a genuine threat to the Canadian and/or American people. Much as I love you, I'm not even prepared to just take your word on that without satisfying myself completely that their execution is absolutely necessary."

Her tone reflected the personal hurt she now felt at discovering that her husband, her soul mate, had been leading a secret life as a clandestine plotter in a different realm to their shared endeavors. She understood that need for secrecy in his military career, but he had left the army years ago, before he had married her. She had not expected he would have continued his old ways in their new life together.

"I would have been disappointed if you had said otherwise," said Parnell attempting to assuage her disappointment. "And that goes for all of you. Don't just take my word on this. Study the files for yourselves. Ask any questions you think need to be asked. Don't just give us the go-ahead just because we ask you for it."

"What you are asking us to do is sit in judgment of these people," said Toulemont. "You're asking us to try them."

"Yes," said Parnell. "And if you find them guilty, I'm going to ask you to sentence them to death."

"Whoa," said the representative from the Florida Regional

Council. "That's a big step to anything we've done before, or even talked about doing. You're asking us to authorize murder."

"What did you think military operations involve?" asked Parnell. "Just blowing up a few pipelines or railroad tracks? We've already agreed we will not get involved in the indiscriminate killing of innocent people. Not only is it immoral, but it's also counterproductive. It would only turn the general population against us. We saw that with the Eielson operation. This strategy tries to avoid that.

"What this strategy does is target the real culprits of the violence being perpetrated against the American and Canadian people. This strategy targets the people who give the legal and political license to the Darcy regime to carry out its brutal repression."

Parnell paused and glanced around the room. Blank stares returned his gaze from the majority. Clear hostility featured on the face of some of the more strident 'peaceniks' especially from Orman reflecting his support for his predecessor's, McCloud's, resistance to anything *kinetic*. His cousin of the same name looked uncomfortable also. Parnell fixed his gaze directly on him and proceeded:

"It avoids killing, or even hurting innocent people, even the foot soldiers of Darcy's armed and police forces and also the multitude of servants and lackeys who work for them who are not doing anything more than trying to make a living," he emphasized. "It keeps the actual casualties to a minimum – to just two hundred people in the whole nation. But if we take out these two hundred, it will put such a level of fear into the remaining several thousand members of the Global Security Commission they will seriously start to consider if it would not be better for their survival to change their ways. Change the mindset of this group and Darcy and his gang will lose their permission to continue their repression."

"I thought you said this was a list of Americans," said the delegate from North Eastern Command. "Who is this 'al Saud' person?"

"He's the pretender to the Saudi Arabian crown," said Parnell. "He escaped that country just as the Islamic rebels stormed Riyadh. He got most of his money out via the so-called 'Sovereign Wealth Fund' in the early few decades of this century. He's an American citizen now and his money is spread right around the world with about twenty percent of it invested here in the United States. But he's been up to his neck in all sorts of skullduggery right around the world since his exile, and several genocides can be linked to him. Read his file. It reads like the key antagonist in an Ian Fleming novel."

Debate on the motion to authorize the strategy raged into the night but by three in the morning, Parnell and Rouleau had secured council approval for their strategy by a vote of eight to two with two abstentions. Approval was in-principle, however. It came with the proviso that no-one would be killed unless and until they had been tried, convicted, and sentenced to death by the Judicial Committee of the APA Supreme Council. Such a body did not yet exist. Forming it was to be the next major initiative undertaken by the Political Wing of the American Patriotic Association.

Assassin

Hardigan did not have to wait until one of his many trips to the United States to sit on the board of one of the fourteen companies he co-directed. Nor did he need to be sought out by his nemesis, the thirty-two-year-old ex-U.S. Marine sergeant who'd dispatched the first target on his list: the New York property tycoon Lot Solamonson. The English peer was dispatched two months after Solamonson, not by an APA operative but by a former Royal Marine Commando acting on authorization from the British Republican Movement, the BRM.

Nor had the trans-Atlantic cousins needed any encouragement or instruction from their North American kinsfolk on how to conduct a targeted assassination campaign. They merely copied the tactics their forebears had learned from the Irish Republic Army a century earlier. At that time the target had been the then reigning monarch's cousin Lord Louis Mountbatten. Neither the tactic nor the target was novel to English military minds. Earl Monvale, Hardigan, in his time, was a natural target: he was a cousin to the newly crowned King George VII, and his known avarice as the largest landlord in Eastern England made him a sure-fire candidate for a British hit list. And his lordship's penchant for grouse shooting made for a perfect cover for the strike to occur. An Englishman's home may be his castle but when beaters are needed to flush out the game, a whole raft of itinerant laborers were bound to enter his estate, so the logistics for the strike were easy.

His Lordship's demise sent shockwaves around the Sceptered Isle and over the Channel to the European Aristocracy. Hasty meetings of security services were convened to meet the growing terrorist threat. Security at royal establishments was beefed up considerably. The 'royals' of all European monarchies quickly reviewed their diaries and culled numerous appearances. Castles became fortresses overnight and peers of realms distant and diverse hunkered down, wondering what on earth was going on. A shooting in the United States of America was not an unusual event but the death of a British 'royal' ... now that *really* piqued the interest of the European elite. Lawyers, accountants, brokers, managers, and all manner of assorted minions grinned and bore the indignity of pat-downs and body searches as they served their elite masters to manage the latter's affairs and earn their commissions.

Initially, few on either side of the Atlantic had made the connection between the New York strike on a Jewish Realtor and the East Anglia strike on a British 'royal', not until the American ex-marine sergeant found his second target.

James Leon Harrison III was not royalty, though his lifestyle might have given that impression. The American aristocrat regularly mixed with both European princes – though rarely with princesses – and Middle Eastern monarchs of all descriptions. His shameless reputation preceded him where ever he went due to his uninhibited and unrestrained lifestyle. He was the great, four times over, grandson of a Southern slave trader whose accumulated fortune had been embellished by several subsequent generations of equally ruthless, but nevertheless, prudent descendants. By the time the accumulated wealth had passed to James III prudence and husbandry seemed quaintly redundant to the aristocrat-in-deed-if-not-in-name and he spent in wild abandon on whatever he fancied, both mortal and material, with scant regard to those from whom it was extracted or in what manner. He had managers and minions to worry about things like that. As a result, both his extravagance and his carelessness well and truly warranted his inclusion of the APA's target list. Its Judicial Committee had no difficulty in authorizing his elimination on the multiple grounds of larceny, corruption, exploitation, criminality, rape, murder, and treason.

The strike, due to its location, pleased Rouleau and Parnell, even though neither had been directly involved in its planning or execution. It came via the deployment of a 50-caliber sniper's rifle from a third-story balcony of The Newport Hotel on the foreshore of the Newport Marina. James III had just steered his thirty-foot tender into its mooring in preparation for his liaison with some obliging ladies in the penthouse suite. The corpulent middle-aged man was alone except for his faithful bodyguard and a three-man crew who would tend the boat until his return. He was unmistakable to the sniper and his spotter, not only because of his large frame and ostentatious transport but also by the scarlet red scarf he had donned atop his tailored sports jack and blue pinned striped shirt, this spotted long before he even boarded the craft at the host yacht club's guest pier. The shot blew his chest apart. Death was instant and his executioner was miles away within minutes.

Flash messages rang alarms worldwide within the hour. At that point, security services made the connections and realized that something quite significant was unfolding. Paranoia now spread from Europe and North America to the furthest corners of the earth. Terror came to the Global Patrician Class.

"It's all very well for you," blurted King George. "No one is gunning for you."

"I don't think that any of us should feel that we are immune from attack," Fifth said calmly. "I can't think of anything that Solamonson, Hardigan or Harrison have in common other than they were all senior members of this Council. All were prominent citizens in their respective countries and all were from prominent families. But that description would apply to almost all our members. Council membership may not be the defining characteristic of this particular terrorist campaign but wealth, influence, pedigree, and industry leadership seem to be defining ones. I think it would be fair to say that many, if not most, of our members could be in the firing line."

"See!" said George, a touch of panic in his voice, "… you are agreeing with me. They're out to get all of us."

"Perhaps," said Fifth, "but that does not mean we need to panic. You, in particular, George … you have one of the finest palace guards anywhere in the world. Don't you have confidence in your own security services?"

"That doesn't guarantee safety," complained King George. "Many royals have been assassinated over the centuries. And so have many of your presidents. The threat is real and we need to do something about it. If they can get to Cousin Jimmy they can get to me."

"Hardigan was an early casualty …" said Fifth, his voice still calm but with just the slightest touch of irritation, "… before anyone realized what was happening. We have all beefed up our personal security since then."

"But it does seem like a well-planned and well-coordinated campaign," chimed in Frazer, keen to lend a professional military perspective to the discussion. "We need to alert some of our more frivolous members that people of prominence are always a target for the disaffected and the envious. Some of our members prance about in gay abandon as if they don't have a care in the world."

"I doubt there are many of those around these days," said van Kleist, a tad sarcastically. "This has spooked many of our people. My executives are refusing to go on any field trips to any of our more remote mines and when they do go, they take whole armies of bodyguards with them."

"Sensible precautions," reassured Frazer. "It's no more than any of us should do – especially the more prominent of us."

"It's alright for you to say that," complained the mining tycoon. "You've got the most powerful military machine in the world at your beck and call, plus a permanent personal security detail in your capacity as a former president. George has got a pretty impressive one too. So has Gerhardt. But I'm a businessman. I've got a company to run. And it's got mines and processing facilities spread across the globe. I can't close down a whole city just so I can pay a visit to one of them. In any case, it's expensive. I've got shareholders to worry about."

"The United States sees this as a national security issue," said Hedley Darcy. "So does the United Kingdom and the rest of our allies. Our security services are available to support your internal security people with advice, equipment, intelligence, and much more should you require them."

"And personnel?" inquired van Kleist.

"Well, I can't provide a battalion of armed marines every time one of your people needs to go bush, but we do have some influence with the governments of most countries where you have major installations. I'm sure we could encourage them to provide security for some of your key people."

"Actually," chimed in Prince Gerhardt, "if you look at the victims to date, they are not the salaried executives of large corporations. They are the prominent owners of large commercial enterprises. Many of them hold extensive portfolios across many industries – they own extensive property and capital assets. No, this campaign is not targeting managers, it's targeting owners. These terrorists are after the owners of wealth, not their servants."

"All the more reason to be concerned," yelped King George. "What twisted mind goes after people just because they have money?"

"People who don't have any," mused Fifth. "This is the politics of envy. But it does not alter the essential nature of the challenge. We simply have to fight this the same way we would fight any insurrection. And we need to be ruthless in doing so."

He turned reassuringly to the British monarch. "Relax, George. The matter is in hand. Hedley is onto it and is liaising with all of our allies, including your people. Just lie low for a while and let them do their jobs. This will all be over in a few months."

It was unusual for Fifth to be wrong about things. He was usually so well informed that he often had solutions before many of the other members of the council knew there was a problem. But he was wrong about this particular challenge. Within the 'few months' that he'd predicted, a further eight strikes had occurred with seven fatalities and one target disabled for life. By then the ex-U.S. marine had dispatched Archie Warren Tuft and was now concentrating on locating his next victim. The ex-Royal Marine Commando had crossed off the second name on his list and was now focused on the third. A second West Coast-based American team had opened its account with the dispatch of a Hollywood film tycoon while in France a second European team had narrowly missed a wealthy Swiss banker as he raced his Ferrari along the winding mountain road from Nice to Monte Carlo.

The tactics employed by the assassins were not confined to firearms. The hit on Muhammad bin Sultan bin Ali was a classic one. The former Bahraini potentate was surrounded by bodyguards 24/7 but that did not save him. The corpulent sultan had long since abandoned his Middle Eastern homeland but he had not abandoned his opulent lifestyle or its sporting pleasures. He died on a falconry trip to the Nevada Desert, poisoned, although no specific agent was identified as the cause of death. Nor was any particular delivery mode identified although fruit, particularly contaminated dates, were suspected. Whatever it was, it was something exotic, and medically undetectable. The influence of the former KGB/FSB was evident in its modus operandi. The State Department blamed the Iranians but Fifth and the GSC inner sanctum suspected otherwise. But nothing could be proved.

The October meeting of the Global Security Commission was anything but a monument to calm and reassurance. It was a hysterical cacophony of wailing plutocrats the likes of which Fifth had never presided over before. He was barely able to calm them enough to maintain order. King George had calmed down somewhat and van Kleist had been reassured but the newly designated pretender to the Bahraini crown was highly agitated and the Saudi princes were also very nervous.

"May Allah protect us," they wailed. But the Almighty delivered no reassuring sign so Fifth tried to substitute for the prophet who appeared to be preoccupied. He did so as respectfully as he dared given that he was not of the faith. He was however somewhat unconvincing. Fifth was quietly unnerved by the experience although, of course, his calm poker face did not display his alarm at their timidity.

Fear stalked those ancient lands and a dark cloud descended over many kingdoms, principalities, duchies, and counties. No-one was trusted. No-one was spared. Republicans prophesized the end of monarchy, and aristocracies everywhere were warned to mend their ways lest they suffer the same fate as their imperial betters.

But Fifth was not distracted from his determination to crush the threat that was now clearly apparent to even the most obtuse playboy. It merely strengthened his resolve. He knew what had to be done and if he could not rely on the members of the organization he had spent half a lifetime building up then he would have to do it alone. He already had the key instruments in place to do so: his second son commanded the most powerful military machine in the world, and his firstborn sat on the United Nations Security Council – its power of veto would keep the foreign governments in line. If push came to shove none would dare refuse to apply whatever dictates Fifth advised them to do.

In private Fifth was different. In a quiet face-to-face meeting with Sixth and Hedley, Fifth was blunt.

"Crush them!" he said with a malevolent hiss. "Crush them completely. Be utterly ruthless. I want them gone by Christmas next year. Any questions?"

Hedley Darcy had none. He knew exactly what to do. All he had needed was the direct order from his Emperor to 'Go' and now he had it.

John Darcy the Sixth was a little less clear about what was expected of him. His role was largely a soft power capability, even if it was backed by his brother's hard power. But he knew not to appear uncertain in front of his father. He would do what he could but, in truth, the actual threats to any errant allies would have to come from his brother's mouth, not his.

Tommy Frazer, Ambassador-at-Large to the President of the United States of America, for his part, did his master's – the President's father's – bidding, but his heart was not really in it. He'd given long and loyal service to the Global Emperor and to be sidelined as he had been caused quiet anguish to him. His promotion to Commander-in-Chief had led him to believe that his days of disappointment were over, but clearly they were not. The Emperor giveth and the Emperor could taketh away, he always knew that. But it did not assuage his sense of betrayal when his dumping came, and his enthusiasm for his service disappeared with his demotion.

He did his job. He set up Fifth's personal retreat on American Samoa and he established a suitable retreat for King George in the South Island of New Zealand. For himself, he retreated to the island fortress of Guam where he was fated by sycophantic subordinates and wannabe up-and-comers amongst the junior officer ranks. There he became one of the old soldiers who never died. He, like pre-consuls before him, just faded away. He died two years after resigning from his presidency and his will bequeathed his presidential library to the people of the Hawaiian Islands.

Several British peers also saw the writing on the wall for the GSC and relocated to the bayside hills surrounding the picturesque city of Dunedin. Several of the French aristocrats relocated to the Marlborough region of the South Island of New Zealand where they poured their millions into lifting the crisp whites, for which its vintages had become acclaimed, into a true nectar of the Global Elite, even if not the Gods.

Several other European GSC members were a little less dramatic in their relocation, opting instead to maintain an air of normality whilst boosting their prestige real estate holdings in the more secluded but strongly defensible locales around Lake Geneva in the

Swiss Alps. Japanese members opted for Guam as their preferred retreat while the remnants of the Middle Eastern monarchies favored Diego Garcia in the Indian Ocean even though Fifth had not specifically designated it as a preferred refuge.

All this relocation was done discretely. Fifth would have it no other way. He did not approve their premature retreat. To him, this was defeatism and he scorned their timidity and caution. But he did not actively dissuade them.

He was not about to throw in the towel himself but was conscious that the worst case scenario might emerge, so he understood their caution. His demeanor and his actions demonstrated resolve and that's what he encouraged amongst his minions. But that did not deter him from quietly making his own evacuation plans – just in case. Sixth was wary also but said nothing. He quietly aped his father's preparations.

For Hedley Darcy, however, the thought of retreat never entered his head. He was quite sure the power he now held at his command could vanquish without difficulty the rabble that dared challenge the ruling class. The thought that it may not succeed was an absurdity to him. And Fifth did nothing to suggest otherwise. He needed a believer leading his forces and the more ruthless his lieutenant was in prosecuting his task the better it suited the Emperor.

"How many are there?" inquired Hedley.

"Fourteen that we know of," said General Atkins.

"Where are they now?"

"Back in Trois Rivieres, sir," said the General. "We spotted them on satellite within minutes of the fireball going up. They were in three pickups and a minivan. They were the only vehicles in the area so it had to be them. They split up as soon as they got back into town. Two are parked outside this motel ... here, one has gone into a garage in this house here ... and the minivan is parked outside this apartment block ... here. We think the six or seven people from that van are holed up in these two apartments here and here."

"Waste them," commanded Hedley.

"We might have to be a little more subtle than that, sir," suggested the General. "The motel has about twenty rooms, most of which seem to be occupied; I can get an exact count within the hour. The apartment block also has fourteen units in the complex, and the two units I've indicated both have apartments on the second floor above them. The house is stand-alone, of course."

"Waste them!" repeated Hedley. "You have drone launch missiles on hand, don't you? So use them! That's what they're for, isn't it?"

"Well, yes, sir," hesitated the General. "But if we just fire them at the targets, we're likely to hurt an awful lot of innocent people."

"Innocent?" scoffed Hedley. "These people are all collaborators of these terrorists! They know what these terrorists have been up to. It's a small town. Everybody knows what everybody else does in a small town. They're all in it even if they don't actually plant the bombs themselves!"

"But, sir," protested the General, "if we just fire and cause multiple non-combatant casualties, the public relations fall out could be disastrous."

"Public relations be damned!" yelled Hedley. "It will be an object lesson to the whole town, to the whole country. It will send a very clear message to everyone, north and south of the border – we will not tolerate these attacks on the vital infrastructure of this country! Waste them," I said. "That's a direct order, General!"

"Yes, sir!" said the General. Raising the hand piece to his ear, he issued the order in a quiet, almost whispered, tone. The respondent on the other end of the phone either did not hear him or did not believe that he had heard. The General repeated the order, this time firmer, and in a more deliberate tone.

Global Revolution

The Aleutian meeting in 2038 between Parnell, Macintyre and the regional commanders of the APA had not been called to form a world-wide dissident movement, but both Russian and Chinese dissidents had chosen to send observers, which widened the scope of the struggle. Chinese dissident Li Chai Tung and his revolutionary army, which drew heavily on Uyghur and Tibetan rebels as well as displaced workers from his native Hunan province, was busy launching an assault against the energy supply corridors from Central Asia to the Chinese east coast population centers to unseat the Chinese Communist Party. The Russian dissident Alexey Medlevkov and his Eastern Ukrainian, Crimean and Tartar-dominated resistance movement was causing significant disruption to the Muscovy and Belorussian-dominated Russian Federation and to Russian energy customers in Western Ukraine, Poland, and Germany.

In Europe, the relatively affluent but embryonic dissident movement in Germany, was in turn inspired by their French and British counterparts and their apparent success, and who, in turn, took their inspiration from their North American cousins and their stoic endeavors. Their collaboration became circular and reinforcing in an increasingly positive feedback loop. The Western Europeans were pressuring the various European royal families to abdicate and were seeking to destroy the power of the residual European aristocracies who still dominated local industry and finance. The European rebels' efforts were having an impact on their quarry, as Fifth was learning in his GSC inner conclaves with his European 'royal' and common associates, King George, Prince Gerhardt, and van Kleist.

At the same time, the increasingly successful rebellions in the Middle East and North Africa were heralding the impending demise of the remaining Arab monarchies, some of which had already fallen. The dictatorial Egyptian military regime had also already fallen. The Middle Eastern rebels were not yet in a position to render significant logistics and materiel support to their Northern and New World colleagues, but the Arab rebels were well equipped with heavy weapons once supplied by Western governments in the support of the twenty-first century wars against the Libyan, Syrian and Iranian governments. Mohammed Ishmael's Egyptians, in particular, were well stocked with anti-armor and man-portable anti-aircraft weapons, and he had not forgotten his old friend who now headed up the North American rebellion.

In North America, Parnell's far-flung military command was not the only form of resistance against the Darcy regime. Indeed, it was not even the largest or most diverse. Many APA supporters across its sprawling cell-like network, and amongst council members both at national, regional and district levels, had not agreed to military-type operations to enforce a return to democratic government. They feared resorting to violence to achieve social change would result in imposing military discipline, both during and after war's end, and that was the least like democratic governance they could imagine.

As Gillian McCloud had so eloquently put it at a private corridor meeting during an APA supreme council conclave: "We don't want to remove one fascist regime in Washington merely to replace it with another. This so-called 'Military Wing' just might emerge as a new fascist regime itself and 'General' Parnell just might become the new dictator."

"She's right," said the usually reserved Wyoming headmaster, Richard Scales. "After all, Robespierre's Terror succeeded the French Revolution and was itself succeeded by the Bonaparte regime. Lenin's Politburo emerged from the Russian Revolution; and Mao's Chinese Communist Party was the Chinese variant that emerged from its civil war with the Nationalists. Even Cromwell's role as Lord Protector in England in the mid-1600s was a military dictatorship," he said, expounding world history. "Military victors have a habit of becoming tyrants after the success of their revolutions. In fact, history tends to suggest it is more the norm than the exception."

Many APA members took note of their warning and shunned the more kinetic urgings of Parnell, Rouleau, and the rest of the rebel military leaders.

Beyond the confines of clandestine meetings of would-be revolutionaries, but largely inspired by them, across the continent protest movements of all shapes and sizes became increasingly active. Citizen groups, whose militancy was confined to non-violent activities, emerged everywhere: from merely boycotting certain goods and services; to comedians and pranksters lampooning and ridiculing public figures and public policy; to vocal cynics dismissing government propaganda. The underground press flourished, with distribution mainly by hand and often just by word-of-mouth, a modern-day version of the wandering minstrel, since formalized electronic communications were heavily monitored by government overseers. Spies and informants were everywhere and dissidents had to be careful who they confided in. But that did not dim the enthusiasm of the critics. Subtle civil disobedience became almost an art form amongst the disillusioned and discouraged population. So too did deliberate sabotage: quick setting glue squeezed into the keyholes of government offices; "do not pin, spike or fold" warnings on official forms became an invitation to do just that. Tax evasion became a national sport and regulation ignorance almost a civic duty. The creativity of the masses to frustrate the government was unbounded and resistance was pervasive and willful.

Not without pain though. Fines and penalties escalated dramatically. Courts became intolerant to delinquents. Jails bulged at the seams. Police, inspectors of all kinds, and almost any government official became persona-non-grata in social settings. Their isolation enraged them and enhanced their vindictiveness. The gulf between *us* and *them* grew wider day by day; week by week; month by month, with no respite in sight.

The harder Hedley Darcy cracked down on the rebellious, the more isolated he and his minions became. Little more needed to be done by the covert dissidents to widen the gap between leaders and the led – Hedley Darcy himself was momentum enough. The masses became enthusiasts and persisted. Defiance became a way of life even if the penalties were high and retribution harsh.

Although the security services controlled almost every checkpoint, every road, every bridge, port and airport in the major cities, at the least, there were neighborhoods where the more experienced officials knew it was unwise to go. They stayed away from them if they could. The countryside, and particularly the wilderness, belonged to the APA. Even crack army units would not go there unless they were specifically ordered to and even then, they went in great force.

Despite the pervasiveness of the dissent though, Parnell and his military lieutenants realized that protest and civil disobedience would not be enough. Some aspects of hard power were needed to dislodge the tyrants. Disrupting vital supplies, energy, in particular, was necessary to demonstrate that the regime was not in charge of the economy, and to prove that dissent was neither marginal nor ineffective. The APA needed demonstrable victories. Despite the inconvenience and the suffering, the masses needed to know the resistance existed, was active, was powerful, and was not going to be crushed. The people had to have some hope that the tyranny would one day end. The Declaration of Independence was widely quoted, almost learned by heart by the masses, particularly the section that read:

"When a long train of abuses and usurpations, pursuing invariably the same Object evinces a design to reduce them under absolute Despotism, it is their right, it is their duty, to throw off such Government, and to provide new Guards for their future security."

'It is their right, it is their duty' was often emphasized, or underlined in written text. The story of the Concord Minutemen and 'the shot that was heard around the world' also became a favorite bedtime story for young and old.

Parnell knew the APA needed 'heroes' so he encouraged the underground press. Amateur filmmakers worked overtime to ensure the masses knew of them and their exploits. Rouleau, in particular, became a popular folk hero and so did Chambers. So did the dashing young Australian, Andrew Macintyre.

The 'heroes' gave the people hope, as heroes tend to do. Hope grew the numbers of activists and enhanced awareness of the key issues at stake – freedom, democracy, and the soul of Western Civilization itself. Even though the mainstream media labeled the rebels as 'terrorists' and 'degenerates' and lambasted their triumphs as criminal acts, the people had long since abandoned any trust in the regimes' propaganda. The subtle psychological war of the non-violent dissenters was its counterweight, and the people believed the 'heroes' before they believed Darcy and his gang.

The rebels were winning the war of 'hearts and minds'. Parnell appreciated that the 'peaceniks' efforts were just as important as his own 'kinetic' efforts although he firmly believed both were necessary. He also knew some military-type discipline would be required to make sure traditional animosity and rivalries did not get out of hand and dissipate the collective effort through needless infighting and the personal feuding that tends to pervade most collective human efforts.

Luckily, he had an important ally, albeit an unwitting one. General Atkins' advice to Hedley Darcy about the Trois Rivieres counterterrorism strike had been right, and Darcy turned out to be very wrong in ordering it. Both Parnell suspected, and Rouleau knew as much, even if the incumbent president did not. The young headstrong commander-in-chief had handed the APA a propaganda coup of significant proportions. Had Darcy Junior been a little more familiar with the lessons of history he would have known it would be. What Wounded Knee did in American history, what the Amritsar massacre did to the British Empire and what the Tiananmen Square massacre did for the Chinese Communist Party, Trois Rivieres did for the Darcy Administration.

To punish fourteen Canadian rebels for the sabotage of the Western Greenland pipeline, Darcy brought about the demise of nine rebels and captured three more, but not the leader of the strike team. Rouleau had left immediately on their return to the small lumber town to report to his superiors in Quebec City.

In the process, the strike on the motel destroyed five units in this publicly occupied accommodation. It killed seven innocent guests and seriously injured three others.

The two adjacent units of the two-story apartment block that was struck were also destroyed, killing eight rebels ensconced in the end unit. Also killed was a family of four in the adjoining unit, and the father of the family in the third most southern unit in the wing. The latter's wife and twelve-year-old daughter were airlifted to Quebec General Hospital with third-degree burns to most of their bodies and it was doubtful the daughter would survive. In the remaining single house refuge, the entire family of father, mother, sister, and two young brothers of the last of the saboteurs, plus the rebel himself, were also killed outright.

The nightly news in both the United States and Canada reported that the fourteen rebels responsible for the attack on the pipeline had been killed in a fierce firefight with Royal Canadian Mounted Police units. One officer had been slightly wounded in the exchange but was expected to make a full recovery.

But the dissident press reported an entirely different story. Many local residents had filmed the retaliatory strike and vivid motion pictures of the burning buildings soon appeared on audio-visual devices across the continent. Footage was also smuggled to dissident broadcast sites offshore and to mobile broadcast units onshore. Soon the internet and other news dissemination media were publishing the event. *Global Voice* out of Toronto broadcast to its two and a half million subscribers and the *European Truth Action Group* out of Amsterdam published to its one point seven million members. Graphic descriptions from on-the-spot eye-witnesses, most of them smudged out for personal anonymity, accompanied the visuals. *Pravda* and *Peking People's Daily* gleefully spread the word to their world-wide affiliates.

Hedley Darcy did not care. Fifth showed indifference. But they should have. The atrocity spurred resistance like no previous incident had been able to do. And not just in North America. The story and its visuals found its way to Europe, China, South America, Australasia, and the Middle East. It went viral globally and all oppressed peoples everywhere noted its savagery and identified with its suffering.

"For God's sake!" pleaded Gerhardt. "We can't sustain this type of publicity. You've got to tell Hedley to ease off."

"Hedley knows what's he's doing," Fifth replied calmly. "These people got no more than they deserved. They have to learn that this terrorist activity has to stop."

"I'm getting protests from Government's across the globe," complained Sixth. "I have to tell them something. It was all a mistake. The Mounties exceeded their authority; the rebels used civilians as human shields; something like that," he appealed to Fifth.

"Make whatever noises you think are appropriate," responded Fifth. "Diplomacy is supposed to be your responsibility, isn't it? So do your job!"

"But these events are getting too frequent!" protested Sixth. "Can't you make Hedley be a little more discrete?"

"Hedley's doing the job I appointed him to do," replied Fifth, a little terser than his usual calm self. "You're not going soft on terrorism, are you, John?"

Sixth stopped wailing, and said no more on the subject. But he sulked and glared at his brother.

"I'm afraid the Secretary is right, John," King George supported Sixth's protest "Public opinion does matter, especially in these troubled times. He is also right that incidents like this one in North America have repercussions for jurisdictions elsewhere in the world. The Quebec incident is acting as a stimulus to terrorist activity right across the globe. We've noted a significant upsurge in public support for rebel groups in the United Kingdom, as the Secretary says."

"Then deal with it," snapped Fifth. "Do you want me to come over and reign over your kingdom too?"

Neither King George nor Prince Gerhardt had been used to such dismissal from Fifth. He had always been a monument to courtesy. They wondered if the old man was losing his grip. And they subtly, and only mentally, edged closer to the door. New Zealand was beginning to look more inviting to the English monarch and the Swiss Mountains were calling the Dutch prince.

Respite

The winter of 2038/39 was surprisingly harsh given the elevated global temperatures of recent decades. It dampened, if not all but ceased, military activity of any kind for the deepest winter months, except in southern commands where the weather was more amenable to military operations. Despite its constraint, it did, however, give the bulk of both sides of the increasingly belligerent confrontation some forced rest and convalescence so it was not entirely unwelcomed.

Huddled in his Central Command Headquarters deep in the Clearwater Mountains, Parnell and his staff pondered their accomplishments and planned their next moves for the upcoming campaign period. Discussion on strategy, tactics, training, logistics, and other military and political quandaries were rife even if communications with distant commands was difficult. But, in the more relaxed moments, when the day's work had been done, there was also time for camaraderie and friendly banter around roaring log fires. Spirits were lifted by retrieved stashes of old malt generously shared with close comrades.

The operational constraint was mainly on the Military Wing of the APA which was a tight-knit, very collegiate group of dedicated patriots; although some minor operations were maintained in some southern commands to maintain the pressure on the regime. But the Political Wing of the network was far more disbursed. About the only thing that really united them was their disapproval of the regime that had taken control in Washington D.C. but the creativity of their protests and defiance grew rather than diminished, especially through social media platforms.

A similar situation existed in Canada. Military activity was severely hampered by weather constraints but political activity still possible although also much more constrained than in the south. Fortunately, many of the more grassroots dissident movements spanned both countries and some also further southward into Mexico to effectively form a North America-wide constituency. So southern-based operations of some kind were still possible by some trans-border organizations.

Key among these embryonic groups was New Valley Forge. The name of the organization was chosen to stir the hearts of patriots throughout the American republic by reminding them that, although the nation was experiencing a bleak winter in its long-cherished quest for freedom and democracy, spring would come and with its arrival the nation would once again sprout forth in all its promised abundance. It was a network of community-based political activists spread right across the nation, with sympathetic counterparts north and south of the border, which met discreetly locally, and occasionally nationally, in low key gatherings by invitation only. In many ways, it was similar to the early Christian movement in the time of the Roman Empire, but it was strictly secular in its philosophical orientation. Its unofficial leader was Californian activist and coordinator Gary Knight.

Knight, in the bitter winter of 2039/40, was the most active of the APA leadership. From his California base, right across the more clement states, he traveled endlessly and spoke calmly, eloquently, and persuasively to dozens and dozens of low-key groups of concerned citizens from many walks of life. And his message was essentially the same to all: we have to do something; we have to be non-violent; but, above all, we must not be passive. Knight encouraged them to be daring in their local activities, to use their initiative and not wait for directions from above. He believed in grassroots activism, revolution from below, a 'people's' revolt, not a 'dictators' one orchestrated from above.

Not all rebel military activity ceased during the winter recess.

While the bulk of the APA political and military wings rested, Parnell still knew he had to keep the regime off balance so he had quietly instructed that it continue where possible. His instruction manifested itself dramatically in the late winter of 2039 when the left-most great oak door of the GSC boardroom burst open and a breathless, ashen-faced Prince Gerhardt burst into the room.

Fifth rose quickly from his seat at the head of the board table and moved with cheetah-like speed to his distressed deputy. "Gerhardt, what on earth is the matter?" he asked. "You look terrible." He motioned the distraught man to the nearest chair at the foot of the table. "Here, sit down."

"They got Scherlinger!" Gerhardt gasped. "They blew him out of the sky right in front of me."

"What?" demanded Fifth.

"Scherlinger," gasped Gerhardt again. "He was right behind me waiting for my bird to clear the heliport. They just blew him out of the sky. I knew he was in holding pattern waiting for me to land so I waited for him at the edge of the pad to accompany him down here. He was just coming in to land when something streaked in from the west, a missile or something. It turned his chopper into a fireball right before my eyes!"

"Try and calm down, man," Fifth soothed, moving to the drinks cabinet to the left of the board table. He poured a double-shot of scotch from the decanter. "Here, drink this," he said.

Gerhardt grasped the tumbler with trembling hands and gulped its contents down. Slowly the color returned to his face, and his breathing eased a little.

"Now," said Fifth in calm, consoling manner, "Tell me slowly once again … exactly what happened? Take your time."

Slowly, more calmly, Gerhardt recounted his story. This time he added: "I tell you, John, they must have people here on the inside. They must know when and where we are going to hold our meetings."

Fifth rose, grim-faced. He moved to the telephone at the end of

the room, lifted the hand piece, and punched in three digits –
connected to the President's personal line. He paused, then barked:
"Hedley, get up here, now!"

He was about to hang up when an afterthought occurred to him.
"Fly into McGuire then come the rest of the way by road," he
added. "It looks like the APes have got their hands on some
MANPADs."

Pressure

General Atkins's regular Northern Command troops still held almost all key strategic points in the United States, but guerrilla activity, while mostly deferred in northern states and Canada, continued throughout the most clement environments in the American south. They were so frequent and so effective in those regions that the movement of key supplies and personnel between most of his strongholds was risky. Even within the stronghold cities – Los Angeles, Houston, Miami, most large Southern and South Western cities, and predominantly African American and Latino neighborhoods – government forces only ventured as part of larger, well-armed and well-supported military operations. No regular patrols were carried out in these areas. Even the capital, Washington D.C., had its no-go zones.

Major military operations were nevertheless carried out by Government forces mainly on Hedley Darcy's direct orders but with the full approval of his father. Fifth was not about to abandon the United States to 'the mob'. He still felt he had to demonstrate who was in charge even if the majority of the American population did not know who he really was.

But his firmness, his unbending determination to prevail, only inflamed the situation. With the privations emanating from the fuel blockade, the lack of fuel for everyday transport plus the disruption of deliveries of everyday consumer items, especially food, only served to further enrage an already enraged population.

One operation, in particular, fueled the fire.

In South Central Los Angles on 29th September 2039, the Federal Bureau of Investigation, with the full support of the Los Angeles Police Department and the California National Guard, mounted a four thousand strong foray in residential neighborhoods, aimed at flushing out a suspected chapter of the APA-affiliated Sons of Atzlan. The government intelligence was good and the disruption ascribed to the group accurate. It had been responsible for numerous armed holdups and two daring bank robberies in the previous several months and the group's leaders were holed up in the area cordoned off by security forces. But the locals were not about to give them up. Their leader, Ferdinando Marquez, had read his Mao Tse Tung well and learned that gaining the loyalty of the local people was vital to the survival of any guerrilla movement. He had been generous to a fault with the widows and orphans of his home district and they were not found wanting when the time came to support him. He may not have achieved notoriety amongst Parnell 'hero' stories but he was a legend to Mexicans north and south of the border.

Had General Atkin's field commander on this operation – Brigadier General Bart Houbertz – been a little older, and had served in some faraway places like Iraq or Afghanistan where American forces had tried to win the hearts and minds of civil populations, he might have understood that brutality breeds resistance and not compliance, especially when the host population feels the soldiers confronting them are alien to their country and their culture. But the young general had not. He was the product of an Eastern establishment commercial dynasty and a West Point graduate. His military experience so far had comprised mostly an endless round of debutante balls, cocktail parties, and the occasional military exercise to justify the wearing of his uniform. He thought he was up against American gangsters, despicable human garbage, and traitors to the American ethos. He was wrong. He was up against Mexican patriots who just happened to be born north of the border – he was up against local heroes.

His reception proved an education to him and his officer corps. His civilian advisers, local LAPD officers, and local FBI agents knew better, of course, and said so. But to the ambitious young general, this was a military operation. As the senior military commander in charge, he knew better.

General Houbertz's *Operation Thunder Clap*, would have made any 'shock and awe' military enthusiast proud. It had all the fire and brimstone of biblical retribution, with inhabited and drone strike aircraft, fixed-wing and rotary, flying hundreds of sorties against insurgent positions. It had armored vehicles, heavy and light, supporting heavily armored ground troops. National Guard troops carried automatic and semi-automatic weapons and were also equipped with grenade and rocket launchers. It was the best on-the-job training for war they could have wished for. Police units also sported armored vests and carried automatic weapons and shotguns while FBI personnel confined themselves mostly to armored personnel carriers fitted with remotely controlled heavy machine guns.

It was not certain how many of the Sons of Atzlan were killed in the operation, the best approximation was forty-three. And three badly wounded insurgents were taken alive. The collateral damage, however, was considerably more than that. Here again, it was difficult to gain an accurate score because no-one was exactly sure how many people had been in the two-square-mile area sealed off at the start of the operation. The exact body count of civilian corpses at the end of the three-day operation was four hundred and twenty-seven: one hundred and thirty-eight men over sixteen years of age; one hundred and eleven adult females, and one hundred and seventy-eight children under the age of sixteen.

Local church groups, who did most of the tallying, were considered the most reliable statistically by aid groups and national and international human rights observers. Official accounts of the operation cited 'one dead National Guardsman, three seriously wounded police officers, and several unfortunate civilian casualties that had been caught in the crossfire'. No mention was made of Marquez from either source but his survival became the stuff of legend in Latino communities north and south of the border. South

Central Los Angeles was ablaze from end to end with smoke visible for hundreds of miles around.

The entire South West erupted as the news of the massacre spread. All towns and cities of any significant size reported rioting, looting, arson, and wide-spread protests, as Mexican Americans voiced and actioned their revulsion. The president, state governors, city mayors, church and civic leaders, and school principals called for calm. But a fuse had been lit and no-one was quite sure how far the fire would spread. Civil disorder also broke out in the South East, mainly street marches and sit-ins, but with the occasional car fire and store looting. In the North West and around Washington D.C. a similar story emerged but with a little less heat than in the Southern regions.

Hedley Darcy ordered a state of emergency, over and above the already ensconced martial law. And he ordered the rebellion to be suppressed at all costs. But the entire military command of the country was not as naive as the young Brigadier General who had sparked it all. They cautioned the President to be more conciliatory. They ordered their field commanders to deploy at a distance and not to issue live ammunition to troops tasked with crowd control duties. They also urged State Governors and Police Chiefs to constrain their National Guard and police forces, urging them to ensure the personal safety of their personnel but to take only such limited offensive operations as was required to protect lives.

Fifth, however, was having none of it. He wanted the rebellion crushed. He ordered Hedley Darcy to appeal directly to the nation to support the government in restoring order. His presidential address to the nation was accompanied by stirring patriotic music and a backdrop festoon with stars and stripes.

"In these difficult times," the president intoned, "it behooves all loyal Americans to stand up and show their true colors. I appeal, in particular, to those of you who wear the uniforms of those services that have served this country so well and loyally since the founding of this great nation. All of you, soldiers, sailors, air force personnel, marines, coastguards, police officers, homeland security personnel: the country needs your loyal service now more than ever. And I also appeal to all civilian patriots: teachers, public servants, inspectors, state and city officials, all of you who have sworn an oath to defend and protect this nation and its people, I appeal to you to stand up for America, today, now and in the future. Rally around your leaders – without you they are powerless but with you they, and you, are invincible."

Some did rally, as the president had urged, but in the main, the response was lackluster, unenthusiastic, and tame. The very people Darcy appealed to were amongst the most disillusioned. They obeyed their orders but their actions were slow and uninspired. They had heard the rhetoric all before and they no longer believed it. If they remained loyal at all it was because they feared the chaos that might ensue if they abandoned their posts. But they were in no mood to risk life and limb to defend the tyrant.

President Darcy backed up his public appeal with presidential directives by the score. He left no doubt to his subordinates exactly what their orders were: crack down hard on anyone who showed sympathy for the rebels. And some of his subordinates obeyed these direct orders. But the regular military's response was tepid at best, insolent often; disobedient at worst. The regular armed services took their cue from those who wore uniforms like theirs, and who had brass on their shoulders. They had mysteriously developed feet of clay. A few National Guard commanders, particularly those with close social, family and commercial contacts with the more belligerent state governors, rallied their troops but at the rank-and-file level the response was also subdued. None actually mutinied but many were 'missing in action'. Service personnel began deserting in their thousands, disgusted and repulsed at their orders to decimate their own people.

"Gun jammed, sir," was often heard, only to be reiterated from an accompanying comrade to whom an alternative order was addressed.

"Out of range, sir," was also common.

"Civilians in the line of fire," required no further justification for failing to obey an order to 'fire'.

And a few bolder junior officers even dared to respond: "I'm sorry, sir, I'm unable to give that command." Some even added, by way of justification: "My men will simply not obey it."

Judgement Day

By the first week of summer in 2040, well-rested after the forced winter break and well supplied by sympathetic locals, Rouleau recommenced operations against the energy supply routes from the West Greenland oil fields, through his native Quebec. At the same time, Chambers recommenced operations in Alberta and British Columbia. Both experienced a significant upsurge in volunteer numbers from incensed Canadians still resentful of the brutality of the Mounties in the Trois Rivieres massacre.

American recruitment had skyrocketed after Los Angles also.

Further west, Alaska Command of the APA commenced operations against the dwindling Prudhoe Bay installations and its southward Trans-Alaska Pipeline down to Valdez. All three operations brought oil and gas supplies from Canada and Alaska sources to the United States to a virtual standstill.

Despite these privations, however, in the end, it was neither the rebel energy blockades nor the civil unrest that finally brought the Darcy regime down. It was Parnell's targeted assassination campaign that delivered the coups de grace.

By the end of September 2040, the body count of that terrorist campaign stood at twenty-one.

Strike Team 1 led by the ex-Marine Corps sniper had crossed off seven of the ten names on his list, one attributable to the British BRM team.

Strike Team 2 was targeting its sixth victim.

Strike Teams 3 and 4 had both dispatched three victims and were now searching out their fourth.

Strike Team 5 had dispatched its first two victims and was now homing in on its third.

Strike Team 6 had attempted its first strike but had been foiled by a particularly astute FBI counterterrorism unit. Its striker had been killed minutes before their strike and its observer captured. The hapless school teacher revealed the identities of the team's researcher, financier, and logistics specialist but died soon after interrogation. The remnants of Team 6 were now on the run.

Strike Team 7 had also gone to ground.

By now the FBI and Homeland Security had both realized this was a coordinated and professionally run campaign and began to hone their investigatory and counter-strike doctrine to more effectively combat it.

APA Strike Teams 8, 9, and 10 had been formed but were still in the final stages of training and yet to be operationally deployed. With the stepped-up counterinsurgency effort, Parnell advised them that it might be unwise for them to have any further contact with their loved ones until this battle was over.

Across the Atlantic, the British Republican Movement's first strike team had two hits to its credit and was seeking out its third.

The BRM had a further three strike teams in the field and two more in training.

French and German movements also had three teams each in training and their liaison with Medlevkov's Russian dissidents was proving useful in terms of weapons supply, access to Russia's ex-KGB and ex-FSB defectors with their dark secrets, and particularly their more subtle non-kinetic, but equally deadly, strike options.

In the Far East, the Chinese rebels were continuing to pursue a largely kinetic campaign. The Chinese Communist Party was far from beaten but it was on the defensive.

Ishmail's Egyptian rebels were now on a roll in the wider Middle East region and had supplied some heavy weapons to the Chinese rebels via its connections up through the Central Asian Muslim republics and the New Silk Road that the Germans, Russians and Chinese governments had so generously developed during the earlier decades of the century.

GSC cohesion was now in tatters as members raced to save their skins. Fifth was still defiant but those around him had become extremely nervous. Van Kleist was a persistent advocate for mediation of some kind. The global mining empire over which he presided was almost at a standstill. He could neither ship ore nor stockpile production. His skilled workforce was reluctant to venture into the far-off wilds where most of the group's assets were located. Insurance companies refused to cover his travel risk and premiums on all life cover for his field staff skyrocketed.

Both King George and Prince Gerhardt advocated a negotiated solution. As royalty, they were under pressure from republican movements in their respective countries, King George being urged to abdicate, Gerhardt under pressure to advise his sovereign to do the same. The Duke of Westminster had been number one on the list of the second BRM strike team. He had narrowly missed a strike by a rocket-propelled grenade fired at his bullet-proof limousine as he returned from a family get-together at the Palace for King George's birthday.

Hardigan's successor, a minor English peer named Cardogan, experienced similar problems to van Kleist, the fossil fuel conglomerate he presided over having far-flung well-heads and refining facilities in distant lands. Its Middle Eastern assets were under daily attack from Ishmail's sponsored forces either through daring raids over the desert or from sabotage from its diverse workforce – the screening of staff was difficult given its diverse ethnicity, source and religiosity. His African assets were similarly at risk, as were his South American ones.

Other less prominent GSC members had also grown nervous, their apprehension spurred on by their lack of access to GSC inner circle intelligence. In the past, they had trusted Fifth – he had served them and their interests well. But now the world appeared to be falling apart and Fifth was not particularly forthcoming in enlightening them as to what was happening or what was being done about it. Dozens had relocated to more secure locations, with Switzerland being the favored by the Europeans, Guam by the East Asians, and American Samoa by the Americans. Bermuda and New Zealand were also popular for the British and Canadians. Hundreds of members that had not relocated their domicile had nevertheless made serious inquiries and personal visits to distant safe zones.

That John Davyd Darcy the Fifth ever saw the light was directly attributable to Rouleau's North Eastern Sector targeted assassination campaign, aided and abetted by the other forces evolving within the North American political space. The revolt by the military high command was a direct result of Hedley Darcy's ruthless attempts to suppress and punish the rebellious masses and to the reluctance of his Northern Command generals to obey the orders of their Commander-in-Chief, the American president. They added significantly to the Global Emperor's change of heart, for it was those very generals who subtly set up the personal strike on the Commander-in-Chief, even if it was APA Strike Team 4 that actually launched the attempt.

"Are we sure this is genuine?" Parnell frowned as he scanned the cryptic note from the military insider. "It could be a trap."

"Unlikely," replied Rouleau. "It would be a little over-the-top just to capture one strike team. In any case, our intelligence is that the military high command is far from happy with the course of events. Indications are that many of them see a mutiny in the making and they're keen to see that one does not occur on their watch."

"But ... I mean ..." fathomed Parnell, "... this effectively leaves Hedley Darcy wide open to attack. I mean, they're basically handing him to us on a platter."

"Oui," said Rouleau, smiling. "It looks like the professional soldiers are far from impressed with the orders they're getting from their commander-in-chief. Apparently, he is riding roughshod over their advice and they don't like it."

"So, you think we should go for it?" queried Rouleau, not that he needed any further convincing, nor, he suspected, did Parnell.

"Alright," said Parnell. "Let's go for it. Who have we got available?"

"Team 4 has now been blooded and since we're talking about a sniper strike, they have an excellent man at their point, I worked with him in Newfoundland. They haven't yet commenced their run on Oberton, their next target, so they could fit Darcy into their schedule without disrupting it too much."

"Fine," said Parnell. "Team 4 it is then."

As assassination strikes go, this particular operation was not particularly complicated. Hedley Darcy himself made it comparatively easy. He was a notorious philanderer and he frequently had affairs with obliging ladies keen to add a presidential conquest to their brag sheets. He was somewhat discrete since he did not entertain his partners in the White House as some of his predecessors had done. Rather, he had a quiet apartment several blocks away. It was continuously under secret service surveillance, and he was always transported to and from the location by a three-car multi-configured motorcade of the type of vehicles normally frequenting Washington streets. *His* vehicle was usually armored but looked no different from the usual runabout the upper-middle-class mandarins of Washington D.C. might drive.

The strike took place in late November 2040 as Hedley Darcy stepped from the rear door of the nondescript sedan. He headed towards the front door of the seven-story apartment block.

The shot came from the fourth floor of the corner apartment of the adjoining block immediately to the right of his destination. The bullet struck him in the left upper shoulder about four inches to the left and above the heart. As a professional strike, any expert in the field would have described it as a botched job – perhaps the seniority of the target had unnerved the shooter – perhaps there had been a last-minute distraction, who knows. Even the most experienced of this unique and elite profession would readily admit that 'things can always go wrong'.

Whatever the cause of the failure, it was not due to the quick and heroic action of the secret service, or of the presence of his personal bodyguard. The normal surveillance detail in the destination building and the adjoining buildings on both sides of the street were mysteriously absent that night. The bodyguards had retreated to the front and rear of the president's vehicle immediately his door had been opened. They had apparently ducked for cover immediately after the shot rang out. But a more observant spectator might have noticed they were well clear of their charge long before the loud report shattered the serenity of the evening. The president himself had not noticed anything unusual either. He had been more focused on the delights that lay ahead within the building.

Hedley Darcy did not die that night. His security detail had gathered around his frame as it lay on the ground, most with guns drawn as they scanned the building to the right and its upper floor windows. They saw nothing. The gunman was gone in an instant after the shot. Then someone leaned down and tested the president's pulse and cried: "He's still alive."

There was a moment's pause – what to do? Their orders had been clear enough: "Stand down immediately the president leaves the vehicle!" No more than that.

"HEDARCY is down. I say again, HEDARCY is down."

The security chief lowered his wrist from the side of his mouth. He had no intention of becoming the scapegoat from this little piece of skullduggery. Twenty-three minutes later Hedley Darcy was in the intensive care unit of the Bethesda Naval Hospital. Doctors reported that his condition was serious but stable.

Four days later Parnell received a note via the Danish Embassy that Fifth would like to meet with him at that county's four-story mansion in Washington's lavish diplomatic quarter.

Democracy Returns

Parnell felt an overwhelming sense of rage and disgust well up inside him as he sat down at the table directly across from John Darcy the Fifth. This was the man who had betrayed him last time he'd sat down to parley. This was the man who had ordered the torture of him, his wife, and his friends – who was directly responsible for the murder of his closest comrade and personal mentor, Father Andre LeMonte.

Parnell's loathing of this suave, urbane psychopath was almost irrepressible. Almost, but not quite. With supreme mental effort, the disciplined warrior overcame his instincts and composed himself to face the more important task that lay immediately ahead: the negotiation of Fifth's surrender.

For his part, Fifth appeared relaxed, composed, and even amiable. He had, unusually for him, dressed in a low-key business suit, impeccably tailored, with a white shirt and pale blue tie, his neatly groomed hair and tanned countenance looking as though he'd just stepped from his private yacht after a pleasant cruise around the Caribbean. He smiled warmly at Parnell.

Parnell almost lost his composure, but managed to restrain himself.

To Fifth's immediate left sat General Atkins in his capacity as Commander-in-Chief of Northern Command. To his right sat John Darcy the Sixth in his capacity as U.S. Secretary of State. To Atkins left sat Tobias Korman, formerly President of UltraDynamics Corporation, but more recently newly installed as Vice President of the United States of American, deputizing for President Hedley Darcy who was still convalescing in the Bethesda Naval Hospital. Across the table from them to Parnell's right sat Piers Rouleau, as

Field Commander of all APA military forces, to his right Gary Knight, leader of the APA Political Wing, and to Parnell's left sat Elsie Chambers as representative of the APA's Canadian affiliates. The head of the table was taken by Gerrard Kniesten, Danish Ambassador to the United States, as host of the meeting.

Collectively the gathering looked absurdly small with its modest table and nine chairs sitting amidst the European splendor of the grand ballroom of the Danish Embassy in Washington DC. The nine were now alone in the room with the respective security details of the antagonists, and the host's service staff, having withdrawn behind the now-closed ceiling length double doors that graced the venue's entrance.

Silence prevailed, somewhat awkwardly for a minute or two. Then Kniesten, sensing it might continue indefinitely if not broken, commenced the discussion:

"Since it is you that requested this meeting," he said looking directly at Fifth, "perhaps it is you who should commence the discussion."

"By all means," said Fifth smoothly. "As you know, Lady and Gentlemen, our respective forces have been engaged in a conflict for some years now which, at best, one might describe as inconclusive in its projected outcome but which, I'm sure we would all agree, is rendering great hardship to the peoples of this North American continent. We, for our part, are appalled at this state of affairs and would like very much to bring these hostilities to an end. We were wondering if you might not have similar sentiments."

His last sentence was framed as a statement but the inflection in his voice suggested a question.

"We do," said Parnell, "but it depends on the terms you are offering. We, for our part, are in no mood for capitulation."

"No, of course not," said Fifth in his silkiest, softest tone focusing on his steepled fingers. Then he looked up and scanned the group before centering his attention on Parnell. "To avoid a long and protracted discussion, perhaps you could outline, in essence, what your main concerns are so we can move directly to exploring how they might be addressed?"

"Simple," said Parnell. "Return to democratic government."

"The United States of America has always been a democracy," said Fifth. "So has Canada. But, as you know, it has been necessary in recent years to operate under emergency conditions due to the disruptive activities of numerous terrorist groups. If that terrorist activity ceases then there is no reason why emergency measures need to be maintained.

'Now, I understand that you have some influence with many of those groups carrying out this illegal activity. So, if you want to see speedy return to democratic principles of government, it would help considerably if you would exercise your influence over these groups." Again, Fifth's tone was friendly, reassuring, and even fatherly.

"Yes," said Parnell, his voice quiet and measured but by no means friendly or subordinate, "we do have some influence over some of the dissident groups, not all of them by any means, but a good number of them. We are reasonably confident we could bring out a significant degree of passivity to the current environment but before we are prepared to lessen the vigor of our approach we would require some clear, and very solid, assurances from both the United States and Canadian Governments that they will both submit to democratic elections for both the Presidency and both houses of Congress, and for the national government in Ottawa."

"We see the main impediment to that occurring as the present ongoing terrorist activity," said Fifth. "If you can guarantee that activity will cease, we can see little in the way of practical impediment to proceeding to hold national elections in both countries in early course. There would be some procedural work to be done beforehand, of course ... for example, the electoral roles would need to be updated in both countries, but these are not insurmountable problems. I think elections could be held within, say ..."

He paused and looked inquiringly at Korman.

The Vice President squirmed. He'd only been in the job for seven months and having come from the private sector was not well acquainted with government processes or the vagaries of electoral campaigns.

Fifth gave up on him and returned his gaze to Parnell:

"… within two years?"

The estimate was couched as a question, not so much to seek confirmation of its practicality but rather as a negotiating point.

"One," said Parnell bluntly, the finality in his tone asserting what he and Fifth were well aware of – it was he that held most of the aces in this game of poker.

"One," repeated Fifth, apparently pondering the estimate. "Yes, I think that's doable. It might be a little tight but with goodwill all around I think that could be achieved."

"There are more than just the electoral procedures to be considered here," chimed in Knight, aware that it was he and his political wing of the APA that would be most involved in ensuring a satisfactory political outcome to the long years of struggle. "We also have to be assured that there will be no obstructions to political campaigning, or any disruptions to the elections themselves on polling day. And we would expect that international observers will be allowed access to all election materials and to any and all polling stations on Election Day to ensure these elections are free and fair."

"The United States has a long history of holding free and fair elections and so does Canada," said Fifth. "Indeed, we are world leaders in such procedures. That expertise may have been a little dormant of late but I have no doubt it still exists. We see no major impediment from that quarter."

"There is another issue." From Rouleau this time. "There has been significant criminality within government in recent years. We would expect redress for those who have suffered from it."

"There have been excesses on both sides throughout this conflict," said Fifth. "We can go forward in the spirit of making a new start or we can saddle this continent with years of revenge, recriminations, and spite. We suggest it would be in the best interest of all to let bygones be bygones. Otherwise, we will become bogged down in these negotiations and without any outcomes that may ensue from the political climate that emerges."

Parnell was little annoyed that Rouleau had raised this issue of retribution at this stage of the negotiations. Getting the Darcy regime out and a democratic government in was his primary focus. If Fifth was prepared to reinstate the democratic process, other judicial issues would follow in due course.

"We cannot commit or bind any future government in either the United States or Canada to any course of action in respect of what had preceded its election," he said. "Therefore, the issue is, in my opinion, irrelevant to the current discussion. I suggest we move on."

Fifth did not object. Nor did he seek any guarantees of amnesty. He would not have even been there had he not realized the game was up. He knew the future security of his person, and his fortune, lay outside the North American continent. He had no doubt that any incoming American government had a long reach – God knows he had exercised it enough. But he also knew, as did Parnell, even if the truculent French Canadian did not, that he still had considerable power and influence at his command even if he no longer controlled the North American continent. He was quite sure a future American government would be content to let sleeping dogs lie rather than stir up a new clandestine war with the rump of the GSC after it had departed Washington.

The meeting lasted another thirty-seven minutes, followed by a half-hour refreshment break, not jointly but in two distinct venues in adjoining anterooms. The resumed meeting lasted eight minutes while the heads of agreement drafted by Ambassador Kniesten, based on the essence of the verbal agreements in the earlier meeting, and a brief bout of shuttle diplomacy during the refreshment break, was read, briefly discussed then signed by the eight negotiators and witnessed by the Dane. There were no handshakes at its conclusion. But the deal had been done and the rest was now up to the long-suffering peoples of the beleaguered continent.

The election for the Presidency, the Senate, and the House of Representatives of the United States of American was held on 3rd November 2042, a few months later than Parnell's specified 'one year'. Jackson Parnell and his wife walked hand in hand to the polling station in Kooskia, Idaho on polling day.

"I've waited a long time for this day," said Parnell as they entered the school hall where the ballot boxes awaited.

"It seems like a lifetime," said Elsie as Parnell approached the electoral roll official.

He collected his ballot papers – APA had insisted on paper ballots and manual counting given the GSC's known skullduggery; he headed to a curtain-covered polling booth. There he exercised his democratic rights as an American citizen. Elsie had already dispatched her ballot paper by mail to the Canadian Electoral Office in Vancouver in a Canadian federal election held a month earlier.

"I do solemnly swear that I will faithfully execute the Office of President of the United States, and will, to the best of my ability, preserve, protect and defend the Constitution of the United States."

With those words, Gary Knight was sworn in as the forty-seventh president of the United States of America on 21st January 2043. His vice president, also sworn in on the same day, was Ferdinando Gonzalez, a forty-three-year-old Cuban American from Miami. Both had been leading members of New Valley Forge with Gonzalez also being the president of the Southern Florida Natural Justice League, a seventeen thousand strong community-based organization that had been mainly fighting for better treatment of young Latino offenders who had been harshly treated by local law enforcement authorities. New Valley Forge candidates also fared well in Senate elections with eleven new senators officially being members of the organization. A further thirty-two new senators were affiliated with various organizations, societies, clubs, associations, and parties that fell under the broad umbrella of the American Patriotic Association, including seven high ranking members of its national and regional command councils.

The Republican Party secured twenty-one senate seats, eleven of them former senators from the pre-suspension period.

The Democratic Party won twenty-three senate seats, with fifteen of its newly elected members being former senators.

American Greens won eight senate seats and there were a further five new independent senators.

The house was similarly structured but with APA affiliates winning a near majority of two hundred and eleven seats, seventeen of which were held by former APA national and regional command council members. Republicans won one hundred and four seats; Democrats one hundred and twenty-two seats; American Greens eleven seats, and five independents. APA Eastern Regional Command Council chair Christine Kagel became House Majority Leader and veteran Republican congressman Robert Scalise Junior, nephew to a former notable party leader, became House Minority Leader.

President Knight immediately set about forming his cabinet and his first attempted appointment was to offer the post of Secretary of Defense to Jackson Parnell.

"No one has done more to earn this post than you, Jackson," he said two days after the election result had been declared.

Parnell declined. He may have been tempted had he been offered Secretary of State, since reform of the United Nations Organization was a task Parnell believed was urgently needed. He might have been more successful in that endeavor had he been the foreign minister of what was still one of the most powerful and influential countries of the world. But Knight had decided not to offer that post to a political ally. After almost two centuries of political cronies or commercial stooges representing the interests of the United States in foreign affairs, Knight believed a period of professional representation from within the ranks of the State Department might be in order. The rest of his cabinet followed fairly traditional lines in its selection and confirmation but with considerable talent drawn from a wider field than just leading industrialists, bankers, and party hacks. Two of his first initiatives as chief of the new administration, however, were to order new inquiries into the events in New York City and Washington D.C. on 11th of September 2001, and into the financial frauds of the early decades of the 21st century.

Parnell was not disappointed or disapproving of the new cabinet appointments. He saw the logic of Knight's policy and, in any case, he already had a broad agenda set for himself, and U.N. reform was only part of that. He did not want to become bogged down in his primary task by having to divert himself to address every political crisis that cropped up throughout the world, for which the world's leaders would instinctively turn to the United States to at least address, if not resolve. Idleness was not his most immediate goal but flexibility and freedom of movement was. There was much to do if his most immediate success was going to bring a lasting beneficial legacy to the whole world as well as to his people. Those long nights of philosophical musings had not been just idle banter for him. His search for a universally acceptable moral code continued and a recent discovery in that quest, in the form of a 2007 book by Canadian writer Rodrigue Trembley entitled *The Code for Global Ethics*, looked promising if somewhat dated. He pressed on undaunted.

King George abdicated the British throne twenty months later and it was not offered to any of his successors from the incoming British Government which was dominated by the English Republican Party. It immediately moved to create a federated union to replace the old United Kingdom with significant administrative powers devolved to the Scottish, Welsh, and Northern Irish parliaments. Enhanced regional councils were set up in seven key English regions plus an enhanced Greater London Council.

The Dutch monarchy followed its British counterpart six months later. Several other European monarchies remained in the small European countries but the Spanish throne looked shaky, and across the Gibraltar Strait, so too did the Moroccan one. Also, several leading French industrialists suddenly felt the lure of the South Sea Islands, and numerous German Junkers took a shine to the clear mountain air of the Swiss Alps.

Fifth retired to American Samoa, as did a considerable number of his North American GSC compatriots. There the nights were cool and the days balmy and there was a significant boom in the local real estate market which Fifth had prophetically anticipated. His global empire was considerably diminished but not altogether destroyed. He was still one of the wealthiest men in the world and his health was excellent for a man of his middle-aged years. His garden became the envy of horticulturalists everywhere and his seed bank second to none anywhere in the world.

Epilogue

Parnell's decision not to accept a cabinet post and instead concentrate on a broader international reform agenda was based mainly on his convictions and his well-experienced judgment of the futility of armed conflict to resolve disagreements. But it was also based on his respect and reverence for his late friend Andre LeMonte, the lapsed Catholic priest who had, after a lifetime of service to his faith and humanity, finally concluded that religion was largely myth and that man's salvation lay in resolving disputes in the secular world rather than relying on supernatural intervention.

Toulemont's receptions of the uncertain nature of the physical universe, along with Nanakinilli's insights into Eastern philosophy, also spurred Parnell's appreciation that any universally agreed global, political, social and philosophical creed would also need to accommodate a wide range of beliefs, customs, and practices to be acceptable, in large measure, to the great majority of humanity. The task seemed daunting but Parnell could see no greater opportunity in his remaining years than to try, even if his efforts only initiated trends that others might continue after his demise.

After years of service and struggle many of his contemporaries were of similar view, including his wife and soul mate, Elsie Chambers, and his old mate, the former Australian Prime Minister, Talbot Macintyre. Rouleau too had grown in stature and conviction into a more inter-nationalistic orientation both having been forced to broaden his horizons from his previous parochial focus on his beloved Quebec to a wider North American perspective and also, via the APA's international affiliations, into a more global one. He had been heavily influenced by the late cleric first introduced to him by Parnell, and increasingly familiarized with via Chambers' close collaboration as the two coordinated the eastern and western realms of the Canadian resistance movement. LeMonte's death had deeply shocked him. It had initially spurred him on in seeking revenge for the prelate's treatment as well as his own. But now the ordeal was over he was more resolved to honor the man by continuing his work than to wallow smugly in self-satisfaction of his triumph or to focus on retribution from his vanquished foes.

The North American rebellion and their coordinating role in the global network of international insurgencies had given them all an insight and an appreciation of the commonality of human needs world-wide, and a desire to further human cooperation beyond the kinetic means that had been necessary for overcoming tyranny in so many diverse cultures.

Parnell and his compatriots, however, largely met with frustration in their attempts to reform the only still existing institution for coordinated global governance, the United Nations Organization, and its operating offshoots. Criticism of the structure had abounded for a century but no-one seemed to be able to bring about reform. The four intrepid veterans of the North American rebellion persisted but with growing frustration, disillusionment and despair. Saving a country was one thing but saving the whole world was a decidedly different proposition. It would not be fair to say that they gave up but growing age and increasing dispiritedness dulled their vigor.

In truth, Parnell knew that his race was also largely run. A new generation would herald entry into the new world as those who had fought the fight grew old, their lives drawing to a natural close. But, the quest would go on, Parnell firmly believed that. If not, what had it all been for?

*****

Appendix 1:
An Overview of a
National Resistance Movement

According to Mao Tse Tung, there are three classic phases to the successful overthrow of a hostile government. They are:

Phase One: the guerrillas earn population's support by

- Distributing propaganda and
- Attacking the organs of government.

Phase Two: escalating attacks are launched against:

- Government's military forces and
- Vital institutions.

Phase Three: conventional warfare and fighting are used to:

- Seize cities
- Overthrow the government, and
- Assume control of the country

This document considers the appropriate tools and tactics for a movement employing both non-violent resistance and fully armed guerrilla warfare for Phases 1 and 2 above in the earnest hope that Phase 3 will not be required.

Overall Organization Structure

APA Supreme Council

↙   ↘

Military   Political
Wing   Wing

Military Wing Activities

Scope of Operations

The following presents an analysis of the possible composition and scope of operations and lists the tools available to each wing of an organization utilizing both approaches. The tools chosen will be a policy decision for the movement's top leadership. The policy-making group will need to appreciate that guerrilla operations are often widely disbursed, uncoordinated, undisciplined and, often clandestine, so the enforcement of policy at senior levels may not always be possible on more junior operatives. Most are considered illegal by the government they are targeted against.

Military Wing Activities

Economic Warfare:

Armed blockades of vital supplies and reinforcements at critical times

Commerce raiding to acquire vital weapons, ammunition, supplies and funds

Electronic Warfare:

Broadcast signal jamming or disruption

Cyber electronic warfare of all types including:

- Cyber electronic attack
- Denial of service
- E-mail jamming
- Computer hacking
- Spy-ware and Viruses
- Google bomb
- Electromagnetic pulse
- Chaff

Guerilla Warfare:

Armed assaults against:

Banks and credit establishments
Commercial and industrial enterprises, plants for the manufacture of weapons and explosives
Military establishments
Commissaries and police stations
Jails
Government property
Mass communications media
Foreign firms and properties
Government vehicles, including military and police vehicles, trucks, armored vehicles, money carriers, trains, ships, and airplanes.

Armed raids and penetrations of key Government, commercial, military or police installations

Occupations - especially media outlets

Ambushes to:
Capture weapons
Inflict casualties
Snipe at high priority human targets
Unnerve the enemy, promote insecurity or instill fear into the regime leadership

Street tactics such as:
Agent Provocateur

Organizing riots

Counteracting and frustrating police cordons
Frustrating arrests
Frustrating resupply or reinforcement of deployed police
forces
Sniping

Encouraging and facilitating desertions, diversions, seizures,
expropriation of weapons, ammunition, and explosives by:
Military personnel
Police personnel
Government employees
Industrial employees

Liberation of prisoners by:
Riots in penal establishments, correctional colonies or
camps, or on transport or prison ships
Assaults on urban or rural prisons, detention centers,
prison camps, or any other permanent or temporary
place where prisoners are held
Assaults on prisoner transport trains or convoys
Raids and penetrations of prisons
Ambushing guards who move prisoners

Executions of:
- Foreign spies,
- Government agents
- Police or military torturers
- Regime leaders
- Stool pigeons
- Informers
- Police or military provocateurs

Kidnappings, either for ransom or prisoner exchange, of:
Regime leaders and their family members
Government sympathizers and apologists and their
families
Sporting, scientific or artistic personalities known to
support the regime
Foreign dignitaries or tourists of countries sympathetic
to the regime
Industrialists and commercial leaders

Sabotage of:

      Agricultural or industrial production
      Transport and communication systems
      Military and police systems and their establishments
      and depots
      The firms and properties of avaricious resource or
      commercial exploiters of the country
      The financial system such as:

- Domestic and foreign banking networks
- Exchange and credit systems
- Tax collection systems -

      by:

      Kinetic effects – explosives, direct fire, incendiaries,
      explosive booby traps, etc.
      Non-kinetic effects – non-explosive booby traps,
      caltrops, tunnels and undermining, etc.
      Contamination of fuel, lubricants, power supplies,
      strategic supplies
      Physical obstruction of key transport corridors like
      roads, railways, ports, airports
      Damage or destruction of key transport vehicles –
      road, rail, sea and air vehicles and their support
      facilities such as fuel storage facilities, repair facilities,
      marshalling points, etc.
      Damage or destruction of key military installations such
      as arsenals, supply dumps, communications facilities,
      recruitment and training facilities, support facilities, etc.
      Damage or destruction of key telecommunications
      facilities and networks

Terrorism: against the elite and the ruling regime only, and never
against the general population or even the junior ranks of the
military or police unless they are actively involved in torture, war
crimes, significant corruption or serious crime, by:

      Targeted assassinations
      Extortion of money from target organizations
      Personal intimidation of the regime elite and their close
      supporters
      Creation of economic losses for individuals and key regime
      supporting businesses
      Provoking a disproportionate response from the regime
      against the civil population

Armed propaganda: such as forced confessions and recorded executions

War of nerves such as:
> Telephone, mail, e-mail threats to key regime leaders and personnel
> Deliberate misinformation to authorities as distractions, diversions, frustrations, etc.
> Rumor creation and dissemination to discredit key regime leaders and personnel

Psychological Warfare such as:
> Counterfeiting official documents
> Penetration of key organizations
> Character assassinations of key regime leaders and supporters
> Persecution of collaborators and apologists
> Establishment and support of international front organizations

Selected Targets

Transportation routes:
> Land
> Sea
> Air
> Space
> Virtual

Individual groups of police or military installations and structures:
> Bases
> Convoys
> Units
> Key personnel
> Key institutions

Economic enterprises:
> Businesses (especially Government contractors)
> Civil institutions
> Political establishments
> Judicial system

Targeted civilians:
    Politicians
    High net worth individuals supporting the government
    Opinion leaders supporting government policies

Civilian Support Structures Required

Provision of Shelter:
    Safe Houses
    Weapons stashes
    Escape routes
    Training bases
    Supply routes
    Mobile headquarters and medical facilities

Provision of Supplies:
Essential supplies include:
    M-money
    A-ammunition
    F-food
    F-fuel
    E-equipment
    M-mechanization
    E-explosives
    W-weapons
    S- Shelter

The movement will require an extended network of supporters to provide these vital resources.

Financing:

Sourcing funds will need to include the following:

    Extortion
    Patronage of wealthy supporters
    Bank raids (physical and electronic)
    Foreign supporters including sympathetic governments
    Donations from the general public

Applications will need to include expenditures for:

    Weapons
    Supplies and ammunition

Bribes
Food
Fuel
Civil support
Travel

Intelligence Gathering:

Observation, investigation, reconnaissance, and exploration of specific targets
Infiltration of sensitive enemy installations
Compromising information on key enemy entities
Identification and prioritization of key enemy industrial, financial, economic, political, cultural, military, and police targets including detailed biographies of key enemy powerbrokers, influencers, funders and leaders
Counter-intelligence including identification of enemy spies, infiltrators, quislings and apologists

Recruitment and training:

Stimulation of interest in active participation through underground media, hero stories, etc.
Careful selection and screening of potential candidates
Attraction of personnel with specific scientific, technical, military, police, medical, etc. skills
Compromise and cooptation of key regime insiders and influencers
Desertion of government personnel preferably with weapons, ammunition, supplies, equipment and/or intelligence
Liberation of prisoners, particularly political prisoners
Training in the arts of guerrilla warfare including:
    Investigation and intelligence gathering
    Observation and vigilance
    Reconnaissance or exploration of the terrain
    Study and timing of routes
    Mapping
    Mechanization and vehicle maintenance and repair
    Careful selection and assignment of personnel
    Selection of firepower
    Weapons and explosives training

Study and practice in success in similar operations
Use of cover
Retreat
Dispersal
Liberation or transfer of prisoners
Elimination of evidence of guerrilla involvement, personnel and locations
Rescue of wounded
First aid and other medical training especially attention to wounds
Intelligence analysis and operational planning
Identification and development of leadership personnel

Operations should feature:
Impermanence and mobility
Hit and run, conservation of forces
Dispersed and cellular organizational structure
Distract, confuse, frustrate, wear down and demoralize the enemy
Independent and self-motivating
Surprise
Terrain awareness, penetration points and escape routes
Superior intelligence
Initiative and decisiveness
Disruption of the enemy transport and communications systems
Widespread, audacious, uncoordinated and persistent operations
Monitoring of police and military response facilities

The seven deadly sins of the guerrilla operative:

Being intimidated by an overestimation of regime strength, courage or resolve
Boasting achievements or guerrilla membership
Lack of consideration for the consequences of operations on others, particularly comrades and complementary organizations
Overconfidence in guerrilla capabilities, reliance on luck, recklessness or lack of adequate planning, training, preparedness or capabilities
Rash or spontaneous action, impatience or failure of nerve
Losing one's temper or arrogance in the face of superior

situational strength
Unwarranted or avoidable violence, brutality or economic
damage to the general public's persons, property or
livelihoods or to popular champions of non-violence,
freedom and human rights

Political Wing Activities

Political Activism

Formation of alternative public forums, political parties and
action groups
Leadership recruitment and policy structure formations
(committees, boards, councils, etc.)
Recruitment of memberships to these alternative power
structures
Recruitment of prominent, respected persons thereto
Formation of research and administrative structures to
support these alternative structures
Research issues, draft policy statements, draft speeches, make
declarations, and recruit experts and celebrities to support
these public pronouncements
Arrange petitions, solicit signatories thereto and formally
present them to authorities
Create slogans, caricatures and symbols and develop banners,
posters, displays, leaflets, pamphlets, broadsheets, newspapers
and other print publications to promote key issues and
suggest solutions
Create audio, video, electronic text messages and broadcast
them via electronic media, by conventional mail, by parcel
services and by hand
Paint, post, stick, write or otherwise superimpose slogans in
prominent locations and by novel media such as skywriting,
earth writing, light projections, etc.
Encourage symbolic public acts by supporters such as flag-
waving, tee-shirts wearing, tattoos, badge-wearing, uttering
distinctive sounds, words or names, symbolic destruction of
own property, public disrobing, rude gestures or disrespectful
behavior, etc.
Heckling politicians, taunting authorities, fraternization with
other known dissidents
Writing and performing humorous songs, plays, skits, street
performances, pranks to ridicule authority structures and

institutions
Arrange occupations and sit-ins of key public assets such as
buildings, roads, bridges, etc.
Ambushes of politicians with persistent and embarrassing
questions
Arrange protest marches and demonstrations, hold public
meetings, provide information and training workshops, and
conduct house-to-house information and advocacy campaigns
Stage walk-outs, call for silence pauses, encourage back
turning, encourage denouncing honors
Arrange deputations, group lobbying, picketing, mock awards
and mock elections to embarrass or frustrate authorities in
their own symbolic and administrative promotions
Hold vigils, mock funerals, homage meetings and political
mourning to honor dead heroes (real or symbolic)

Economic Warfare:
Consumer boycotts: local, national and international goods
and services, austerity advocacy and/or consumption
minimization, rent refusal or delay
Workers' boycotts; middlemen (wholesalers, retailers,
transporters) boycotts, delays or disruptions
Producers' and/or traders' boycotts, "merchants' general
strike, deliberate spoilage, refusal to supply
Property owners' refusal to rent or sell or only to supply on
specified conditions
Refusal to repay debts or pay interest, fees, dues, levies, fines,
penalties or tax assessments
Withdrawal of bank deposits or other financial patronage
Advertising or exposing key product and service deficiencies
and immoral or illegal practices
Naming and shaming rapacious suppliers, businesses or
institutions, blacklisting errant suppliers
Demanding government embargos or other sanctions on
rapacious or immoral suppliers

Electronic Warfare:
Broadcast interruptions and event intrusions

Non-violent Guerilla Activities:
Unarmed raids and penetrations of key Government,
commercial, military or police installations
Counteract and frustrate police cordons, frustrate arrest

attempts, frustrate or delay resupply or reinforcement of
deployed police forces aimed against protest action
Organizing strikes and work stoppages to:
    Disrupt economic activity
    Facilitate other guerrilla activity
    Involve the general public in the resistance effort
Organizing desertions, defections, whistle-blowing and leaks
by:
    Military personnel and veterans
    Police personnel and veterans
    Government employees, politicians and supporters
    Industrial and commercial employees
Liberation of prisoners by:
    Legal aid
    Fundraising
    Government embarrassment
    Invoking international law and support
Seizure of incriminating evidence of wrongdoing

Sabotage of:
Government media and propaganda campaigns
Unfair, immoral or illegal laws, government policies or police
or military practices by:

- Shame campaigns
- Strikes, go slow, work-to-rule and similar disruptive activities
- Poor maintenance and deliberate neglect
- Obstruction of key transport corridors and supply routes like roads, railways, ports, airports

Public exposition of those actively involved in torture,
war crimes, significant corruption or serious crimes

War of nerves such as:
Exposing corruption, mistakes and failures of the
government and its representatives
Presenting denunciations to foreign embassies, the
United Nations, international commissions and NGOs
defending human rights or freedom of the press

Psychological warfare activities such as:
    Underground press
    Paid sponsorship and testimonials

Penetration of organizations
Vilification of regime collaborators
Establishment and support of international
organizations promoting freedom, democracy and
human rights
Supporting sympathetic political and social
organizations
Exposés of discreditable activities by wrongdoers

Propaganda Techniques:
    Media manipulation exposés
    Supporting anti-war productions
    Supporting anti-exploitation campaigns
    Atrocity exposés

Public Relations Techniques:
    Media clips
    Hero stories
    Appeals to patriotism and human rights

Focus international attention on the resistance cause
Clearly explaining resistance strategic goals and
operational objectives

Scope of Operations

Transportation routes:
- o Land
- o Sea
- o Air
- ▪ Space
- ▪ Virtual

Public installations and structures:
Government institutions and facilities
Industrial and commercial government contractors
Public transport infrastructure especially when supporting
government activities
All levels of government and law enforcement but
particularly federal government facilities
Key public institutions that support the status quo

Economic enterprises:
    Businesses (especially Government contractors)
    Civil institutions that support the ruling regime
    Political establishments that support the ruling regime

Targeted civilians:
    Politicians
    High net worth individuals particularly known owners and
    managers of organizations and institutions supporting
    government
    Other opinion leaders supporting government policies

Civilian Support Structure Required

Shelter and facilities:

Office accommodation
Transport facilities
Offices supplies
Telecommunications equipment
Coordinated and public organizational structure

Supplies:

Conventional office facilities and support
Donations in kind
Financing:

Sources:

Legal fundraising activities of all kinds
Sales of underground press and media products
Event attendance fees
Patronage from sympathetic supporters amongst the general
pubic
Donations
Endowments
Foreign supporters (but with scrutiny of ultimate funding
sources)

Applications:

Key personnel and supporters fees, reimbursements, allowances
and costs

Secretarial, printing and distribution costs
Travel costs of key supporters and advocates
Accommodation expenses

Intelligence:

General situational awareness including international initiatives
Observation, investigation, reconnaissance, and exploration of specific targets
Infiltration of key administration installations
Compromising information on key regime entities
Detailed biographies of key regime powerbrokers, influencers, funders and leaders
Counter-intelligence including identification of regime spies, infiltrators, quislings and apologists

Recruitment and training:

Stimulation of interest in active participation through underground media, hero stories, etc.
Careful selection and screening of potential candidates
Attraction of personnel with specific scientific, technical, military, police, medical, etc. skills
Compromise and cooptation of key regime insiders and influencers
Desertion of government personnel preferably with useful intelligence
Training in active civil resistance techniques including:
Investigation and intelligence gathering
Observation and vigilance
Reconnaissance or exploration of the target venues and facilities
Study and analysis of successful non-violent resistance movements elsewhere
Intelligence analysis and operational planning
Identification and development of leadership personnel

Tactics should feature:

Permanence of establishment
Unrelenting activity
Coordination locally, regionally, nationally and internationally

Be well advertised and promoted
Superior intelligence
Boldness and resolution
Widespread, audacious and coordinated operations
Monitoring of police, military and political responses

The seven deadly sins of the non-violent resistance movement:

Violence, brutality or deliberate economic damage to the general public's persons, property or livelihoods or to public assets or facilities
Being intimidated by an overestimation of regime strength, courage or resolve
Lack of consideration for the consequences of operations on others particularly comrades, complementary organizations and the general public
Overconfidence in resistance capabilities, reliance on luck, recklessness or lack of adequate planning, training, preparedness or capabilities
Rash or spontaneous action, impatience or failure of nerve
Losing one's temper or arrogance in the face of superior situational strength

Appendix 2: 911 Research Report;
An Australian Perspective

By David Frank Palmer*

The following summarizes the outcome to date of my ongoing investigations into the events of 911, the destruction of the twin towers of the World Trade Centre in New York City on 11th September 2001 and the implications flowing therefrom:

1. A peer reviewed scientific paper authored by Professor Niels Harrit and eight co-authors published in the Open Chemical Physics Journal[1] in 2009 reports that traces of a highly energetic (explosive) material known as nano-thermite was found in dust collected from four sites in Lower Manhattan shortly after the collapse of the South Tower (the earliest being 10 minutes later, two samples several hours later and the fourth sample one week later). This high technology nano-scale material is only produced in very sophisticated laboratories like the Lawrence Livermore and Los Alamos laboratories which service the American military-industrial complex.

2. The twin towers (WTC 1 and WTC 2) were not the only buildings to collapse in New York City that day. A third building, WTC 7, also collapsed. It was not struck by any aircraft. Furthermore, WTC 7 collapsed seven hours after the collapse of the second tower (the North Tower, WTC 1) falling in a manner highly similar to that usually observed in controlled demolitions.[2] The collapse of this third building was not even mentioned in the first published report of the 911 Commission.

---

[1] Harrit, Niels H., Farrer, Jeffrey, Jones, Steven E., Ryan, Kevin R., Legge, Frank M., Farnsworth, Daniel, Roberts, Greg, Gourley, James R. and Larsen, Bradley R., *Active Thermitic Material Discovered in Dust from the 9/11 World Trade Centre Catastrophe*, The Open Chemical Physics Journal, 2009, 2, 7-31.

[2] Numerous citations including those cited in this paper. This is now a well-recorded and verified fact even from official sources.

3. A French language video clip entitled "Demolition Controlee" presents visual evidence indicating that all three buildings, WTC 1, WTC 2 and WTC 7, all collapsed at near free fall speed ("chute libre" in French) and concludes that "C'est un demolition controlee" – which translates as: "It was a controlled demolition".[3]

4. A three-hour video record of a seminar hosted by the organizations Architects and Engineers for 911 Truth and Firefighters for 911 Truth in California on May 7th 2010 presents extensive evidence and expert testimony from a structural engineer, a demolition expert and a fire-fighter corroborating the evidence cited above regarding the collapsed WTC buildings. This video presentation also features the convener of Architects and Engineers for 911 Truth, American architect Richard Gage, and by American fire-fighter Erik Lawyer. It is entitled "Fire-fighters, Architects and Engineers expose 911".[4]

5. On May 16th 2010 I attended a conference in Santa Cruz, California, entitled "Understanding Deep Politics". At that conference ten keynote speakers presented information confirming and corroborating much of the evidence cited above. All speakers appeared to be highly educated, highly articulate, highly credible people – retired university professors, journalists, media commentators and professional practitioners. They did not appear to me to be "crazies". A full video record of this conference is also available at a cost of US$12 so readers of this paper can also view and judge for themselves the credibility of these speakers.[5]

6. I have read extensively over the past eight years articles and books on American Foreign Policy, American History, Current Affairs, and International Relations (I have over two dozen books and over a thousand articles in my library of these subjects). Two specific books relevant to the above evidence are Michael C. Ruppert's book "Crossing the Rubicon[6]" and David Ray Griffin and Peter Dale Scott's edition "9/11 and American

---

[3] Available at http://www.dailymotion.com/video/xbhyvw_911-demolition-controlee_webcam. Extracted 29th June 2010.
[4] Available at http://enlightenedfilms.com/. Extracted 13th July, 2010.
[5] Available at http://enlightenedfilms.com/.
[6] New Society Publishers, Gabriola Island, 2004.

Empire: Intellectuals Speak Out"[7]. Ruppert is a former Los Angeles Police Department narcotics investigator and at the conclusion of his book he says that if he had been in charge of a criminal investigation into the mass murders that were committed on 911 he believes that he has sufficient evidence to proceed with laying charges against the senior members of the Bush Administration for mass murder. Griffin and Scott were both keynote speakers at the Santa Cruz conference referred to above. In their work cited here is a chapter by Professor Emeritus Steven E. Jones entitled "Why Indeed Did the World Trade Center Buildings Collapse?" in which he proposes that explosives were used to demolish these three buildings. Jones is also featured in a video entitled "Nanothermite: What in the world is High-Tech Explosive Material Doing in the Dust Clouds Generated on 9/11/2001?" This video contains the illustrated lecture given by him in Sacramento, California on 30th April, 2009.[8]

7.   David Ray Griffin is also the author of "The 9/11 Commission Report: Distortions and Omissions". Since publishing that work he has summarized the 115 distortions and omissions reported in that work in an article entitled "The 9/11 Commission Report: A 571-Page Lie".[9]

8.   At a seminar co-hosted by the Lowy Institute and the Australian Institute of International Affairs at the University of Western Australia Club on 28th June 2010 I engaged in a casual conversation with another AIIA member (I won't name him since I have not obtained his permission to cite this evidence) in which I outlined my experience in Santa Cruz and opined that it looked like the United States Government was complicit in the events of 911. He looked at me in surprise and said:
"Of course, everyone in France knows that. There have been two or three documentaries aired on French television showing that."

He did not elaborate on the details of those documentaries but it does appear that the French people are well-informed on the

---

[7] Olive Branch Press, Northampton, Mass., 2006.
[8] Available from 911TV.org.
[9] Available at http://www.911truth.org/article.php?story=20050523112738404
Extracted: 10th August 2010.

above cited evidence whereas the Australian people are largely ignorant of it. It was this casual conversation that prompted me to start searching the world wide web using the French wording for "controlled demolition", "demolition controlee", which resulted in me locating a twelve-minute video clip referred to above.[10]

9. On 17th July, 2010 I attended a lecture at the Sydney Mechanical School of Arts given by the same Professor Niels Harrit referred to above. There he reiterated the essence of his above cited paper and summarized his findings and conclusions that explosives were used in the destruction of the World Trade Centre buildings. I met Professor Harrit and spoke with him personally. His academic and professional credentials appear to be impeccable particularly in respect of the chemical evidence which forms the basis of his paper in a field in which he is an acknowledged expert. He was later joined on stage by one of the other co-authors of the paper, Dr Frank Legge, a chemist, and also by Dr David Leifer who is an architect and "incorporated" engineer and a senior lecturer at Sydney University, and David Andressen who is a civil engineer. They also confirmed Professor Harrit's conclusions.

On 18th July 2010 I accepted an invitation from Mr. John Bursill, a licensed aircraft engineer, to a barbeque at his home in Helensburgh, N.S.W. Mr. Bursill is a member and key spokesperson of the organization Architects and Engineers for 911 Truth in Australia and was also the convener of Professor Harrit's lecture. He is employed by QANTAS and specialises in avionics for Boeing 767/737 and 747 aircraft. At that barbeque Mr. Bursill introduced me to several other members of AE911Truth movement. Dr Legge was also present. All in attendance generally corroborated the conclusions outlined above regarding the controlled demolition hypothesis. The group also declined to speculate on who might have been responsible for 911 preferring instead to concentrate only on that evidence that they believe can be proved scientifically. However, subsequently in a review of this paper Dr Legge commented: "Although we don't say who did it, we are not afraid to point out the impossibility of gaining the necessary prolonged access

---

[10] Available at http://www.dailymotion.com/video/xbhyvw 911-demolition-controlee webcam. Extracted 29th June, 2010.

without inside help."[11]

10. On the question of how could conspirators gain access to the World Trade Center buildings for all the months that would be required to place explosives, American chemist Kevin Ryan[12] has analyzed the tenancy lists of all three buildings in the years and months prior to 911. In a four-part paper entitled "Demolition access to the World Trade Center towers" he outlines the extensive interconnection between the tenants, service providers, contractors and renovators that had access to all three buildings in the years and months before 911. The close affiliations of these organizations to the Bush Administration and to the US military-industrial complex are striking.

He also points out that many floors in the Twin Towers had renovation work done on them in the months and years prior to 911 and that a major overhaul of the central lift systems was also conducted during this period. He concludes:

"If we look at the companies that occupied the impact zones of the WTC towers, and other floors that might have played a useful role in the demolition of the towers, we see connections to organizations that had access to explosive materials, and to the expertise required to use explosives." And:

"It seems that, if certain management representatives of the tenant companies listed above wanted to help bring the WTC towers down, they would have been well suited to do so. The companies mentioned were located at well-spaced intervals in the buildings, and some … had a reputation of being secretive. In fact, a number of the executives from these firms were either on the board of intelligence firms … or were closely related to others who were. Others were connected to the CIA itself, and to some of the largest defense contractors in the world, like Lockheed Martin, Raytheon, General Dynamics, Halliburton, and SAIC.

---

[11] Review note to the author from Dr Legge on 11th August, 2010.
[12] Kevin Ryan was actually employed at the time of the 911 events by Underwriters Laboratories Inc., the company that certified the steel that was used in the construction of the Twin Towers of the World Trade Center in New York, in their subsidiary Environmental Health Laboratories Inc.

There are also strong connections to those who benefited from the 9/11 attacks, most notably the Bush family and their corporate network, including Dresser Industries (now Halliburton) and UBS, and to Deutsche Bank and its subsidiaries, reported to have brokered the insider trading deals. There are links between these tenant companies and the terrorist-related fraudulent bank BCCI."[13]

With respect of WTC 7, Wikipedia reports:

"At the time of the September 11, 2001 attacks, Salomon Smith Barney was by far the largest tenant in 7 World Trade Center, occupying 1,202,900 sq ft (111,750 m²) (64 percent of the building) which included floors 28–45. Other major tenants included ITT Hartford Insurance Group (122,590 sq ft/11,400 m²), American Express Bank International (106,117 sq ft/9,900 m²), Standard Chartered Bank (111,398 sq ft/10,350 m²), and the Securities and Exchange Commission (106,117 sq ft/9,850 m²). Smaller tenants included the Internal Revenue Service Regional Council (90,430 sq ft/8,400 m²) and the United States Secret Service (85,343 sq ft/7,900 m²). The smallest tenants included the New York City Office of Emergency Management, National Association of Insurance Commissioners, Federal Home Loan Bank, First State Management Group Inc., Provident Financial Management, and the Immigration and Naturalisation Service. The Department of Defense (DOD) and Central Intelligence Agency (CIA) shared the 25th floor with the IRS. Floors 46–47 were mechanical floors, as were the bottom six floors and part of the seventh floor."[14]

With the CIA's New York office, Defense Department offices and the Securities and Exchange Commission tenanted in the building one can also presume that this was one of the most secure buildings in the city accessible only to those with

---

[13] Ryan, Kevin R., "Demolition access to the World Trade Center towers: Part one – Tenants", available at
http://911review.com/articles/ryan/demolition_access_p1.html
Extracted 27th July, 2010.

[14] Available at http://en.wikipedia.org/wiki/7_World_Trade_Center.
Extracted 28th September 2010.

appropriate security clearances.

11. It seems that it is not just the French that are better informed than the Australians on this issue. Woodworth reports eighteen case studies of main stream media coverage being given to the 911 Truth Movement in Britain, Canada, Denmark, France, the Netherlands, New Zealand, Norway, and Russia. She concludes:

"This more open approach taken in the international media ... might be a sign that worldwide public and corporate media organizations are positioning themselves, and preparing their audiences, for a possible revelation of the truth of the claim that forces within the US government were complicit in the attacks – a revelation that would call into question the publicly given rationale for the military operations in Iraq, Afghanistan, and Pakistan.

The evidence now being explored in the international media may pave the way for the US media to take an in-depth look at the implications of what is now known about 9/11, and to re-examine the country's foreign and domestic policies in the light of this knowledge."[15]

12. It has become customary within Australian society to dismiss those who inquire into this issue as "conspiracy theorists". The label is not intended as a compliment. However, as Griffin and Scott point out in their edition cited above: "the official narrative about 9/11 is itself a conspiracy theory, alleging that the attacks were orchestrated entirely by Arab-Muslim members of al-Qaeda under the inspiration of Osama bin Laden in Afghanistan"[16] The more relevant question in respect of this matter would therefore appear to be not "Are you a conspiracy theorist?" but rather "Which conspiracy theory do you believe is most plausible?" To answer that question confidently one would have to review the evidence for each theory under consideration and to decide which alternative appears to be the most credible based on the evidence available.

---

[15] Available at
http://www.globalresearch.ca/index.php?aid=17624&context=va.
Extracted 26th July 2010.
[16] Op cit, page vii.

The above research leads me to conclude, with a high degree of confidence, that:

a. The official version of the events of 911 by the United States Government, and particularly its key instruments in the matter, the Fire and Emergency Management Authority (FEMA) report on 911, the National Institute for Standards and Technology (NIST) report on 911 and the 911 Commission report, are, at least, inadequate, if not a complete whitewash. They are simply incredible – that is, not believable.

b. An alternative hypothesis that the collapse of WTC 1, WTC 2 and WTC 7 was due to a controlled demolition is at least as credible as the official version – in fact, more so, in the light of the Harrit paper and the other evidence cited above.

Less certain are any conclusions that might be drawn with confidence about who might have been responsible for this crime although the above evidence suggests that some agencies of the United States Government may have been involved in some way.

Since this issue is so important to the future governance of the United States of America and to International Relations generally, a new, fully independent, competently staffed and objective investigation of the events of 911 is needed. This investigation needs the powers of subpoena, to take evidence under oath and to have authority to investigate deep into the American political and national security establishment. Anything less will only serve to perpetuate the ongoing distrust of the American Government – the former Bush Administration in particular but also its successor the Obama Administration and also the legislative and judicial arms of the American Government. It will also continue to foster distrust of those governments allied to the United States including the Australian Government.

The implications of the above evidence are extremely serious for Australia. The whole of Australia's Foreign Policy posture and its Defence strategy is built around the ANZUS alliance. Therefore, the maintenance of good, co-operative relations with the United States of America is vital to Australia's national security. However, it is also incumbent upon Australia's national government to defend its citizens and to seek justice for those who have been wronged by other governments. Ten Australians are known to have died in the events relating to 911 in New York and Washington on that day. Moreover,

Australia has participated, and is still participating, in two wars since 911 which have been justified on the basis that it was Islamic extremists who were solely responsible for this crime whereas the above evidence strongly suggests that this is not so.

Whilst this is undoubtedly an embarrassing, difficult and unpalatable issue for the Australian Government, Australia cannot proceed in its relations with the United States, or any other government for that matter, on the basis that some of our citizens are expendable in the pursuit of our national goals and aspirations or those of our allies. All Australian lives must be protected and defended by our government no matter what the cost or discomfort of doing so. Australia's credibility is also at stake here since it is evident that the above information has now been widely disseminated in Europe and is well understood throughout the Islamic world even if Australians and Americans are still mostly ignorant of it."

** This paper was first written by the author in 2010 and circulated to the main political parties in Australia and to other selected addressees. It is referred to in this novel in the chapters entitled Betrayal and New American Patriots.*

Appendix 3: 911 Research Report–
An Australian Perspective (Addendum)

Further to my 911 Research Report that I first penned in July 2010 and selectively distributed in November 2010 I now report two further developments in my ongoing research into the events of 11th September 2001 in New York City and Washington DC:

1. On 13th November 2010 I was invited to the home of Dr Frank Legge, a co-author of the Harrit/Jones nano-thermite paper referred to in my earlier report. Dr Legge personally reaffirmed the findings of that paper and his belief in its integrity and he persuasively answered all of my questions about its findings.

2. On 4th May 2011 I met Professor Amparo Sacristian Carrasco at the Hotel Universal Barcelona in Spain. At that meeting I showed her the Spanish language version of her report of 26th March 2003 entitled (in English) "Analysis of the Images of 11 September 2001" and asked her if the report was an accurate version of her original. She said that it was. I then showed her the English language version of the report and asked her if it was an accurate translation of the Spanish version. Apart from a small typographical error (SR RR erroneously transcribed as RR) she said that it was. I then asked her if she had had any reason to change her opinion or the conclusions of her original report in the seven years since writing it. She said "No". I then asked her if she would confirm the authenticity of her report and that she still stands by its findings by signing the Spanish language version that I had shown her. She agreed to do so and signed the report in my presence. I now have that signed copy next to me as I write this addendum.

    I then asked Professor Carrasco if she appreciated the implications of her report – that it effectively proves that the aircraft that struck the South Tower of the World Trade Centre on 911 was not a commercial airliner. She said "Yes". In fact, the only thing that she seemed perplexed about was that anyone should be interested in inquiring into this matter so long after she had completed her report. She considered it to be ancient history. This further suggests that Europeans generally are well acquainted with the information contained in my earlier paper and have difficulty understanding why others are not also as well informed.

For those readers not familiar with Professor Carrasco's abovementioned report, the English language translation of it is available at http://www.amics21.com/911/report.html. The Spanish language version is available by hypertext link from that document also. The report confirms that the apparent cylindrical shapes noted in several images of the aircraft that struck the South Tower of the World Trade Center on 911 are real physical objects and not aberrations of the light. The report also notes that commercial Boeing 767-300 aircraft do not have such attachments. This leads to the obvious conclusion that the aircraft that stuck the South Tower of the World Trade Center on 911 was not a commercial airliner.

I did not ask the lady that I met at the abovementioned meeting to show me any official identification but I recognized her immediately we first met in the foyer of the Hotel Universal from a photograph of a blonde-haired woman contained in the top left-hand section of the second page of a website article contained at this address:
http://www.goyadiscovery.com/images/COVER_GOYA.pdf.

The juxtaposition of this picture to the content of the accompanying article suggests that this is a photograph of Amparo Sacristian Carrasco. Two of my other travelling companions who were with me in the foyer of the hotel when I met this lady also agreed that the woman I met was the same person shown in this article. The signature my interlocutor wrote on the Spanish language version of the abovementioned report reads "A. Sacristian". I first contacted this lady via her Linkedin network page under the name of Amparo Sacristian Carrasco. As a result, I have no reason to doubt that the lady that I met in Barcelona was anyone other than Amparo Sacristian Carrasco.

This paper was written by the author in 20th May 2011 and forwarded to the office of the Prime Minister of Australia on that date.

Acknowledgements

My thanks go to Ann Harth for structurally editing this manuscript, to Professor Graeme McQueen for reviewing it, and to Helen Iles for a final review and copy edit at a very generous fee.

About the Author

DAVID PALMER is a retired seventy-one-year-old former management consultant who specialized in strategic business planning for twenty-five years. He is also the 'old man' referred to in the chapter entitled New American Patriots and the author of the 911 Research Report; An Australia Perspective, which is contained in Appendix 2.

To date, David has published one philosophical essay, entitled *A Thesis on the Nature of Religion,* on the Centre for Globalization Research website. He has written and self-published a non-fiction book on mature-age entrepreneurship, entitled *Creating your Self-Employed Third Age Career.* He also published a speculative fiction novel, entitled *Armaginning,* through Zeus Publications of Brisbane in 2009 which drew on his technical strategic planning knowledge of forecasting methodologies, his travel experiences, his two business degrees and a Graduate Diploma in International Relations.

www.ingramcontent.com/pod-product-compliance
Lightning Source LLC
Chambersburg PA
CBHW072004180726
48291CB00002BA/596